SURVIVE?

How

Ray Wilcock

Random Survival

Ray Wenck

Rebel ePublishers
Detroit New York London

Rebel epublishers
Detroit, Michigan 48223

All names, characters, places, and incidents in this publication are fictitious or are used fictitiously. Any resemblance to real persons, living or dead, events or locales is entirely coincidental.

Random Survival
© 2015 by Ray Wenck

For information regarding permission, email the publisher at rebele@rebelepublishers.com, subject line: Permission.

ISBN-13: 978-1-944077-00-6
ISBN-10: 1944077006

Book/Cover design by *Caryatid Design*
Cover image: Shutterstock/tankist276

This novel is dedicated to survivors everywhere.

Prologue

THEY WOULD COME FOR him soon. It was just a matter of time. They would come. And if they found him they would kill him. He didn't doubt that for an instant. He could only hope that he would have enough warning to hide before they discovered his existence.

KCHUK. "UNH." *THUNK. KCHUK.* "Unh." *Thunk.* The sound repeated endlessly. His back ached from the constant strain. How many times had he sunk the shovel into the hard mixed earth of dirt and clay? How many times had he placed the sheet-wrapped bodies into the shallow graves? *KCHUK.* The sound droned on as he tried to lose himself in thought. If he kept his already dulled mind occupied, he wouldn't concentrate on just how exhausted he was. He sunk the blade. "Unh." The sound escaped his lips as he struggled to lift yet another shovelful and toss it aside. *Thunk.* The heavy, moist clod struck the pile and scattered down the slopes on all sides.

"Almost there," he said to no one; no one alive. Another one laid to rest. Truly, how many had it been? How many days straight? He would have to figure it out when he was all done – if he ever did get done. The task seemed endless, but had to be done. The alternative was unthinkable.

Mark lifted two more shovelfuls, his eyes burning from the sweat running down his face. Wiping his eyes, he forced his muscles to an erect position and leaned on the shovel. He squinted into the sun enjoying its heat, then glanced back at the hole he'd dug. Judging his work sufficient, he stuck the shovel into the ground. His shirtless body glistened with sweat; his once snug jeans now sagged from his tightened and smaller stomach. Not what they called washer board, but at his age, and in this short time, it was close.

Grabbing the sheet by the feet, Mark pulled the expired shell of one of his neighbors, into the pit. The body dropped the four feet with a solid thud. Leaning on the shovel, he once again said a silent prayer. With sudden guilt Mark realized, he did not know his neighbor's name. He'd said "Hi" to him three or four times a week in passing, for over five years, but never knew his name. It made the unpleasantness of burial even more so. He sighed and finished his prayer with an apology to God. If there truly were a God, which lately he had his doubts, He would know the name.

Plucking the shovel from its berth, Mark set about filling the hole. When it was done, he patted the mound down, then stomped on the pile. It was important to pack the dirt down as tight as possible. He didn't want any animals digging up the bodies. He stood back and looked at the four graves, all in a row. Two dug two days ago, the mother and the little boy. The little girl was planted yesterday and now the father. He had watched them die knowing there was nothing he could do for them. An entire family lost in three short, painful days. He was beyond sadness. All emotion had faded at least a week ago. He could bring no more feelings to the surface. Whatever emotion he'd possessed lay buried in the graves he had dug for his wife and youngest boy. He couldn't afford to feel. And yet, unbidden, the memory returned.

AS THE LAST SHOVELFUL of dirt hit the grave, Mark dropped to his knees, devastated. *What could I have done differently? How could I have saved them?*

One week earlier, people all over the country – he wasn't sure if it was the world – had begun getting sick. The symptoms were flu-like: fever, then cramping, and then chills. Within two days, the bodies had piled up. Hospitals and medical facilities were overwhelmed. In the first few days, there was still media coverage showing the crisis. News helicopters captured video of out-of-control mobs. What made it worse was not knowing what the illness was. The government didn't even seem to know what the population faced. Their only words were to remain calm and they were working on whatever it was.

They hadn't worked fast enough. Not for Sandra. Not for Ben.

He'd tried to get to the hospital with Sandra and Ben moaning in the car. But no matter which route he took, he couldn't get through. Crowds and police barricades blocked the roads. After an hour of slamming the steering wheel, honking the horn, and swearing at anyone in the way, Sandra touched his arm.

"Just take us home, Mark. It's where we belong." She must have known then that the end was close.

Mark could only comfort them as their life ebbed from their bodies. Unable to ease Ben's pain, Mark crushed two sleeping pills into a glass of water. Even in sleep, his son's face contorted in pain.

Sandra went first. Mark held her until the end and thought his heart would explode as he felt her exhale her last breath. Ben never woke and followed his mother hours later. He had been so strong, had fought so hard.

3

Whatever the devastating illness was, it had taken them in less than three days, but their suffering made it seem like an eternity.

Mark didn't bother calling the authorities. They had too much death and chaos to deal with for them to even care. In the end, he went out behind their beautiful suburban home and dug two graves. Becca and Bobby, his other two children, were both away at college. All his efforts to contact them had failed.

What is left to hope for?

He rubbed his hands together to clear off the dirt and strode toward the house. When he returned, he carried a pistol. Mark dropped the gun between the two graves and picked up the shovel. He pushed his foot down on the blade. With the hole half dug, a warm and comforting breeze caressed him, as though someone had touched his cheek. In an instant his actions ceased and a soothing calm enveloped him. The breeze transferred its warmth through his body as though he had taken a drink of warm tea. A scent, carried on the wind, sparked a memory. A picture of Sandra danced before his eyes.

Whether imagined or not, Mark released the shovel. This time his tears flowed without pain, just sadness. Had it been real or just an illusion?

He chose to believe it was Sandra because that thought brought comfort when he needed something to give him hope.

There must be a reason I'm still here.

One

MARK HIKED TOWARD THE small city. In the distance, a glow lit the night sky. It gave Mark hope. If there was light, someone had to have turned it on. His pace quickened, as did his heart rate. As he drew nearer the main downtown street, he heard a *crack, crack, crack.*

Mark stopped.

Fireworks?

For an instant he was excited. Someone had to have set them off. Then he realized the light was orange and danced in an unsteady way. The glow didn't come from electric lights. The city was on fire. He moved on with caution.

As he drew closer, he heard another *crack*. This time he recognized the sound. Gun shots. Still, it meant someone was alive. A few steps more and the strong scent of the fire was upon him. Mark stopped. Was it worth exploring further? He heard a woman scream.

Someone else was alive. But perhaps not for long.

The scream came from somewhere to his left. Whoever that someone was, was in danger. Perhaps hurt. Thinking of Sandra and spurred by the fact he was unable to save her, Mark ran in that direction in hopes of helping whoever was out there.

When she screamed again Mark stopped and listened,

hunting for a more exact direction. He rounded a corner, slowed to a walk. Two blocks away, the glow of the fire played across the buildings on the far side of Main Street. There were no people, just bodies in various stages of decomposition.

Staying to the shadows, Mark edged forward. At the first corner he stopped and looked down the street in both directions. It was dark so he wasn't sure if anyone moved or not. He jogged across the street and closed in on Main. At the next corner, Mark pressed himself to the building and peered around it. The entire middle of the block was in flames. Bodies lay all over the street. Fleeting shadows and forms moved in and out of the buildings, carrying armloads of worthless items, big-screen TVs, dolls, speakers, and DVDs, as if there were an actual need for any of it.

"Let go, bitch!" The shout drew Mark's attention across the street. A man stood over a prone woman, trying to wrestle a two-liter pop bottle from her hands. As he watched, the man stomped on the woman's chest. She shrieked, but refused to relinquish her prize.

Rage flared through Mark. Without thinking, he sprinted toward the man. Just as the man managed to wrench the bottle free, Mark hit him. He drove the man off the woman and slammed him into a brick wall. Mark fired his fist into the man's face. Days of pain, anger, and frustration rushed to the surface, unleashing a flurry of crushing punches until the man slid down the wall in a heap, his face a bloody mess.

Mark stared at his fist, appalled. Was he capable of such violence now? Then he looked for the woman. She scrambled on her knees to retrieve her precious pop bottle, the bottle that had almost cost her life. Once she had it in hand she crouched defensively, pointing a small paring knife at Mark.

"You stay back. It's mine. I'll kill you if you try to take it."

Mark was so astonished he was unable to speak. The woman fled with the pop like she was carrying a baby.

6

What had happened to humanity in the short week since the plague had descended?

They are willing to kill for a bottle of pop?

He walked to the corner and watched what was left of humankind. There had to be fifty people out there. There was still hope. As he stepped from the shadows into the street, a building crumbled and collapsed, raining fire and debris onto the street.

A woman carrying a case of water ran past. Mark was about to call to her when from down the street a man yelled, "Hey!"

"Oh, shit," said the woman and ran faster.

As the first shot was fired Mark jumped, his heart pounding hard against his chest. He ducked, turned, and ran after the woman. Another shot followed.

"Bring that back here!" The man shot at her again.

Mark pulled up next to the woman. With the water pressed against her chest, the woman ran on. She bumped into Mark as she turned the corner, but tripped on the curb. She went down, skidding on her knees, the water sliding on the sidewalk.

Mark reached down to help her up. She hesitated, but took his hand. He hauled her up and started to run, but she dragged her feet.

"No!" she screamed and wrenched her hand free. "The water!" She ran back to retrieve the plastic wrapped case.

"But—" Mark was dumbfounded. *When someone shoots at you, you run. Was the water worth dying for?*

The woman stooped to pick up the case. Some of the bottles had come free and were loose on the street. Mark ran back to help, picking up two bottles. The woman stood as the shooter rounded the corner.

Mark threw one of the bottles, striking the man in the chest. They wouldn't get much more time. He grabbed the woman's hand and took off with her in tow. Two more shots sounded. The heat of one round passed near his cheek.

7

Another shot came just as Mark skirted another corner. The woman tripped again. Mark raced on, dragging her.

"Come on, get up, or he'll catch us."

The woman didn't reply. Mark reached down to lift her and felt wetness on her back. He looked into her eyes and she blinked once. Then she exhaled a long breath and her head lolled backwards.

The whole world has gone crazy!

Mark gave her one last saddened look and ran into the darkness. He ran until his lungs felt they would explode. By the time he stopped, he was nearly home. He gasped for air, looking over his shoulder for pursuit. The shooter must have been more interested in the water than in him.

He walked on, his thoughts coming like a flood, battering his brain.

What's happened to people? Don't they understand that we are all we have left?

They were so willing to kill each other over water instead of working together to salvage and share what they could. It was more than he could take.

He turned his face upward. "How could You let this happen? What were You thinking? I will never believe in You again."

Mark stopped outside his house until his breathing returned to normal, if anything in this mad world could be considered normal. He stared at his house. It could never be home again, but he had nowhere else to go. Besides, Sandra and Ben were here. He'd had no contact with Becca and Bobby since this plague had fallen upon them. If they survived, this is where they'd come. This would still be home to them.

Mark dragged his weary body up the steps and entered the house. The steps to the second floor seemed to go on forever. Without undressing, he flopped on the bed. The pillow still held Sandra's scent. He pushed her memory from his thoughts for a moment.

If he was to survive, it would take some planning. He would to have to toughen up and think things through. Those animals he'd seen in the city tonight would come looking for food when theirs ran out. Mark was determined to get it first. He would need it to survive. There had to be others like him alive somewhere. If he found them, he wanted enough food and water to share. Maybe there was still hope. Yes, it would take some serious planning or that wild horde would kill him and take it.

His thoughts returned to Sandra. Mark hugged her pillow to his face and inhaled.

Two

SINCE HIS WALK INTO town, Mark hadn't seen anyone living except his neighbor, Summer. It seemed strange that everyone in the subdivision had died except for two people who lived next door to each other. If there was a connection there, Mark wasn't smart enough to find it. Mark had buried Summer's husband in their backyard the day before Sandra had died. Since then he'd tried several times to convince Summer to move in with him, for safety reasons only. But Summer could no longer be reasoned with. The loss of her husband and the chaos into which the world had descended had affected Summer's mind. She had become unresponsive and spent most of her time in her own little world. Mark made a mental note to check on her tomorrow.

Mark's gaze moved from the grave in Summer's yard to the two in his own. How many times had he placed sheet-wrapped bodies into shallow graves? The children were the hardest because they made him think about Becca and Bobby. Mark had become the self-appointed gravedigger, priest, and mourner of his neighborhood.

There was no one else left to do it.

Darkness fell fast, matching the darkness in Mark's heart. After finishing the graves, he'd packed the van and headed home. He didn't like being out in the dark. He turned into his driveway, parked, and got out. Every day Mark went out, scavenging the neighborhood and stripping it of anything useful. He pulled up the garage door, slid back in the van, and drove inside. There he closed and locked the overhead door.

Mark moved the day's finds from the van into the house. Finished, he grabbed the rifle, checked the side-door lock, and went inside for the night. He walked through the laundry room to an interior door, which he locked, then continued down the basement stairs. To the average eye, it looked like a full basement lined with shelves, but it was actually larger.

Mark pulled a set of shelves forward. He tugged on the section of paneled wall behind it, revealing a twenty-four by twenty-foot area. Against the far wall was a fold-up bed. Next to it was a small nightstand with a lamp and a book. Along the wall to the left sat a dorm-size refrigerator powered by an inverter and charged by a generator, which was housed and vented in a separate space.

Mounted to each wall was a rifle rack, each full of shotguns and different caliber rifles, including an old Marine sniper rifle he had discovered along with two full boxes of 7.62mm bullets. In his days in the Marines, he had trained on the same model. Through the wall to the right, another secret door fitted into the paneling. It went into what used to be his work and tool room. You could no longer reach the room from the main basement because he had blocked it off and paneled over the doorway.

The small four by ten foot room was now where he stored his collection of food, water, and medical supplies. Next to the door was a stack of twelve car batteries. They supplied the power for his lights and the security cameras placed around the house, inside and out.

Mark took a five-gallon can of gas recovered from his day's hunt and left it next to the generator. There were barely two gallons in it. It wasn't worth taking out to the storage tank he had buried in the backyard. Today he'd found twenty-four cans of food, two partial cases of bottled water, three cases of assorted pop, and a bag of potatoes. He placed the new items in their appropriate spots in the storage room.

All in all, not a good day on the collection front. He had spent too much time digging graves. It needed to be done, but he would have to make more time tomorrow for collecting.

The one interesting item he had found was an AK-47 with three full magazines. What had Malcolm, one of his neighbors, been doing to need a gun like that? He added the AK to the other guns.

In a short four-foot exterior sidewall, he had cut a door. He was digging out a cave underneath the deck at the rear of the house for further storage and to vent the generator. A crude vent created by a plastic pipe aired the fumes. When complete, it would serve as a place for propane burners and kerosene heaters without worrying about the exhaust vapors. It could also be used as an escape hatch when completed, in case he was trapped inside by intruders. The excavation was about two-thirds done with the treated lumber from his son's old backyard play set carefully bracing the ceiling. He needed more wood to finish the job. The floor was lined with large square patio blocks, but was still eight to ten short of covering the space.

Tired, Mark pulled a beer from the refrigerator and walked toward the large desk that sat in front of the escape route he was building. Deprived of human interaction, these projects were how Mark kept himself from going crazy. Mark entered the small cave, placed his beer on the dirt floor, and picked up the shovel he'd left there the night before. Remembering the security system, Mark walked back to his living quarters and hooked wires to the battery terminals, activating the alarm.

Three hours later, Mark was done for the night. The space was almost as large as he needed it to be. Maybe two more nights of good digging should do it. Tomorrow night he would haul in the wood necessary to support the dirt ceiling then begin work on his escape hatch. Mark took off his boots, peeled off his socks and shirt, and slid into a clean shirt. Checking his security system once more, he laid his exhausted body down. As his muscles relaxed and formed his frame to the bed, a wave of physical relief swept over him. His final thoughts before he drifted off were of his two remaining children. He hoped they were safe, but more importantly, Mark prayed they were at peace.

I love you, Bobby. Love you too, Becca.

THE NEXT MORNING, Mark fixed a pot of coffee, heating the water on a small propane burner on the deck. He ate a hunk of cheese and an apple. He wanted to eat all the fresh produce before it spoiled. Mark scaled the deck to the roof, using the heavy overhanging beams that ran from the house down to the front posts.

Sandra had used them to hang plants.

In the summer, Mark rolled sheets of black shade-cloth over the beams so they could sit outside. From the beams it was a simple process to get up on the roof. Once there, he crawled to the peak and used binoculars to scan the area. The height allowed him to see quite a distance. Seeing nothing, he climbed back down and headed for the garage. The tools he needed for his foraging were already loaded in the van.

The drive didn't take long. Nothing about the trip

suggested the world had changed – except for the lack of people. The sun shone brightly with the promise of a beautiful day. Arriving at his starting point, he backed up the driveway of the house next to the one where he had stopped the day before. He liked to be able to finish as many houses as possible each day, but a lot depended on how many graves he had to dig. Since Mark had started hunting, he had covered close to ninety of the one hundred and forty-five houses that made up his subdivision.

Mark decided to change his routine starting today. When he finished these houses, he would drive to the next subdivision and just strip the houses as fast as he could. His life might very well depend on collecting as fast as possible. Since almost being shot in the city, Mark never went anywhere unarmed. Opening the rear doors, he slipped a 9mm automatic into his belt at the small of his back; his knife was in a sheath on his belt. There was a fanny pack with assorted small items he might need on the opposite side of the knife. After grabbing the shovel, his toolbox, a five-gallon gas container, and the shotgun, Mark went around to the back of the house.

This house had two back doors. One came out of the garage while the other was on the deck and opened up into the dining area off the kitchen. He set the toolbox down by the garage door then walked up the deck to peer through the windows. He couldn't see anyone. He no longer expected to, but it didn't hurt to check.

Using a heavy pry bar and a long thin-bladed screwdriver, Mark popped the garage door and went inside. His and hers BMWs were parked alongside each other. A variety of gas-powered tools hung around the garage walls. The first job was to siphon the gas tanks. He found another five-gallon container in the garage that was half-full. Inserting a flexible plastic line into the first BMW's gas tank, he sucked on it until the gas was inches from his mouth.

That was why he now used clear hose. He'd tasted gas before and needed no reminders of how nasty it was.

While the gas flowed into the container, he loaded a small propane heater into the back of the van. Hauling four empty ten-gallon containers from the van, he returned to the garage and switched out the nearly full five-gallon one.

Mark set up to drain the second car in the same way. With that in process, he went out on the deck where he removed the propane tank from the grill and stowed it in the van with the first five-gallon container. He fell into a rhythm, having done these same actions nearly a hundred times.

After draining the cars, he moved on to the mower. Mark found a gas-powered chain saw, but decided to take that without draining the gas. The net gain was over twenty gallons of gas – a good beginning. Some houses had no cars at all.

Inside the house, Mark emptied the cupboards of anything that would keep, including another bag of potatoes. In a drawer he found a large pack of AA batteries. He found a case of bottled water and half a case of diet cola in the pantry, along with several boxed meals. Overall the score on the food and supplies was not very good. He cleaned out the medicine cabinet of anything that might prove useful, like vitamins, aspirin, and decongestant capsules. There was also a box of Band-Aids.

The good news was there weren't any bodies. Where could they be since there were two cars in the garage? As long as he didn't have to bury them, he didn't dwell on it. He moved to the next house. There, to his dismay, he found a family of five. Mark sighed and walked out back. He pushed his feelings aside and began to dig.

He'd given up digging separate graves after the first

day. To save time and energy, he dug one grave for the parents and one for kids. In the first he laid the father and the mother, wrapped in sheets and a quilted comforter. Her body, having been dead for more than a week, was bloated. Mark had no idea how many more burials he could do. The bodies were only going to get worse. The children were placed in the second grave.

He'd just begun to cover them when he heard a growl. He looked up. A large pack of dogs in a variety of shapes, sizes, and breeds moved out of the woods thirty yards from the split-rail fence at the rear of the property. A large German Shepherd stepped forward from the pack, lowered its head, and growled. The others joined in, sending a chill up Mark's back. The pack bolted forward, coming full speed toward him. The sight was unnerving, causing a momentary bolt of panic shooting through him.

Their sickly thin bodies strained as they sprinted for him. With matted and mangy coats, they looked like demon hounds released from hell. Mark threw the shovel down and ran to the fence, where he propped the shotgun and took aim at the lead dog. He loosed a round. The German Shepherd let out a yelp, landed face first, and flipped over several times. Mark pumped another round into the chamber and fired again. This time the pellets struck two dogs, taking one down, slowing the other. Several of the pack, seeing defenseless fresh meat, started tearing into the wounded animals. But a dozen or more continued on.

Mark fired three more rounds. Three more animals dropped. He fumbled another cartridge into the gun, but dropped the next. He wouldn't be able to stop them all before they got to the fence. If he were caught in the open, they would take him down for sure. Fortunately, metal fencing had been secured to the wooden cross-rails. Most of the dogs would not be able to get in the yard. He had to hope they would not be able to clear the fence. That hope was dashed, however, when the first dog bounded over it in one long leap.

The gun bucked again, catching the dog in mid-flight, but now he was out of shells. Mark dropped the gun and ran for the house, pulling the handgun in his belt free. He fired on the run as he reached the door on the deck. He'd left it open when carrying the bodies out. Mark slammed it shut just as one of the larger dogs launched at his back. The beast hit the glass with such force that it knocked him backward and cracked the double-paned glass. The door slid open a few inches.

The dog bounced off, stunned, giving Mark time to regain his feet and lock the door. Even locked, however, how much more would the glass withstand? Mark backed away, breathing as if he had run a marathon. Leaning against the refrigerator, he fought to keep from shaking.

From the garage a smaller, but just as vicious, dog pushed the unlatched inner door aside and bounded in. Mark let out a startled cry, raised his gun, and in a panic, fired six rounds into the dog. A Golden Lab followed, leaping at Mark before he had a chance to aim. The wild animal snapped at his neck. Mark's only defense was to sidestep and pistol-whip the beast on the side of its head. Its nails slid on the wooden floor as the beast scrabbled for purchase.

Mark ran toward the open door, slamming it shut before any more dogs could get in. The Lab came at him again. There was nothing left of the family pet it had once been. Spinning, Mark took aim and fired once as the animal gathered for a leap. The bullet caught the dog in the top of the head. It skidded to a stop at his feet, whimpered once, and died. Mark let out a relieved breath and pushed the beast with his toe to make sure it would not come back at him when he walked away.

At the kitchen window, Mark watched the dogs feasting on the dead. A few had jumped into the graves and ripped at the dead flesh. Some, not large enough to hurdle the fence, were still outside digging at the ground or attempting to scale the links. A quick check of his magazine told him he only had six rounds left. He would have to make a run for the van to reload.

But Mark could not leave them alive, or they would be back. Perhaps next time he would not be so lucky. Opening the front door a crack to make sure none of the pack had scaled the fence, he ran to the van and hopped in. Once there, he reloaded the 9mm, grabbed a handful of shotgun shells, and picked up the rifle. Forming a plan of attack, he took a deep calming breath and exited the van.

Mark took his time picking off the dogs outside the yard as they feasted on their dead pack mates. He liked dogs, but these were no longer man's best friend. Mark felt no remorse putting them down. It was a very close shot for a rifle that was made for long distances, but it did make the shot easier than using the handgun.

The sound of at least two more dogs ripping flesh and snarling at each other came from inside one of the graves. From where he stood he had no angle for a shot, so he climbed the fence. Approaching with caution, his heart pounding, Mark picked up the discarded shotgun and reloaded it. No sound came from the first grave, so Mark bypassed it. In the second, however, were two dogs. One of them, a large Chocolate Lab, saw him and snapped threateningly. As it lifted its blood-covered muzzle to reissue the warning, Mark pulled the trigger.

The second beast was not in sight, but Mark could hear it snarling and tearing at the rotted flesh. He had to inch closer to the edge of the grave to see it. Its teeth were buried in the man's face, tearing the flesh away. Holding the shotgun over the top of the dog, Mark pulled the trigger again.

Mark decided to check the first grave, just to be sure. As he came to within three feet, a Pit Bull bounded up and out of the hole and threw itself at him. Mark stumbled backward, surprised, firing as he fell. The pellets caught the animal in the mouth, ripping its face. The shock of the attack and the recoil of the shotgun pushed Mark over the edge of the second grave. He fell into the gore below.

"Aw, yuk!"

Three

AFTER CLIMBING OUT OF the grave, Mark went to get a toy wagon he'd seen in the garage. He couldn't leave the carnage for other scavengers, so he loaded up the carcasses and deposited them inside the graves. Afterward, Mark went inside, stripped off his clothes, and found replacements to wear home. He called it a day even though there were still at least two more hours of daylight left.

After emptying the van of his day's plunder, Mark decided to waste some of his water supply on a sponge bath. If he wanted to bathe more often, he needed to put out barrels to catch rainwater, rather than waste what drinkable water he had available to him.

As the sun went down, Mark took the weapons he'd fired out back. He stripped, cleaned, and oiled them while enjoying the sunset. It annoyed him that the grass was so long, but to cut it would announce his presence to passing strangers. A mild wind blew, bringing with it the scent of roses. Although the breeze mingled with the smell of the gun oil, memories of happy times flooded him. A smile crossed his sun-creased face until his gaze fell upon the two graves at the back of the yard.

Normalcy was now an abstract concept.

Just then, his neighbor opened her door. The one connection he still had to the recent past walked to the grave Mark had dug for her husband. Summer knelt next to it, made the sign of the cross, and prayed. After a while, she sat and talked to her husband. Mark tried not to listen. It was the same routine three or four times a day.

Before the madness, Summer had been vice-president of a marketing company. She'd never had kids and from the few times they'd spoken, children didn't seem to be an interest of hers. Now, she was not eating well and no longer made an effort to take care of herself. Not that there was any reason to change, but she went for days wearing the same clothes.

"Hi, Summer, how are you today?"

She didn't always respond, but when she did, the reply seldom matched the question.

"Oh, we're doing fine. Theo is resting. He's had a very hard day. We were trying to decide where to go on vacation this year. We love Cancun, but we've been there so many times now, I thought it might be nice to try someplace new."

"That would be nice. Are you eating all right? I'm worried about you. Do you need anything?"

"No," she said absently. "No, I think we're doing just fine. Thank you for asking, Mark."

"I could fix you something."

She leaned over the grave and whispered something to her husband, then straightened up and said, "Maybe some other time. We're going out to dinner tonight."

Mark packed up his weapons and went inside for the night. He went through his nightly security routine, which included making sure he'd locked all windows and doors. Next, he used binoculars and scanned the surrounding area for any signs of movement. Last, in his secret room, Mark set up his alarms.

21

After eating a quick meal, Mark went into the cave to dig. Five hours later he had made good progress in the cave, placing support beams. Mark estimated it could be finished in two more days if he could find the materials. When that job was finished, he would be looking for another project to occupy his time and his mind. Anything that would keep him from thinking too much.

Mark went to the plot map of the subdivision laid out on the desk. Checking off the houses done that day, Mark counted what remained. A few more good days and he would be done.

Four

MARK RETURNED HOME EARLIER than usual the next day. After a successful day of collecting, he decided to use the remaining daylight to plant the garden he'd been planning. He had just pushed the shovel into the ground when he heard a sound that drove heart-stopping fear throughout his body: a car engine, and multiple engines at that.

Mark tossed the shovel into the trees, grabbed the rifle, and ran to the deck. Like a monkey, he climbed to the top of the roof. Mark's worst fears were realized. A platoon of men scurried through the neighborhood, smashing down doors and pillaging what they could find. How he had not heard them approach sooner, Mark didn't know, but some were already across the street. Others were in the driveway next door.

He did a quick count of the people he could see. There were at least twenty men in five vehicles: two pickup trucks, a van larger than his, an SUV, and an older full-sized red convertible. The pickup trucks were half full of assorted unimportant items, such as dressers and dining room tables. Mark couldn't see what was inside the step van. They couldn't be finding much food or anything useful because he had already stripped the houses at the front of the development.

Mark slid down the roof until he was halfway between the peak and the bottom edge. He had to get Summer to safety. There were too many intruders to take on.

Peering through the small hexagonal window on the side of her house, Mark found Summer lounging on her sofa and staring straight ahead, oblivious to everything around her. He was about to slide down and try to get her out the back door when the room filled with men. For a moment, no one moved or spoke. Summer's shocked look turned to fear.

Reality had intruded on her small world. Viciously.

They pounced on her. She screamed until one of the men slapped her. Mark heard the contact up on the roof. One man yanked her head backward over the arm of the sofa by her hair and pressed his mouth to hers, cutting off any more screams. Several men muscled her legs apart and fought over who would be first.

Mark's head pounded like it would explode. He rose up on one knee and sighted the rifle through the window.

Just then, all the men stepped back as an enormous man in bib-overalls and no shirt strode into the room. He had a great round bald head and muscles on top of muscles. He spoke a few words to the men. By the looks on some of their faces, they weren't happy with whatever was said. Several backed away. Still others argued with the huge man until he drove a massive fist into one protester's face. He dropped out of sight. No one else protested.

For a brief moment, Mark hoped that this man would be Summer's savior.

The men cleared a path as the large man came forward, his massive chest glistening from the day's work. His head moved left and right, admiring Summer's body. He fondled one of her large breasts and some of the men laughed. Then he stepped behind her, his massive body blocking the view. The man unfastened his bibs.

On the roof, Mark lined up the shot again, his sights on the back of the big man's head. At that moment, the rear patio door opened and two of the animals came outside. Mark ducked away from the edge so he wouldn't be noticed.

Seconds later, two more men came into Mark's yard from the front of the house. The men talked over the fence.

A man in Summer's yard said, "We found us a new plaything."

His partner added, "Yeah, Buster's with her now."

Another man said, "Who's he gonna give her to when he's done?"

"Don't know," replied the first man. "But it's gonna be Christmas for someone."

The men laughed.

Mark was desperate to help Summer, but it would do neither of them any good for him to commit suicide.

Mark risked another look through the window. The large man had finished with Summer. He was patting her bottom and caressing her back, like he had just test driven a car and was admiring its lines. Someone tied a belt around her neck and they led her out of the room.

They weren't going to kill her.

There were worse things than death. He gritted his teeth.

If only she had moved in with me, maybe we could have hidden before this horde descended.

An air horn sounded, the same type heard at football games. The men came running from all directions, including his house. Mark watched them go. They were leaving with his cutlery. They hadn't been inside long, but if that was the extent of his loss, he'd done well.

Mark crawled back to the peak, watching as the men loaded their prizes in the step van. They sat Summer on the side wall in the back of one of the pickup trucks. He watched as the caravan pulled out. The convertible, with the large man driving, led the way, followed by a pickup truck, the step van, and the pickup truck with Summer in it. The SUV brought up the rear. He considered their route. On the next street there was a vacant lot between two houses. The caravan would have to pass that lot if they went back the way they came.

That spot offered the best chance for him to save Summer.

Mark had trained as a sniper in the Marines, but he'd never actually had to shoot anyone. As the first truck came into view, he tracked it. With all the furniture and men sitting in the back, they were not moving fast. He would only have, at best, three to four seconds to take the shot. He lined up one of the men in the back of the first pickup truck. He took several deep breaths, letting his last one out slowly. As the second truck came into view, Summer looked up as if she were staring directly at him. Mark almost lost his resolve.

He hurried to refocus. Through the scope, a red dot appeared above Summer's left eye. Without hesitation, Mark squeezed the trigger. The truck jerked to a stop. Summer's lifeless body tumbled backward, over the side, and landed in the street.

Men scurried from the truck and took up a defensive position behind it. He didn't think anyone out there had the skill to track where the shot had come from but wasn't about to take a chance. He slid down the roof and climbed onto the wooden beams. Swinging down, he dropped to the deck and ran inside the house to the front windows. If they were coming, he'd still have time to get to his hiding place.

Should he have tried to take several of the men out to even the odds?

But if he'd done that, they might be more determined to find him.

Mark watched for fifteen minutes, but no one appeared, so he made his way to the safe room and shut himself in.

He sat on the bed.

There was no way to avoid the guilt of killing Summer, but he would not regret taking the shot. Shooting her was a mercy killing. In this horrid new world, shooting her was the right thing to do and the only way to stop the endless abuse she would have to endure. After dark, he would creep out and retrieve her body. He would lay her to rest beside her husband.

Mark would miss her.

He had been unable to save his family, and now he'd failed to protect Summer. He'd failed them all. He had played God, and he cursed himself for thinking he had the right.

Five

THERE WAS NO MOTIVATION to rise the following morning, no urgency to hunt. Sleep had eluded him for much of the night. He kept seeing Summer's face through the scope.

Mark would never forget that moment, but he had to move on. The one thing he was certain of: the Horde, as he now referred to them, would be back. They had come, as he always knew they would, but they'd still caught him off guard.

With that thought playing in his head, Mark found the determination to continue. He'd have to be ever alert now. Mark had to salvage as much food and water as possible. As he went through his preparations, he decided to forgo any burials for the next few days until he had a chance to search the remaining houses. Then he would go back and take care of the bodies

Mark went through ten houses before noon.

By his estimation, there were about thirty houses left to search. He decided to do ten more then head home to see about increasing his defenses. Four houses later, as he was popping the patio door open, he thought about a couple of alterations he could make to the cave. When it swung free, Mark froze.

From somewhere in the house came a noise, a scurrying sound that made him think there was a house pet still alive. After his recent narrow escape from the dog pack, he wasn't taking any chances.

Mark set his tools down and pulled out his gun. Closing the door behind him, he advanced into the kitchen, stopped, and listened. The sink and counters were full of dirty dishes that looked recent.

Perhaps someone else was alive here.

Again he thought he heard a faint sound, this time from the floor above. Moving from room to room, Mark cleared each one before stopping at the foot of the stairs.

He took them slowly, thankful they were carpeted. At the top of the stairs, Mark paused again. Typical of most of the houses in this area, it had two bedrooms to the left, two to the right and a bathroom across from him. Both rooms on his left were small and empty. Perhaps it was just his imagination, but there looked to be a recent body print on one bed in a boy's room.

The bathroom was empty but smelled. Lifting the toilet lid, Mark could see it had been used, a lot.

Someone was here.

Standing in the hall between the last two doors, Mark put an ear to each, trying to pick up anything that might tell him what to expect. Choosing left again, he turned the knob and pushed the door open. There were dolls and stuffed animals lined up on the pink bedspread. Checking under the bed with a baton, he found assorted shoes and toys. He moved the clothes around in the closet. No one was there. One room left to check.

As soon as he pushed the door open, the odor hit him. The smell made him step back away from the door to catch a clean breath. His eyes watered. Four bodies lay on the king-size bed, the mother and father and two small girls who couldn't have been more than five or six years old. Someone had laid them together.

There were three other doors in the room. One led to a bathroom. He checked the first door on the left. It was a large closet, wide, but not too deep. He squatted down to try and peer in under the hanging clothes. Although he could see most of the contents, it was difficult to see it all without actually entering. He checked the other doors before venturing inside. The next door was a walk-in closet, the father's. This one was narrow but deep. Mark did the same there, but again, nothing moved. The bathroom was also empty.

Standing in the doorway, he looked at the bed. Maybe he had been mistaken; the place seemed vacant like all the others.

Unless someone is hiding under the bed.

Stepping toward the bed, Mark thought he heard a sound like soft growling. He had no desire to deal with any more dogs. He moved off to the side, readied his gun, and reached forward to grab the bedspread.

"You leave them alone!"

Mark turned. A young boy squeezed out from between a large dresser and the wall and charged, swinging a baseball bat. Mark jumped back to avoid the swing, but it caught him on the back of his hand. The frightened child was screaming and wild-eyed. Mark stepped forward, caught the bat in both hands, and ripped it from the youth's grip. The boy hesitated, then launched himself at Mark, beating his arms against Mark's chest.

Mark caught the boy's arms and held them until he calmed down. The boy kicked and screamed, but Mark held fast. Soon the screams turned to sobs. He twisted and turned to pull his hands free. Stepping back, he tried to kick his captor. It was like trying to contain a wild animal.

"Stop. Stop. I'm not going to hurt you. Stop it."

But the boy continued to struggle. Mark pulled him

close and held him. The boy continued to strike out, but his blows had lost most of their force. He looked into the boy's eyes and repeated, "Settle down. I am not going to hurt you."

The boy buried his face in Mark's chest and cried.

"It's all right, son, you're no longer alone."

The feel of having his arms around a living being was enough to make Mark cry. He held the boy tight, wanting to feel the warmth and to know this was real and not some illusion created by his companion-deprived mind.

He rubbed the boy's head, running his hands through the long greasy hair, sparking a memory. That was how his son would've worn his hair if Sandra had let him. The image pushed Mark over an emotional cliff. Tears dropped on the boy's hair. Mark went to his knees to study him. The boy was about ten years old. How long had the poor child lived alone in this house? The trauma of living in a house with your deceased family would be enough to drive a grown man crazy. It had to have scarred this poor child beyond imagining.

"What's your name, son?"

The tears still flowed and the boy refused to let go, keeping his face pressed against Mark's body. Mark let him go on for another minute before repeating the question.

This time the boy wiped at his eyes and muttered, "Darren."

"My name is Mark. Darren, I'm so very glad to meet you."

The boy looked up at Mark. He lifted his dirty T-shirt and wiped his face with it.

"That's my mom and dad, and my two sisters. They're dead."

"Yes, they are. I'm sorry. A lot of people are dead, including my wife and my son. You know what we have to do for them now?"

He shook his head.

"We have to bury them. It's what they would want. It's a way for you to honor them."

Darren's head lowered and his little body shook as a fresh wave of tears let loose. Burying his family was going to be hard for the boy, but it was the best way for him to move forward.

"We're going to have to hurry though because it's getting late. We don't want to be here after dark. I'll go down and get started so you can say good-bye to your family. But then I need you to gather a bunch of sheets, okay? Can you do that?"

He nodded. Mark patted his shoulder and went down to the van to get a shovel. More than an hour later, he finished the graves and went inside. Darren was standing in the kitchen, watching him. He fidgeted nervously.

Mark asked, "Did you find the sheets?"

The boy nodded.

"Do you want to wait down here or do you want to help me?"

He shrugged.

"Stay here for now. I'll call you if I need you."

Upstairs, Mark found the stack of folded bed sheets on the floor and wrapped the bodies in them. When he'd finished, Mark had four mummies. He dragged the father down the steps first, pulling him outside and placing him as gently as he could in the first grave. The boy watched from the kitchen, his eyes going wide when his father disappeared into the hole.

Mark returned with the mother and set her in the second grave. He placed one of the girls on top of one of the parents. When he looked up, Darren was standing in the open doorway, crying. Mark's heart went out to him, but there was nothing to be done about it. Darren would have to be strong in order to survive in this new world.

With the first shovel full of dirt, Darren dropped to his

32

knees. Mark set the shovel down and went to the boy. He squatted next to him and rubbed his back.

"Darren, I know this is hard for you, but it has to be done. You've been strong for so long but I need you to be strong a while longer. When I'm finished, we'll have to leave. I'll take you to my house. You'll be safe there. There are a lot of bad people roaming this area now. We can come back to visit in the daylight, but for now I need you to collect whatever you want to take with you and put it in a bag or suitcase or something. Go on now. I want to leave in about fifteen minutes."

He had to lift him up but still the boy refused to budge. Mark held the boy by the head and looked him in the eyes.

"You are old enough to understand that your mom and dad are dead."

"No," he howled. But Mark would not let go of him.

"Your parents would have wanted you to do this. This is very important. Bad people will come for you soon. You need to be some place safe. Now get moving or you won't be able to take anything with you. Hurry. Go collect what you want to bring with you. Clothes, toothbrush, pictures, whatever … you have fifteen minutes before we leave." He gave him a little push. "Go on now."

Darren moved toward the stairs.

When Mark finished covering the bodies, he went inside to find the boy sitting on a bed in what must have been his room. He had a bunch of things piled on his bed, but it was all loose. Mark's desire to move clashed with his need to be a father.

"Darren, how are you going to carry all that?"

"I couldn't find a suitcase," he sobbed.

Mark ran to the parents' room and hunted through their closets. Finding no luggage, he scooped up the pile of pillow cases Darren had pulled out earlier. He tossed one to Darren. "Start stuffing things in. Whatever doesn't fit gets left behind." Mark jammed the clothes in a second bag.

The sun was setting fast. Fear pushed his parenting skills to the side. When his bag was full, he grabbed Darren's hand and pulled him from the room. He dragged the boy out the front door, led him to the passenger side, and pushed him in. Mark ran around to the driver's side and hopped in, pitching the bag in the back. He sped off with a nervous anticipation of impending doom.

Back at his house, Mark parked and closed the garage door in near panic as the last of the sunlight disappeared behind the trees.

The panic was new. As was the tightness in his chest. A cold chill ran down his spine. He felt he was overreacting, as though he was afraid vampires would come out as the sun set. Only this threat was real and more dangerous.

Darren helped him unload the van. Once that was accomplished, Mark set all the locks and checked the windows to make sure the streets were still clear. Then, Mark led Darren to the basement and opened the secret room.

Only then did he begin to relax. With the day's collection put away, Mark decided they both could use a hot meal. He took the small propane burner into the cave and heated the last two steaks he had. On another pan, he sliced up some of the potatoes and fried them in some olive oil. It had been quite a while since he had tasted hot food.

Pulling out a folding table and two chairs, he set out paper plates and plastic forks and knives while Darren watched. Plating the food, Mark popped a beer for him and a cola for Darren and sat to enjoy the feast.

Mark couldn't help himself; he dug in hungrily. He

34

had to force himself to slow down and enjoy the food. Between bites he tried to coax Darren to eat.

"Darren, I know this has been upsetting for you, but you have to eat. Things will get better. You'll just have to trust me on that. Steak will be almost impossible to find from now on. I suggest you take advantage of it, because we may never get to have one again." Trying to remember how Ben had been at that age, Mark asked, "Do you want me to cut it for you?"

"No." Darren shook his head. "I can do it."

"I thought so. How old are you?"

"I'll be eleven next week."

If he could engage Darren in conversation, maybe he would relax. Mark smiled as the boy sawed at the steak with the plastic knife. He managed to cut a piece free and put it in his mouth. From there he needed no further coaxing. The last morsel consumed, they sat back and looked at the empty plates.

"Well, the nice thing about eating like this is you don't have to do the dishes." Mark scooped up the plates and plastic ware and dropped them in a garbage bag. Mark pulled out a sleeping bag and set it on the floor next to his bed.

"Which one do you want, the bag or the bed?"

Darren shrugged.

Mark smiled. "I'll tell you what, you take the bed for tonight and tomorrow we'll search for another one. You go ahead and get ready for bed. I've got some work to do."

When he didn't move Mark asked, "Problem?"

"I, uh, I have to, uh ..."

"Need the bathroom, do you?"

He nodded.

"Normally, I try to go outside before I settle in for the night. It's a little late for that now. So let me show you what I do in case of emergencies."

Mark reopened the wall and led Darren to the far corner of the basement. There he had a large five-gallon bucket and a roll of toilet paper. It was next to a floor drain. A pile of grocery store plastic bags were next to the bucket with one inside.

"Use the bucket for number one. Put a bag inside for number two then put the toilet paper inside the bag and tie it up. We'll bury it in the morning. Got it?"

Darren nodded. Mark left him and went back to the room. He went into the cave and returned to digging. A short while later Darren was back.

"Did you close the wall back up?"

"Yeah."

"Need anything else?"

"I forgot my toothbrush."

"I'm sure I've got one here somewhere." He checked his supplies and found a five-pack of brushes. "Here you go. Do you know how to brush your teeth without running water?"

"Yeah, it's just like camping."

Mark smiled. "Exactly, only you have to be very careful with how much water you use. If we run out, we may never find clean drinking water. That's very important, all right?"

"There was some water at my house." His eyes dropped. A sad look crossed his face as he thought about home.

"I'll tell you what, we'll go back in the morning and collect the water and anything you forgot. Okay?"

"Yeah."

"Why don't you get some sleep now?"

"Okay." He paused. "What are you doing?"

"I'm making a room where we can cook and get fresh air, or use as an escape route if the need arises."

"You dug all that out yourself?"

"Yeah."

"Do you need any help?"

Mark's first thought was to tell him maybe tomorrow. The boy should sleep. But maybe Darren needed to keep his mind occupied. After all, wasn't that what he was doing himself?

"Sure. Why don't you take that other shovel and scoop up the dirt that I scrape away? Just pile it in those buckets and we'll take them out in the morning."

As the boy worked alongside, Mark thought, *It'll be nice having someone to talk to and share the load with, even if he is only eleven next week.*

Six

THE NEXT MORNING MARK fixed Darren cereal with canned milk. He packed a lunch of cheese, canned fruit, granola bars, and cookies. They were both tired, having stayed up late to finish digging and squaring off the dirt walls. The space added another twelve by sixteen-foot area to the safe room.

They visited Darren's house as promised. Darren had a little more life to him now. The meal, the sleep, and knowing he was no longer alone had done wonders for him.

"I'll show you where all the food is," he said, as they entered the house. He led Mark to a well-stocked pantry. A lot of packages had been torn open by Darren as he had tried to find things he could eat. They loaded up most of a case of water, a half case of pop, and a full case of beer. Darren's mother must have just gone shopping when they fell ill. They filled four bags with food and another two of supplies.

While Mark finished taking things out to the van, Darren went back upstairs and packed more things, including some of his favorite toys, games, and books. Mark emptied the family vehicles of gas while Darren went and stood by the graves. Mark let him be for a while, putting everything in the van himself, but then it was time to move to the next house.

In some respects, having Darren made things easier, but in other ways he slowed the process down. After the fifth house, Darren was ready for a break. Mark would have worked through until the tenth, but Darren was still a child. He gave Darren a granola bar and a couple of cookies and told him to sit and rest. Mark, however, continued to load.

When Darren informed Mark that he had to use the bathroom, Mark decided to take the time to start a grave for the two bodies inside. He was halfway done and wondering what was keeping Darren when he heard a scream. He looked up as Darren ran around the side of the house. At first, Mark feared it might be another pack of dogs. With the gate open there was nothing to stop them from coming in the yard. Two men entered the yard, laughing. They froze when they saw Mark. The only one moving was Darren, who was running right at Mark.

None of them held a weapon. Then, everyone moved at once. Mark grabbed Darren and threw him into the grave then followed him in. It was only three feet deep, but it was more cover than the two men had. The shotgun was out of reach and propped against the fence, so he snatched the gun from his belt.

One of the men ran toward them with a gun. The man got to within eight feet before Mark shot him. Mark shot him again, dropping him in front of the grave. Switching targets, he shot at the other man who leaped behind a small apple tree for cover.

Mark had time to aim now and tried to make his shots count. If he ran out of bullets in the hole, they would never get out of it alive. Fortunately, the other man was not much of a shot. He reached around the tree and fired.

The shotgun loaded with buckshot would offer better

firepower. Mark fired three quick shots, jumped out of the grave, and ran. He grabbed the shotgun without stopping, since a moving target was harder to hit. He ran along the fence while the man tried to track him. Bullets flew behind him. Mark leveled the shotgun at the tree and pulled the trigger. His shot was off target but caused the man to duck, allowing Mark to stop, aim, and blow the shooter away.

Mark ran to the man, made sure he was dead and grabbed his gun. He searched the body and found a second magazine. He dragged the man toward the grave and yelled for Darren to climb out. The poor boy shook with fear.

"Go inside and watch through the front window. If you see anyone else, come and tell me immediately." He grabbed the boy's shoulders and forced him to focus his teary eyes. "This is very important, Darren. Can you do it?"

The boy nodded and jogged off.

Mark dumped the body in the grave and went to get the second one. He dumped the man in with his partner. As he hit bottom, the man let out a low groan. Mark tried not to think about this killer still being alive. These men hadn't come to talk or form an alliance. They had tried to kill him. There should be no guilt associated with the deed.

Yet there was. No matter how he tried to rationalize his actions, burying the man was wrong. Still he did not stop shoveling dirt into the hole. He closed his mind to any sounds coming from the grave. When a soft moan rose from depths, Mark could take no more. He stopped, took a deep breath, and set the shovel down. He couldn't bury him alive. Picking up the man's gun he fired once into the hole and the moaning ceased. Mark hurried to fill in the rest of the dirt.

Mark packed up fast and ran out to the van. He had

no idea if there were more men in the area, but didn't want to hang around to find out. From the driver's seat, he motioned for Darren to come out. While waiting for Darren to join him, Mark searched for any unfamiliar vehicles.

Whenever he saw a car parked on the street, his habit was to siphon the gas and put a chalk mark on the tire so he knew which cars he'd already done. He couldn't see any new cars. That left three possibilities: the men had lived nearby, the men had walked from where the rest of the group was, or the men had been dropped off, which meant others would return. Mark did not want to be on the street if the latter was the case, so instead of continuing their rounds, they went home.

Mark was very cautious about parking the van. He made sure no one was around before pulling up the driveway. He brought the garage door down too fast, crashing to the floor with a bang. Filling his arms with as much as he could carry, Mark instructed Darren to open the house door. From there, he stationed Darren at the front window to stand guard while he locked the garage door and emptied the van. As soon as everything was stowed away, he relieved Darren from his post.

"Have you ever shot a gun?"

"No." Darren avoided Mark's eyes. He was nervous.

"We'll have to make some time to teach you. Do you think you can handle a gun?"

The boy shrugged.

"Darren, I know what you saw back there was upsetting. If I hadn't shot them, they would have killed us. I didn't enjoy shooting those men, in fact, I didn't want to. I would much rather have allies, but some people just don't see things like we do. We were after the same things they were, food and water. If they were interested in sharing, we could have worked something out, but all they wanted to do was take.

41

"I hope you can understand the difference. One day we'll find others like us who want to share. But until then, we have to be very careful. So I'm going to teach you to shoot. You never know, it could save your life someday, or mine."

"I don't think I could ever shoot someone."

"What if it was a choice between shooting him and dying? Would you just let him shoot you?"

Darren rested his head on his arms and stared straight ahead.

Seven

MARK AND DARREN WENT through the next few days with caution. They did not stay out long and traveled in short spurts, stopping and shutting down the engine in case anyone was close enough to hear the motor running. When they entered a house, Darren always stood watch at the front window. Since that day with the two men, they had taken the time to go into the woods a few miles past Mark's house and practice shooting. Darren now carried a .22. The gun had intimidated him at first, but after a while he gained confidence and his fear eased. Darren was only ten – well, now eleven – but Mark hoped if the need arose he'd be able to defend himself. Of course, shooting targets and shooting a person were two entirely different things.

Mark also taught Darren about the security measures he had established in the house. Darren got to the point where he could set the alarms and check all the locks. He learned how to scan the area with binoculars, to cook, how to dig a toilet, and the easiest way to climb on the roof. Mark also taught him how to use a knife safely and gave him one to carry on his belt.

When they went into a house, Darren now knew what to look for that would be important to them. While Mark was in the garage siphoning, Darren would collect food in between keeping watch. The amount of time it took to clear a house decreased rapidly as Darren became more experienced.

Instead of staying out all day they devised a new routine. They went out as the sun rose, did six to eight houses, and then went back home. They would spend the day training or finishing off the cave. Then an hour or so before dusk they would go back out and do a few more houses, returning as the sun set.

The stores were growing, but now with two mouths to feed they dwindled quicker, too. With just ten houses left, they would never be able to stop searching for food and water. To sit back and relax would be a mistake. Only a finite amount of food was available out there and they would have to travel to get to it.

One night, as Mark returned from the outside toilet, multiple gunshots disrupted the peaceful night. The shots came from the north, perhaps out by Erie Road, the main road that passed in front of the subdivision. His first instinct was to ignore the gunfight. Mark didn't need to go looking for trouble. Trouble was sure to find him soon enough.

But what if regular people, like Darren and me, are being attacked by the horde?

Racing motors and screeching tires came next, followed by more shots. A car crashed, the sound echoing through the still night air. Mark picked up the rifle he had set on the deck. Darren was in the house getting ready for bed. Mark had taught Darren never to leave the room when Mark was away. Darren would be safe. Mark ran for the woods behind the house. He took a fast, yet careful, path toward the shots. The twenty-five-foot wide swathe of trees and undergrowth had been left in place during development to act as a buffer between the houses, condos, and senior apartments behind them.

The woods ran the entire length of the subdivision from Erie to Little Road at the back.

Mark moved slower as he drew near the road. There was a lull in the shooting and voices not too far away. Again, the sound of motors filled the night. Was this some stupid form of drag racing? Then another crash occurred followed by a scream and more gunshots.

Mark stopped at the edge of the woods, about twenty feet from the street. Four cars had stopped on the road to the right. All four cars had their headlights on and their engines running, but they appeared empty. A fifth car had crashed head-on into a tree on the far side of the road. About forty feet separated the four cars from another car and an SUV, on the left. The car's engine was off and sat on an angle across the road. The SUV was on its side in front of the car.

In the shadows beyond the lights, people converged on the two vehicles on the left. A shot came from inside the SUV. Answering rounds pinged off the undercarriage.

A woman's body hung out of the flipped SUV's window. Whoever was inside the car was trying to start it but it wouldn't catch. Someone was crying inside the car. A female pleaded, "Oh God! Please."

The engine cranked again but didn't start.

A man shouted, "Start the damn car!"

"I'm trying," the woman driver said.

The crying continued. It was hard to determine how many people were inside the car. In her panic, the driver had flooded the engine.

Mark lowered to a prone position and used his scope to see what he was up against. He had counted seven people when someone entered the woods on his right. He turned his head slowly and spotted two men trying to flank the two target vehicles.

At that moment, no one was firing. The attackers were

closing in on their prey. The people in the car cranked the ignition over and over, but it refused to start. The battery was growing weaker. In the SUV, someone poked his head up.

As the two men crashed through the brush, Mark slid his hand down and drew his knife. The first man stepped right over Mark without noticing him but the second man stepped on Mark's back. Mark didn't move or make a sound. The man was on and off him before his curiosity made him look down. At that instant, Mark lunged up, impaling the man to the hilt. The man yelled but Mark clamped a hand over his mouth.

The other man turned and advanced toward Mark. Pulling the blade free, Mark threw the dying man forward into the second, causing him to fall backward. Before he could catch his balance, Mark was on him. He drove a punch into the man's face, then grabbed the man by the hair and pulled, exposing the neck. He sliced through the throat and pushed the man's face into the dirt.

Mark collected their handguns sticking them in his belt at his back, their weight heavy and awkward. He crawled back to his original position and scanned the scene. One man had worked his way to the underside of the SUV. No one inside could see him, but as he climbed the undercarriage a scream came from within. If that man reached the top, he could shoot down through the windows into the interior of the vehicle. That gunman was the most immediate threat.

Mark lined up the shot and squeezed off a round. The man fell against the SUV and slid to the ground. Without waiting to see if he stayed down, Mark swung to his second target, a man who had just reached the trunk of the stalled car and was readying a shot through the rear window. Mark dropped him on the trunk. A third shooter behind a tree not ten feet from the car's windshield took a bullet to the side of his head.

The remaining targets disappeared. Some began shooting blindly into the woods. They weren't accurate, but the wild shots forced Mark to keep his head down. Backing up about ten feet, he crawled farther to his left to get a different angle.

Four gunmen remained.

A man wiggled free of the SUV, climbing out of the window. Sitting on the door frame, he fired three quick shots at random then jumped down and ran for the car with the people trapped inside. Before Mark could lay down covering fire to protect the running man, two shots struck the man in the back, sending him skidding face first on the road.

Someone screamed from the car. The front passenger door opened and a tall man stepped out, holding a gun. His left arm dangled at his side. He'd been wounded.

A woman shouted from the car, "John, no!"

John ran to the fallen man and tried to pick him up. A flurry of shots tore into his body, dropping him next to the first man.

"John!"

"Daddy!"

The shots exposed one of the shooters and Mark took advantage by dropping him.

Suddenly, to the right, headlights lit up the woods, blinding Mark. With the light in his eyes, it was impossible to see in that direction. Exposed, he had to move. Mark scampered for the slim cover of a small tree and pulled out a handgun. The car moved forward, keeping Mark highlighted. Reaching around the tree, he fired at the headlights. The car stopped ten feet from the tree line. It took six shots to put them both out.

In the meantime, bullets ripped through the trees all around him. Mark moved. He ran to his right, trying to use the stopped car as a shield. The driver slipped out the passenger side, running for the safety of the cars parked on the street. Mark fired until the man fell. Quickly he squatted behind the car and switched guns.

Mark waited for the barrage directed at him to die down, then dashed into the street to the first car. The motor was running, the window down. Mark reached in and put the car in gear. With the headlights now in the attacker's faces, Mark waited for the car to move past him then ran behind it, stopping at the trunk of the next vehicle in line. Staying low, Mark moved along the passenger side to the front bumper.

Shots pinged off the moving car as the men tried to put out the headlights. Switching back to the rifle he steadied his elbow on the hood. Mark sighted on a man sneaking up on the stalled car from behind. Mark shot him.

The rifle was empty. He was down to one half-empty handgun. Movement in his peripheral vision grabbed his attention. A man Mark had not seen leaned out the passenger side window, gun in hand. Mark dove in front of the car as the bullet grazed the left side of his head. The wound burned, but he pushed the pain aside. He wasn't sure if there were any other shooters left. If so, he could be trapped between them and the gunman in the car.

Mark took a quick, nervous look around him. He didn't see anyone else. Maybe there was just the one shooter left. Then, the engine of the car behind him started. The man was going to try to run him over. Mark dove and rolled to his right just as the car shot forward. The front wheel missed his leg by inches.

He stopped his roll and pushed up to one knee. The car stopped as the driver leaned forward in his seat. His head turned as if trying to locate Mark. Mark took the shot as the driver looked straight at him. The glass shattered, the man's head rocked back, and his body slumped over the wheel.

Keeping his gun trained on the body, Mark sped to the car. The man did not move as Mark touched his head with the gun barrel. He reached through the broken window and turned off the engine. The act of shutting down the car ignited a memory. Mark turned around fast.

What had happened to the moving car? It should have crashed into the SUV by then.

The car was no longer where it should have been. The wheels had been turned. There was someone at the wheel. Mark moved toward the turning car with his gun up. Just then the car accelerated, squealing its tires as it straightened out. The driver shot through the open window but was looking down the road. Mark ducked.

With the car pulling away, Mark emptied his gun trying for a lucky shot to stop the man's escape. He stood and watched the taillights get smaller.

Damn!

The escaped man would bring others.

Eight

AFTER MAKING SURE THERE were no more surprises, Mark approached the two target vehicles with caution.

"Hello in the cars," he called. "All of the men who were attacking you are gone. It is safe to come out."

He waited but there was no response.

"Look, if I wanted to harm you, I would have waited for them to kill you and then taken care of them." He walked closer to the SUV, which served as a screen to protect him in case anyone shot from the car.

Other than the woman's body hanging out the window, Mark couldn't tell if there was anyone else inside.

"Is anyone in there?" Mark climbed the undercarriage until his head was even with the body. Soft crying drifted up, like someone trying hard not to let sobs escape.

"Are you hurt?" Mark spoke in a soft, reassuring voice, but he was tense, not knowing if there would be a gun pointed at him.

From the other car, a woman yelled, "You stay away from there!"

Mark crawled along the rear passenger door until he could look down into the interior of the SUV. As his vision adjusted to the darkness, Mark found a second body in the driver's seat. Movement in the back seat brought his focus on a teenage girl. She lay against the opposite door, her body twisted sideways. She held a hand to her forehead. Mark couldn't tell if she was cut or just in shock.

Mark studied her for a moment. Her legs were under the front seat. A portion of the roof had collapsed and the door Mark lay on had buckled when the SUV rolled. The door wouldn't open when he tried it.

The front seat, with a dead man in it, lay across her lap. Careful not to spook her or get himself hurt, Mark climbed in while the woman in the other car continued to scream. When Mark pulled out his knife, the girl's eyes lit up with fear.

"It's all right; don't panic. I'm just going to cut your seat belt so you can climb out."

The girl whimpered. She closed her eyes and turned her head away from Mark. The knife cut through the belt easily.

"Are you able to move? There's nothing broken, is there?"

"I-I don't think so."

"Does anything hurt?"

"Just my head."

A good size gash lined her forehead.

"Take my hand and see if you can pull loose."

She hesitated at first but gripped his hand. Her body moved upwards, but her legs were still stuck. Mark tried to pull harder, but she let out a cry of pain.

"Tell me where you're stuck."

"My ankles."

"Okay, hold on, I'll to move the seat."

Mark angled so he could reach across the dead man's body to the controls on the far side of the seat. He couldn't see where they were but felt for them, found the right one, and got the seat to move forward. Mark

51

climbed back out the window and reached down.

"Give me your hands. When I pull, try to point your toes down if you can."

She winced but otherwise pulled clear. When she was free, she gave him a brief hug. Mark took her hand and led her around the flipped vehicle. When the occupants of the car saw the girl was safe, they called to her and Mark let go of her hand.

"Go on," he said and she limped toward the car. Now that he was closer Mark saw several people inside. The rear door opened and someone reached out to pull her in. The door slammed and the engine coughed again. The driver continued to turn the key but the engine kept cranking while the battery grew weaker.

Mark squatted next to John and the other man. Both men were dead. The woman in the driver's seat watched him, perhaps waiting for Mark to give the final ruling on the two men. Their eyes locked for a moment and Mark shook his head. The woman choked back a sob. Mark stood and walked closer to the car. As if fearing he might get too close, the driver turned the key several times in succession. Each turn drained the battery further.

"I think you flooded the engine," Mark said. "It may not start right away. Do you want me to take a look at it?"

There was no response. The driver tried starting it again. The starter barely cranked.

"It's not going to start." Mark shook his head as the driver tried once more. "Look, I've got a house not far from here. Let's get you all to safety for the night and in the morning I can jump the car and get you going. There's no telling who else might have heard all that noise. Others could be — "

He froze. In the distance were tiny white dots. Multiple sets of headlights were coming toward them.

"Damn! You're out of time. We have to make a run for

it. We only have a few minutes before they'll be here."
No one moved. "Run, damnit!" The driver's door opened
and the woman's head appeared over the roof.

"But what about the food and water?" the woman
asked.

"You can't use it if you're dead," Mark shouted.

The woman looked in all directions, as if searching for
answers there. She wiped her tear-streaked face. "I don't
know what to do."

"I'll keep you safe, but we have to leave now. Grab
some of your food. We'll come back in the morning.
Move or I'll have to leave you here." He started running
toward the attacker's cars. "Get into those woods and
start walking. I'll catch up to you in a minute."

Mark couldn't waste time watching over them; he'd
done all he could. He was not going to die because they
were afraid to trust him. He hopped in a car and started
it. Backing it up Mark turned it around so it was heading
back in the direction of the oncoming cars. Making sure
the wheel was as straight as it could be Mark opened the
door, stepped on the accelerator, and jumped out. He
landed on his hands and feet and scrambled away from
the car. He hoped it would keep moving and stay
straight enough to delay the approaching vehicles. If
nothing else, with the headlights in their faces, they
would not be able to see which direction Mark went.

He repeated the same thing with another car but had
nothing to wedge against the pedal. He ran back to the
car where the group was still trying to decide what to do.
Their lack of progress was annoying. Mark reached into
the trunk, grabbed a case of water, and shoved it into a
teenage boy's hands.

"That way. Go." He pushed him toward the woods.
He repeated the process with a bag of groceries, sending
two teenage girls on their way. The woman took a box of
food. Mark took a case of water.

"Come on. We have to get your family to safety."
Mark looked down the road and yelled, "Hurry, get off
the road! Those white dots are headlights. They'll be here
in minutes. We have to move – now!"

Finally, their movements took on some urgency.
Everyone ran for the woods. Mark sprinted to the front,
ducking branches and dodging trees. "Follow me. Stay
close. And keep quiet."

They might not trust him, but they followed. He set a
fast pace, wanting to get as far away from the wreckage
as possible before reinforcements arrived. The Horde, as
Mark termed the city dwellers, would know that any
survivors had left on foot and would give pursuit. The
woods would be an obvious destination for anyone
trying to hide. Mark needed to throw them off.

About seventy-five yards from the street, Mark moved
right and left the safety of the woods. They came out in a
parking lot of a senior housing complex. Mark said,
"Keep moving along the tree line. You'll be able to move
faster."

The woman asked, "Where are you going?"

Mark ripped two bottles of water from the plastic
wrapped case. "A little misdirection. Keep going. I'll
catch up."

Mark ran about ten yards from the group and tossed
the bottles as far into the parking lot as he could to make
it appear they had gone that way. Then Mark ran back
and caught up to the group. Immediately he increased
his pace, even though the family was dropping farther
behind. If they thought they might be left in the woods to
fend for themselves, they might be more motivated to
move. He went three houses past his house then listened
for sounds of pursuit before crossing through the woods
to the other side and doubling back.

Mark led them to the rear door. He waited until they
were all on the deck before going inside. Darren

wouldn't open the secret room door unless he heard the signal Mark taught him, just as Mark never entered without giving the signal. He wasn't sure yet he wanted to expose Darren and the secret room to these new people.

Once inside the house, Mark said, "The door right there."

He pointed to the basement door. The older of the two teenage girls walked over and pulled it open. Mark nodded to the woman. She hesitated, perhaps fearing they were entering a trap. Then, taking a deep breath as if drawing in courage, she went down followed by a girl and a teenage boy. The first girl looked at Mark and waited.

"Go ahead," he told her, "I'm going to make sure we weren't followed."

She nodded and ran down the stairs.

After fifteen minutes, Mark joined them. In the basement, the group had dropped everything. The children sat together near the watching woman. The boy had an arm around one of the girls. They were both crying.

Mark scanned the dark room trying to decide where best to hide them. They looked at him with some suspicion. He couldn't blame them. They were scared and had just lost family members. For now they were safe. Mark didn't know what to say to them.

"Thank you for helping us," the woman said. She was slender and her dyed blonde hair was a mess.

Mark had to decide if he should show them his inner sanctum. He didn't know these people and wasn't sure it would be smart to give away his secrets, especially if they didn't stay. If he were alone, Mark would be more willing to take the risk, but he had Darren's safety to consider. For now Darren was safe

"Make yourselves comfortable. I'll go dig up some

blankets and things so you can make a place to sleep. Kids, why don't you clear some space here, okay?"

He jogged upstairs and crept through the kitchen. Mark stopped and peered out the kitchen window.

Damn! Was someone out there in the trees?

He watched for several minutes. Nothing moved. Keeping low, Mark moved into the foyer then raced up the stairs.

In the linen closet, he grabbed sheets and a few blankets. There were two extra pillows as well. He went into his son's room and pulled the bedspread, sheets, and pillows off the bed. With his arms full, Mark moved to the first floor. He went through the living room and dining room to avoid the full-length patio door. As he moved into the kitchen, he glanced out the window.

Someone had tracked them. Two men emerged from the trees in Summer's backyard. They scanned the area with flashlights and one pointed at Mark's house.

He dropped to a squat and opened the basement door. Dropping everything he was carrying, he kicked it all down the stairs and pulled his gun, before closing the door and hurrying down the stairs.

"There are at least two men outside. They don't seem to know where to look. We must be quiet."

The decision to unveil the hideout could no longer wait. If anyone came inside the house, there would be little chance to get everyone inside the safe room without making noise. He needed to move the family now. If he didn't, he'd be trapped in the open too with no way to get into the room without being seen. He sighed as his four new charges looked at him.

After risking so much to save them, he couldn't put them in danger now. Mark went to the wall and knocked in the code he'd taught Darren. He doubted the boy would actually shoot as Mark instructed him to do if someone entered without using the code, but he wasn't about to chance it.

Mark pulled open the panel.

"Darren, it's just me and a few friends. It's all right. Everyone, pick up the blankets and pillows and come in here, quick."

The kids looked toward the woman for direction.

Mark looked at her too. "Please, hurry. If someone comes in the house, we won't be safe here."

The woman told the teens to move. The three kids scooped up the blankets and pillows and entered the room.

With everyone inside, Mark closed the door. "Sit on the floor and stay quiet."

It was like being back in elementary school and having to sit in the halls during a tornado drill, except this was no drill.

They waited like that for quite a while. Mark transferred the cables for the security cameras from the generator to the car batteries. The monitor fired up with grainy images of the outside of the house. He separated the screen into four different viewpoints. In the surveillance video from the backyard, two armed men walked from right to left across the screen. They stopped to stare at the house then continued off the screen. When the men didn't reappear in close to an hour, Mark decided it might be safe, at least for the moment.

"I'm afraid you'll have to sleep on the floor for now. It'll be cramped but we should be safe."

No one spoke. They spread out the bedspread first to give some cushion to the floor. When they were all situated as best they could be the oldest girl asked, "What do you do for a bathroom?"

Mark smiled. "It's best that you wait. It wouldn't be too good if you were using the bathroom when someone walked in on you. Can you wait for a bit?"

"I think so," she said. She brushed her hair behind her

ears. Mark could see a resemblance to her mother. The girl looked to be about sixteen.

"Oh, you're bleeding," the red-haired girl said.

Mark's hand went to the graze on his head and he winced. He had forgotten about it.

"May I?" asked the woman. She lifted a sheet as if to tear it.

"Yes, of course."

The woman tore a long strip from the sheet and wrapped it around Mark's head. She had a practiced, gentle touch that sent a surprising jolt through his body. She finished, stepped back, and smiled down at him.

"Thank you," he said. He wanted to introduce himself and Darren. *But if they were leaving in the morning, why bother?*

Nearly thirty minutes later, the stalkers still had not returned. Mark had Darren show the girl the facilities.

As each person took a turn at the makeshift bathroom, Mark switched the wires to the door alarms. They were rigged so a beep would sound in the room but not throughout the house. When everyone was back inside, he sealed the door and turned off the lights.

With sleep refusing to come, Mark listened as someone cried softly. It had been a difficult and tragic night, but Mark was sure of two things. His supplies would dwindle fast with this many people, and the Horde was getting closer.

Nine

MARK WOKE TO THE sound of whispered voices. He opened his eyes and strained to hear what was being said.

A female voice said, "Will he let us leave or are we his prisoners?"

Another female responded. "I didn't get that impression, but no one will hold us against our will."

"And no one *will* hold you against your will," Mark said. He sat up and turned to face the group. "I didn't rescue you to make you my prisoners. If you are not comfortable here, you are free to leave whenever you want."

The mother spoke. "It's not that we aren't grateful for your help. We, uh, there's someplace we're trying to go."

"Okay," Mark said. "But your car will need a jump. Let's eat breakfast first. That will give me a chance to scan the area for any intruders. Can you wait that long?"

She looked at the kids. "Yes, I guess we can."

"Okay. Everyone knows where the bathroom is. You can take turns. Darren and I will prepare a meal. After that, I'll lead you back to your car."

"We can find our way from here. We'll just take what we brought. You don't have to be bothered."

"Well, first of all, it's not a bother. You certainly can take your belongings with you and if you need anything else just ask. If I have it, I'll share."

The woman sucked in her lip and chewed it. Mark thought she was scared.

"I'll lead you back to your car. I will help you start it. Then I'll watch to make sure you drive off safely." The mother started to respond but Mark cut her off. "Please, don't argue. If you want to go, I'm going to escort you. Besides can you jump a car?"

"Yes," she said with defiance.

"Do you have jumper cables?"

She worried at her lip again. "No" she admitted.

"Well then, it's settled."

Mark passed out granola bars and fruit cups to everyone. He poured a box of cereal into a large bowl and set it in the middle of the group. They ate from the bowl like they were eating popcorn. Mark gave each person a plastic bottle of an orange drink.

While they ate, Mark asked, "Where were you trying to go last night?"

No one spoke. Mark frowned. They were afraid to say where their destination was. He gazed at the woman as if to say, *"Really?"*

She blushed. "We were going to Indiana to meet some family."

"Oh. Have you had any communication with them?"

"Not after the phones died, but everyone was all right then."

Mark nodded. He hoped that was still the case. "Well, if things don't turn out the way you hope, you know where to find us."

"Thank you. We'll keep that in mind."

"You realize, I hope, that your belongings have most likely been scavenged by the Horde?"

"The Horde?" the boy asked.

"That's the name we use for the bad guys," Darren explained.

"You mean the people who chased us?" the redhead said. "They're the Horde?"

"It's just a name I gave them. I'm not sure how many of them there are, but they live in the town you passed through."

The woman asked, "Would they take the car too?"

"I don't know. They might. But there are lots of cars around. Of course, they won't have your stuff in them but you can get cars and stuff anywhere now."

After finishing their meal, Mark went to the second floor with his binoculars. He moved from room to room, trying to see if anyone was waiting outside for them. A good twenty minutes later, Mark descended.

"I think it's clear. If you still want to go, now would be a good time to leave.

Mark went into the garage and returned with jumper cables coiled around one shoulder. The binoculars still hung around his neck. The small party, excluding Darren, left the house and jogged into the cover of the woods.

Reaching the end of the trees, Mark grabbed the woman's arm to keep her from walking out in the open.

Mark spoke in a harsh whisper, "If there's someone out there lying in wait, you'll be an easy target. Let me check it out first." He crept on his hands and knees until he was able to see the wreckage from the night before. The SUV and the car were still where they had been. The other cars were still there as well.

That seemed wrong somehow. Why wouldn't they have taken them? The only ones missing were the two Mark sent down the road.

The woman came up next to him.

"Look," she said, excited. "They never touched the cars. All our stuff is still there."

"There is no way they'd leave food and water, just no possible way. I think it's a trap. They're hoping to lure you out."

The mother looked from Mark to the street. She panned right to left and back.

The taller girl said, "What do you think, Mom? What if he's right?"

Mark felt the hair on the back his neck stand up. His group was making too much noise. His eyes flicked in rapid succession, taking in the woman's car, the SUV, the attacker's cars – and that was where he stopped. Something about the green Buick bothered him.

He stared hard, trying to understand what was making him tense. He reached out and took the woman's arm without looking away from the car.

"What …?"

"Shh!"

Mark pulled her slowly back toward him. *If it was a trap, what were they waiting for?* Mark let the cables slide off his arm to the ground.

One of the girls said, "I'm scared."

Mark continued to stare. Something inside the car was wrong. Then he saw what had spooked him. The pendant hanging from the rearview mirror was swaying. Someone was in the car.

Mark pulled the woman behind him. "Get back," Mark commanded, raising his gun. A face popped up in the window and Mark fired.

"Go back!" he ordered. He backed up with his gun ready. All at once a group of men showed themselves and fired. Mark returned their fire in a hurry, more to keep the shooter's heads down than to hit them.

A bullet hit the tree near his head. He ducked. *Where did that shot come from?* A scream brought his attention to the rear. Someone was *behind* them.

They were cut off.

"Get down," he said and rolled on his back, facing the way they had come. A man ran toward them, taking wild shots. Mark shot from a lower trajectory, upward. The bullet went in under the man's chin, exiting the back of his head in a red plume. He dropped to his knees and fell face first not six feet away.

Mark fired several shots at random to make the other attackers seek cover. He scurried forward, snatched the dead man's gun, then reversed direction as fast as he could crawl.

Bullets tore through the trees from front and back. There had to be at least half a dozen men out on the street. No telling how many were behind them. He needed some serious help. He handed the gun to the woman.

"Stay behind a tree and fire shots back into the woods. Space them out so you don't run out too fast. Don't worry about hitting anything. I just want to keep them away from us. All of you keep down and stay behind a tree."

He turned back to the street to see if he could even the odds a little. Mark slid the rifle off his shoulder and rolled on his stomach. He scooted forward for a better view of the street. Three men felt safe enough to leave the cover of the cars and dash toward the woods. Mark sighted and shot the first man in the chest. He swung the barrel and planted another round in the top of a second man's head as he dove to the ground for cover. The third man scurried back behind one of the cars.

The teenage boy crawled up next to him.

"I can shoot if you give me your gun. I'll go back and help my mom."

Mark looked in the kid's eyes and wondered if the boy could actually shoot another human. Even if he couldn't, it was still good to have the extra firepower.

"Make your shots count. We have a limited supply of

ammo." He handed over the 9mm.

From out front, a voice called out, "Hey, you in the trees. Let's make a deal."

Mark didn't respond. Instead, he reloaded the rifle's five-shot magazine.

"I'll let you go if you give me the women. In fact, I could use a man like you, so I'll offer you safety as well, as long as you join us. What'd'ya say?"

"I don't think so," Mark said to himself. Mark looked behind him to see how the others were doing. The two girls hid behind a tree, curled in balls with their arms over their heads. The boy looked to the rear. The woman watched Mark, a frightened look in her eyes as the proposal was laid out.

"Joining us can't be worse than dyin'. We won't hurt the girls ... we'll just use them."

Someone else out front added with a laugh, "Yeah, a lot."

Panic and terror enlivened the girls' faces. Mark leaned toward them. "They're trying to scare you. I'm not going to let them get near you."

Just then, a man ran straight at them from behind a tree not ten feet away. He fired an off-balance shot that hit the tree above the girls' heads. They both screamed while Mark rolled for cover. Two more shots followed, then a loud crash. Someone was crying. Mark crawled to the woman. Her hands shook, tears flowing, but he didn't see any blood.

He grabbed her shoulders. "Listen to me, are you hit?"

She shook her head. From a few feet away the boy said, "We both shot him. I think she's just upset."

"So am I. Do you see any more behind us?"

"No, I think it was just those two."

"Then I need you to lead them back to my house. You think you can do that?"

He nodded. "Yeah, I think so."

"Do you remember how to get there?"

"Yeah,"

"Okay, girls, follow your brother." He turned to the mother. "Hey, pull yourself together, your children need you. Go with them now."

She wiped her eyes and started to follow. "Be strong for them," Mark added.

MARK MOVED TO A new location and used the scope to find the four remaining men. Two were behind each of the two cars, crouching behind the tires. One man sat on the ground with his legs outstretched. Getting as low as he could for a better angle, Mark was at eye level with the space between the undercarriage and the ground. A box of ammunition sat on the ground next to the man. He was reloading and didn't realize his legs were exposed.

Taking careful aim, just as he had been trained so many years ago in the Marines, Mark lined up the shot and fired. The bullet hit the man in the leg. The wounded man howled and rolled to the ground, clutching his leg. Mark was ready. He could see just enough of the man's head to make the shot work. Mark had no angle for a straight on shot so he bounced the bullet off the street inches from the small portion of head he could see. The howling stopped.

All three remaining men were up, shooting and running for the car farthest from Mark. They piled in and the driver floored the accelerator in reverse. Mark tried a shot at the driver, but as he pulled the trigger, the driver swerved the car in a one hundred and eighty-degree turn. The bullet shattered the passenger side window, showering the occupants with glass. They were gone before Mark could get off another shot.

Mark ran after the mother and the kids. When he caught them, he shouted, "Wait!" He ran in front of them and stopped. "They're gone. We have one chance to get your things and get away. Now's the time, so it's up to you. But I'd hate to leave anything for those scavengers."

The mother looked at the children. "I-I don't know what to do."

"Don't think, *do*. Let's go, Hurry."

Mark led them back to the road. No new cars had arrived. They would have maybe fifteen to twenty minutes to take what they wanted and run. With the others hanging back in the tree line, Mark stripped the bodies of any weapons and the box of ammo. When the others came out of the trees, the mother stopped over the body of her husband while the others stood back and watched. Mark said nothing, allowing her a moment to grieve.

She wrapped her arms around her children, but no tears were shed. The redhead stood over the other fallen man. It was time to interrupt. Mark walked to the group. "I'm sorry, but we have to move now."

No one moved. Mark handed his binoculars to the redhead.

"I need you to go down to the end of that last car and keep looking down the road. If you see anything moving at all you tell me immediately, okay?"

"Okay." She took the binoculars. When she looked up at him, tears had filled her eyes. He gave her shoulder a reassuring squeeze.

"I'm sorry. I promise I'll come back and we can bury all of them. Right now though we have to stay safe. Can you to do this?" She nodded and walked off.

"Okay," he said, walking to the other three. "Get in your car. Let's try to get it started before they come back. You two start transferring everything from the SUV to the car. Hurry now."

Mark took the keys from the ignition of the SUV and popped the tailgate. As the kids unloaded, he raced back into the woods and retrieved the jumper cables. He ran to the first car the attackers left, a red Camaro and found the key in the ignition. Mark started the Camaro and moved it to the woman's car. Attaching the cables, he let it run for a bit

He glanced around the hood. The woman stood sucking on her lip. She was obviously afraid, but he marveled at her inner strength and her ability to go on in spite of that fear. Their eyes met and in that instant, he knew he would do whatever he could to protect her.

He nodded at her, then instructed Lynn to start the car. It almost caught. It would need a few more minutes. He went to the SUV and helped unload.

The SUV empty, Mark said, "You two go into the woods. Strip the bodies of anything useful, especially their guns."

The kids raced off without a word.

"Okay, try it again."

This time, the engine caught with a roar. Mark almost didn't hear the girl call to him as he reached under the hood to remove the cables.

"Ah, whatever your name is," the girl with binoculars called, "something's coming."

Mark slammed the hood shut. "Quick, come here," he yelled.

She handed him the binoculars. What Mark saw put a chill into him. There was an entire caravan of cars and trucks led by a semi, barreling down on them.

They were out of time.

"You," he pointed to the girl, "go with the other two. Tell them to run back to the house. Get into the safe room and do not move from there. What are you waiting for?" he screamed. "Go!"

The girl broke into a sprint and disappeared into the woods. Mark ran to the woman's window.

"Go to the next corner and turn left. About a quarter

mile down there is a small shopping center. Turn in there and go all the way to the back. You'll see a senior center back there. Park the car so it's hidden behind the building, then cut through the woods. You'll come out at the back of my house. Keep them quiet. I have a feeling they're going to do a very thorough search this time. Please take care of Darren." Mark tapped a pattern on the roof. "That's the signal to get into the safe room without him shooting you. Hurry!"

Mark started to move, but she reached out and grabbed his arm. "What are you going to do?"

"I'm going to try to lead them away from here."

"Oh God, please be careful. And come back." Her eyes held the fear that he felt.

He smiled to reassure her. "I'll be all right. Now go. Hurry."

She put the car in drive and sped off. Mark climbed in the Camaro and waited a few seconds to make sure his pursuers could see him. He had maybe a mile head start, so he floored it and the powerful car jumped.

Lynn made her turn south. Mark, making sure the pursuit followed him, eased off the gas and pumped the brakes several times, so the brake lights flashed on. Then he sped off straight down the road, heading west. As he drove, Mark tried to recall details of the road ahead, trying to think about someplace to ditch the car. He would then work his way back to his house on foot.

The car was fast, but then he noticed the low gas gauge. He wouldn't make it very far.

As he increased his lead, he looked in the rearview mirror. The semi plowed straight through the cars on the road, throwing them to the side like toys. Several vehicles turned to follow Lynn. There was nothing he could do about it now. He hoped she was already hidden. Mark flew past other subdivisions. Could there be anyone else alive in any of them? About three miles farther, the road made a long curve and he moved into a rural area. A small copse of trees blocked the view from behind, but the road continued on. He eased off the gas, then changed his mind. It would be obvious to those chasing him that he'd turned off. He raced on.

Mark had a location in mind. The road curved sharply to the right, continuing for a short distance before curving back. Farm buildings lined the left side of the road. They wouldn't offer cover for long, but it would do for his purposes. After the first curve, a road came up to the right. Mark took the turn a little too fast, flashing the brake lights to tip his pursuers off that he was slowing for the turn. The rear end swung off the pavement, ending up on the grass at an upward angle. When Mark stepped on the gas, the wheels spun. He had to either get the car out of sight or get out and run. He rocked the car forward and back, trying to get the tire to dig in. "Come on!"

Finding it difficult to breathe, Mark was about to give up and run when the wheels began to pull. The car climbed slowly at first, then jumped forward, almost overshooting the narrow road before he was able to right the car. Forty feet in front of him, a small concrete bridge crossed a creek. The creek was bordered on both sides by large trees with lots of undergrowth, offering cover from the main road.

Mark crossed the bridge and turned a hard right along the creek, behind the trees. The ground sloped down from the road. He drove along the edge of a wheat field that even without proper care from the farmer was growing well. He tore through the fender-high brown plants until he had gone about a hundred yards.

Angling the front end toward the creek and into the brush, Mark cut the engine. He got out and listened. Roaring engines approached. His breathing became short and quick. The convoy passed by on the main road, the sound of engines fading.

Bathed in sweat from panic, he acknowledged how close he had been to capture. But he wasn't in the clear yet. Mark worked the car deeper into the trees near the stream, trying to hide it should anyone double back to check the road he'd turned on.

He grabbed his rifle and binoculars and searched the car for anything else he could use. Jogging along the tree line, he headed back the way he'd come. As Mark ran, he felt for his 9mm. He no longer had it. He'd given it to the teenage boy and never got it back. He pulled the magazine from the rifle. Two bullets left. There were no more rounds in his pockets.

He was in big trouble if he had to shoot it out. His only other weapon was the survival knife he wore on his belt. Mark would have to be very careful. If they found him, the end would come quickly.

Ten

As NIGHT FELL, Mark found himself at the edge of a subdivision. For most of the day, he had stayed hidden in the trees. Now he was only a hundred yards north of Erie Road. Several times he'd seen cars on Erie, running in both directions. They must have realized he'd turned off somewhere and were searching. They were not giving up the hunt.

Mark hopped the split-rail fence that was common to most subdivisions in the area and scurried to a house. He would have to break in and hopefully find a weapon. He didn't want to do it so close to the road. Working his way from house to house, Mark made his way to the center to the subdivision.

He was about to make a dash across the street when he heard a car. Mark dove behind some rose bushes at the front of the house and lay still. The car came around a bend in the road. Two people sat in the front seat, searching for him with a hand-held spotlight that swept from one side of the street to the other.

The Horde must really want him. If they were patrolling the subdivisions and side streets, it would be difficult to get through. Once the car was out of sight, Mark sprinted across the street, ran between two houses, and hopped the rear fence. At the next house, he went to the sliding patio door. Locked. He didn't have any tools to break in without making noise.

He tried hacking away at the lock plate with his knife but it was futile. Most of those types of doors had a deadbolt lock and a wooden stick or metal bar in the base track to prevent exactly what he was trying to do. In the end, he took the butt of the rifle and rammed it through the window. As he reached through to unlock the door, a piece of glass fell and sliced his arm. He swore. He should have found a door that swung inward instead of on a glide. It would have been easier to gain entry. In the end, he couldn't reach the piece of broomstick cut to fit the door and had to knock all the glass out so he could step through.

The first thing Mark did was move to the front window to see if anything was happening on the street. He watched for several minutes and then the same car drove past. How many men were in the Horde? Were there enough to station a patrol in every development? It might be easier to move to another location and not return to his house. Then he thought about Lynn, Darren, and the kids.

They needed him. Or maybe, he needed them.

When the car passed beyond view, Mark went about searching the house. There were no weapons. Probably the only house in the area without a gun and he had to break into it. At least he found some bottled water. He drank one down and opened a can of almonds. Mark found gauze and tape in a cabinet and bandaged his arm.

While he rested, Mark tried to decide his next move. The Horde was no longer just a bunch of people trying to kill each other. Somehow they had organized. They were still killing, but now they were killing other people. The large man at Summer's, could he be the reason the Horde worked more like an army now? He had acted like the leader.

Mark relieved himself in their bathroom then went out the rear door. Two more streets and the subdivision ended. He was at a main cross street. The other side was farmland and wide open for a long distance. The crop was low to the ground. In order to stay hidden, Mark would have to go into the field. If he got caught in the open, he would not survive. The alternative was to move farther down the road and cross by the farmhouse. It all depended on how much he wanted to gamble.

Mark opted for the house. Once there, he decided to break in. Most farmers would have a gun. The large house probably dated back to the turn of the nineteenth century. It had a wrap-around porch and three stories. Three outbuildings behind the house would offer good cover when he moved on.

Stopping at the side door, he took out his knife. Mark fitted the blade under the latch. The door swung open and he stared down the double barrels of a shotgun.

"You best get away from this house now," a man said. He was tall and had a head of wild black hair and a full beard to go with it.

But just as Mark raised his hands and backed away from the door, he heard a car motor. He turned his head and saw the cones of light growing on the street. "Oh, shit."

The farmer stepped forward to see what Mark was looking at. Without hesitation, Mark pushed up the barrels, twisted, and yanked the gun forward, out of the unsuspecting man's hands. Mark stepped into the house and placed the knife under the man's chin. With his foot, he reached back and closed the door.

They were on a small landing with steps going in both directions. Headlights turned up the gravel driveway.

"Damn! Look, you're going to have to trust me on this," Mark whispered. "If you make a sound we're both gonna die. Move down the stairs away from the window." Hoping it wasn't a mistake, he removed the knife from the man's chin.

As the man moved, Mark flipped the lock on the door. A car door shut. Someone approached to check the house. He stepped down the steps and pressed himself against the block wall.

"These people are killers. You don't want them to see you."

"How do I know you're not the killer and they're hunting you?"

"Because, if I were, I would have cut your throat with the knife."

Someone tried the doorknob. A face pressed up against the pane.

"Looks deserted," Mark heard someone say. Shoes crunching on the gravel announced the man working his way around the house.

"Is there any other way in other than the front porch?" Mark whispered.

"There's a back door off the kitchen."

"Is it locked?"

"Should be."

"All right, just hold on a little bit longer. When they go, I'll leave too."

A few long minutes later, the car backed down the driveway and Mark let his breath out in relief. The man eyed him warily.

"Okay, I'll get out of your hair now. Back all the way down the stairs."

"Why?"

"Oh, geez, just do it, would you?"

"You're gonna shoot me when I get down there, ain't you?"

"Look, I'm gonna set your shotgun down and leave. I just want to make sure you're far enough away from it

74

that you don't shoot me in the back while I'm leaving."

The man hesitated.

Mark sighed. "All right, forget it. I'll do it this way." He cracked the shotgun open and pulled out the shells. Then he set it down on the stairs on the far side of the door.

"I'll take these with me," Mark said, putting them in his pocket.

"But them's the only two shells I got," the man complained.

"What? How do you have a shotgun and only have two shells?"

"Well, I kept meaning to go get me another box but I just never done it. Who knew the world was gonna get so crazy?"

Mark sighed again. "When I leave I'll pitch them back inside."

"You really ain't gonna shoot me?"

"No, but those others wouldn't have hesitated."

"Who were those fellas?"

"A very nasty gang of scavengers and killers you never want to meet."

"Why they chasing you?"

"They were trying to kill a couple of families who drove through their territory. I stepped in and stopped them."

"What happened to the families?"

"Well, some were killed before I got there. The others, I hope, are safely hidden at my house. I led the killers away and now I'm trying to get back home."

"Huh, well, come on up and sit a spell," the farmer said, climbing the stairs past Mark. "You want a beer?"

Mark didn't know what to do. The man picked up the shotgun and pushed open the door at the top of the stairs. "Well, come on. I ain't had no one to talk to since my wife passed."

Mark followed him into a large country kitchen. The man set the shotgun down on a counter and walked to a refrigerator. What Mark noticed, though, was the light inside.

"You have electricity?"

"Yep. Got me a windmill. Keeps things running pretty good. Got water too. There's a pump and a well and it's all hooked to the septic system."

"No shit."

The man laughed as he popped open a beer, setting it down on the table. "Got plenty of that too. Got some cows, pigs, and chickens so the shit does tend to pile up."

"Sounds like you're doing all right out here then."

"I guess, 'ceptin my wife, a'course." He sat down and took a swallow of his beer. "Well, go ahead, take a load off. I ain't gonna bite you, leastways not now that I know you ain't here to kill me."

Mark drank from his beer. It was nice and cold.

The farmer asked, "So, can you tell me what's going on out there?"

"I'm not sure myself. Something happened that caused people to die. Everyone thought they had the flu. Whatever it was, it killed them pretty quick. Until a couple of days ago I was beginning to think I was one of the last ones alive. Now I'm meeting all kinds of people, although most of them seem to want to kill me. I think I liked it better when I was alone."

"Well, there's something to be said for that, but every once in a while it's nice to hear another person's voice."

"Yeah, I agree."

"So how many others have you found?"

"Just a handful. Right now, they're staying with me. It'd be nice to find enough people to create our own little community. You know, to look out for each other and share the work. The only large group of people I've seen so far has been this group of killers. Other than looking for women, they don't seem to be interested in adding to their ranks."

"How many you think there are in this group?"

"Don't know for sure. I've shot a bunch, but they still have a lot more. A whole convoy of vehicles chased after me. I figure even with just two in each vehicle there had to be thirty or so."

"Huh, most likely crazy city folk. They tend to be a little more aggressive than us laid-back country folk."

Mark finished his beer. "Well, I guess I should be going. It's safer to travel at night. Funny, I used to fear what came out at night. Now it's the best time to move."

"How far you gotta go?"

"Guess about three miles. I need to get there before first light. I want to thank you for your hospitality."

"No problem. Stop by anytime. Just leave all the bad guys behind."

"Yeah, believe me, I'd like to."

Mark opened the side door and looked out.

"By the way, the name's Jarrod." The farmer stuck out his big hand.

Mark smiled and took it, putting the two shotgun shells in Jarrod's hand as he did. "Mark."

"Safe journey to you."

"Thanks. Maybe I'll see you again."

Mark trotted to the far side of the barn. The sounds and smells of animals hit him. The thought of fresh meat made him smile and his mouth water. Perhaps, if he survived, he could find something to trade the farmer for one of his livestock.

Working his way along the buildings, he stopped at the last one. There, he took out his binoculars and scanned the fields in front of him and the road to the right. A lone car traveled the road at a slow pace. Evidently they hadn't given up. If they were searching houses and roads, they must have found the car.

Otherwise, they'd still be looking for it.

He waited until they were well past him, then took off at a fast jog toward the far side of the field. On the other side was another subdivision, the houses larger and more expensive than his had been. For the most part, the rest of the way would be one development after another. Along the road, headlights appeared. He threw himself to the ground and watched. This one had a hand-held spotlight. Maybe the same car as before. The beam played along the ground. However, it wasn't powerful enough to reach him.

But it did emphasize how important he seemed to be to them. Even if he made it back tonight, he would be looking over his shoulder the rest of his life.

Eleven

IT TOOK THE REST of the night to work his way to the main cross streets. Erie, the street he'd fled on, ran east and west. Walden went north and south, a quarter mile behind his house. His house sat south and east of his current location. He was in a yard that backed up to a big chain pharmacy. The building sat on the corner across from where he needed to go. The Horde had busted into the pharmacy, evidently in the process of rummaging for anything of value that might still be left.

At least ten men went in and out of the store, and two cars blocked the intersection. To get across, he would have to go around. By his estimation and the halo of light over the eastern horizon, it was close to six in the morning. He needed to find someplace to hole up. It was too dangerous to move anymore.

Mark hopped the fence, heading north along the back of the pharmacy. He continued past a line of houses until he reached a creek. Sliding down the bank put him below street level, which gave him an idea. He kept to the creek and crossed under Walden Street through the drainage tunnel below. The creek bordered the back of the subdivision that was directly across Erie Street from his. Staying close to the creek bed, he made his way to a spot he thought aligned with the middle of his development and climbed the bank.

He hopped another fence and ran from one house to the next until he hit Erie, placing him about a quarter mile past the blockade at the intersection and two long blocks from his house. He just needed to cross Erie. However, from his current position and with the sun peeking over the horizon, he could see the people and cars down the street. If he could see them, they would be able to see him if he tried to cross.

Even moving farther from the intersection, crossing Erie would still be difficult. It was getting lighter. As he tried to decide what to do, a car turned out of his subdivision. He now knew they were patrolling there too. Could they be waiting for him? Did they know where he lived? And, more importantly, had they found Lynn and the kids? The smartest thing for him to do would be to hide in one of the houses until dark. However, Mark was hit by sudden fear for Darren and their guests.

Mark had to know for sure they were safe. He felt responsible for them now, as though they were his new family. He wasn't going to lose this family too. Smart or not, he moved.

Mark backed up and cut through another yard, hopping the fence. He would have to get farther away from the roadblock until he was sure no one could see him cross. His mind preoccupied with thoughts of his new family, exhausted from his night's journey, and his aching body, Mark didn't pay enough attention to what he was doing. As he ran out into the next street, a bullet ricocheted off the concrete in front of him.

Startled, he jumped, then dove behind a small tree. Two men got out of a parked car and ran toward him. Mark cursed; he was getting careless. As more gunshots followed, Mark knew the sound would summon others. He had to move before he was trapped.

Trying to save his last bullets, he made a mad dash for the driveway of the house he was in front of. Bullets flew all around him, but they were shooting on the run. Mark ran around the attached garage and turned behind the house, running as hard as he could to the far side. Glancing around the corner to make sure his pursuers had passed, he jumped the fence and ran back out front. The two men had followed him up the driveway, disappearing around the house. Before they could figure out he had doubled back, Mark sprinted toward their car.

His heart fell as he pulled open the door and the keys were not there. However, in the back seat, he found two handguns. He reached over the front seat and grabbed both. Next, he ran to the side of the nearest house, which was two down from where he had been. There, he stopped to listen for his pursuers. He didn't want to run into them. While he listened, he pulled out the magazines of both guns. One only had one bullet in it; the other was half full. They were both 9mms, so he slid the single bullet out and placed it in the half-full magazine, then dropped the empty gun in the bushes. Mark slung the rifle diagonally across his back and moved to the back of the house. Now that he had a weapon, it was his turn to hunt.

He steadied his breathing and glanced around the corner. Neither man was in sight. He waited, listening for any sound that would give him a direction to follow. Creeping along the back of the house, he moved closer to where he thought they might be. What he heard startled him. The two voices were behind him, back on the street.

"We know he's here someplace. Let's drive back and gather everyone up. That way we can search the entire section."

They were back at the car, but Mark could not afford for them to get away. He crept along the side of the house until he had them in sight. When the driver had his back to him, Mark ran at him. Keeping low, with the gun in his right hand and the knife in the left, he tried to keep the man's body between him and the second man, who was on the passenger side. Mark had just hit the street when the soft scraping of his shoe drew their attention. The driver, with the car door open, turned in his direction. Mark took two more steps and lunged, the knife like a spear, out in front of him. The man, unprepared for an attack, had placed the gun in his belt at his back. He fumbled for it and tried to fall away, but Mark got there too fast. The knife sliced into the man's belly, doubling him over. Mark's momentum pushed the man inside the car into a sitting position. Mark landed on the door frame and banged both knees. A sound of pain escaped his lips. He pushed it from his mind and focused on the second man.

The driver was still alive and struggling to hold the knife still. The second man had pulled out his gun and leaned in the passenger's door trying to line up a shot. Keeping the knifed man between them, Mark shot the outside gunman before he got the chance to fire. While that man fell backward, Mark brought the gun down across the other man's nose. He hit him three times before the man relaxed his grip and went still. Mark then finished the job with the knife.

Running through the man's pockets, Mark found the key. He popped the trunk and dumped both bodies inside, relieving them of their guns first. He started the car and drove to the corner. This would be a very bold move, but he hoped anyone seeing the car cross the street would recognize it and pay it no attention. He pushed the pedal down and raced across the street entering the subdivision to the east of his. Glancing out the passenger side window, he noticed a car from the blockade moving in his direction. Someone had heard the shots and was responding. He had to hide before the chase car got there.

The street wound to the left, then back to the right,

before coming to an intersection. He turned left because that direction would take him farther away from where his house was. If the car was discovered, he didn't want it to be obvious where he was going.

The houses in this area had been stripped already, leaving many of them with open doors. He found one with the garage door up and drove in. Mark hopped out and yanked the door down. If he hadn't been seen, the car and bodies should remain hidden for quite a while.

It was daylight now, but he wanted to keep moving. That meant being extremely cautious. Mark knew at least one car had seen him and most likely there was another patrolling the area. He didn't want to stay in the house for very long. If he had to hide somewhere, he didn't want it to be where the car was hidden.

First, Mark went to the window to make sure no one was in front of the house. The streets looked clear. Next, he went out the back door and crept along the rear wall. Almost too late, he saw a car and jumped behind the exterior chimney. It didn't offer complete cover; it only stuck out from the house about a foot. He held his breath, sucking in his gut to make himself as small as possible. Anticipating an alarm being sounded at any second, he held the gun ready.

The car drove past. If they'd been looking harder or in the right direction, they would've seen him. As soon as the car was out of sight, Mark turned and fled to the backyard. It was easier to stay hidden behind the house. Between the two houses facing the next street, he watched another car go by. He had to move before he was trapped.

Mark bolted for the houses across from him. He ran between them, opened the gate to the yard, ran to the rear fence, leaped it, and sprinted to the back of that house. Mark squatted, leaning against the vinyl siding, and waited while he caught his breath.

By his estimation, he had to go four or five more blocks

before he got to the street that bordered his subdivision. Although he should lie low until darkness fell again, Mark was feeling a strange sense of urgency about getting back to his house.

Have I already lost my new family?

Once again, he moved to the side of the house, scanned both directions, then sprinted across the street.

Mark moved up between the houses and stopped behind a bush. The coast was clear so he ran once more and his luck ran out. One of the cars came to the corner as he dodged between two houses. The tires squealed as they braked hard.

With one hand on the top cross beam, he hurdled the split rail gate and dashed toward the rear fence. There were voices behind him. The next fence passed easily under him. As he ran for the house, shots landed around him. He made it to the side of the house and stopped. Waiting until he heard the fence creaking, Mark stepped out and shot the first man while he still perched on top of the fence.

The second man dropped to one knee and hammered shots into the vinyl siding, forcing Mark to duck back. Another car screeched to a stop on the street in front of him. He was about to be surrounded. Trying to find any advantage, he moved to the front of the house and saw one man head toward the far side. A second stepped out of the car. Mark aimed and took the second man down. Everything was happening so fast. Even though his heart was pounding, he felt calm when he needed to kill.

Have I become as much a cold-hearted killer as these men?

Dodging left, staying undercover of the bushes and small trees that landscaped the next house, Mark dove to the ground on the far side of the porch. No shots followed him. Mark knew he couldn't stay there long. The remaining men would be closing soon. He lined up a shot and waited for someone to poke his head out from between the houses. A head did pop out and duck back, but too quick to get a shot off.

"Where'd he go?"

"I think he's hunkered down next to the porch. Leastways, I didn't see him move on."

"Keep him pinned down. I'll go 'round behind him."

There was no reply, but bullets began ripping overhead.

Could the front door be open since most of the houses had been ransacked already? He doubted they would have bothered to lock them. The trouble was, if he got up to check and it was locked, he'd be standing in the open, an easy target.

Knowing he was about to be outflanked, he fired two shots to keep the man in front of him down, then jumped up on the small concrete porch and turned the door knob. A shot whistled past a second later and a smell of rotting flesh hit him as he pushed through the door. He shut and locked it then ran for the back. When he found the rear door, he went through it, vaulted the deck railing to the right and moved with stealth to the side of the house, hoping to come up behind the flanking man.

"He's in the house. He went in the house," the voice called from out front. As he looked around the corner, the man stopped. He turned his head and Mark ducked back. He counted to three then jumped out, ready to shoot, but his prey was no longer there.

A chill ran up Mark's spine. He turned and stepped to the side of the house. He had no idea where the men were. If they came at him from both directions, he had no cover. Mark had outfoxed himself.

Sliding toward the backyard again, he glanced around the corner in time to see one of the men coming around the deck in a crouch. He noticed Mark a second later and tried to shoot and duck. Mark got his shot off faster. It hit the man in the shoulder as he dove for the cover of the deck. Before Mark could finish him, shots ripped long furrows in the siding near his head, forcing him around the corner to seek protection. Reaching back around the corner, Mark shot one round to keep the man from being too aggressive in his pursuit. Hoping the wounded man would not be able to get off an accurate shot, Mark ran for the deck and climbed over the rail.

The wounded man tried to sit up high enough to take a shot. The bullet went wild. Mark ran down the far steps and to the end of the house. As he rounded the corner, he almost ran right into the second man. They both raised their guns, fired off target, and ran back the way they came.

The wounded man fired another round, which shattered the window above him. Mark ducked, and without thinking, ran out beyond the deck and fired repeatedly. He kept moving toward the wounded man. The two men exchanged shots until the man was down and Mark's magazine was empty. He threw down the gun and pulled out the next one.

Mark grabbed the dead man's gun and searched the body for extra ammo, but found none. When he opened the gun, he discovered the man had been down to his last round. As quietly as he could, Mark climbed on the deck. The sliding door stood ajar and he inched it open enough to slip inside. He didn't have enough ammunition to trade shots, and by now, others must have heard the gunshots and would be on the way. Mark needed to locate his target before reinforcements came. Getting trapped in the house, would be a death sentence. Mark tiptoed from room to room, peering out the windows. He found the man sneaking up on the opposite side of the house. Knowing he would give himself away if he tried anything from there, Mark went upstairs to the corner bedroom and eased the window open. A screen blocked him. Mark took his knife and sliced a large X in it, then waited for the man to break cover.

It only took a moment. "Charlie. Hey, Charlie, you still there?"

When he didn't get an answer, the man crept around the corner in a crouch and made his way to the side of the deck. He was now below Mark and to the left. Mark pushed his gun through the X inch by inch. The man below froze. He tensed and turned back the way he came. Mark pulled the trigger without proper sighting, and the first shot hit the deck. The man dove to his left as the second shot hit his leg. Without hesitating, he came out of his roll and fired up. Mark's third shot hit his left arm. His fourth found his enemy's chest and the gun went dry. The man fell back, staring straight up.

Mark dropped the empty gun and took out the first man's weapon. Slipping the lone bullet out he placed it in the last gun. He had eight shots left. He needed to get the dead man's gun. Sprinting back down the stairs he came out of the sliding door with his gun up and ready. He looked over the railing. The body was gone.

Damn!

Mark stepped off the deck and walked around it, watching the side of the house. It was the only direction the wounded man could've gone. He walked a wide path to get a view. With one step to go, Mark dove to the ground, rolled, and came up on one knee ready to fire – but there was no target. A sound back by the deck made him drop to the ground as a bullet tore into his calf. He grunted in pain as fire shot up his leg.

Mark couldn't afford to let the wound distract him. From a prone position, Mark found the man wedged halfway under the deck.

Both men fired one shot after another. When the bullets stopped, Mark wasn't sure if it was because the other man was dead or, like him, had run out of bullets. The man's head was down and looked bloody. The gun was still in his hand but his hand was on the ground. Mark couldn't risk checking. And now, he heard cars approaching on the next street. It was time to run.

With the bullet wound in his calf, running was painful. But if he got caught he would die, so he pushed the pain from his mind and ran for all he was worth. He crossed the street, hopped three fences, and crossed the next one. He kept repeating the move until he found himself on the road that bordered the eastern side of his subdivision. This street was wider and more traveled than the others; the houses were farther back from the road. Once across it, though, he would only be four blocks from home. He prayed the safe room hadn't been compromised. His stomach knotted as a picture came to his mind of bodies strewn around the basement.

No, I won't think that.

He looked to the right as a car passed on Erie Street. The gunfight had spurred a lot of activity all around him. If he stayed there, sooner or later he would be discovered. He darted across the street and flung himself over the first fence. It took another twenty minutes to get to his backyard and hide in the trees.

Twelve

THE HOUSE LOOKED THE same from where he was, but Mark dared not approach until he was positive no one had followed him. He both longed for and feared what might await him in the basement. Thirty minutes later, he crawled out of his hiding place and advanced toward the house. As he drew near, he could hear the muffled rhythmic beating of the generator even from underground. He thought that was a good sign, but made a mental note to work on a way of deadening the sound.

Once inside, he crept through the house and squatted at the front windows. The house was not ransacked, so either no one had been there or it was a trap. The street was deserted. He paused at the basement door and said a silent prayer that everyone was safe. The thick wooden steps made no sound as he descended. He held the rifle out in front of him, ready to shoot and run if he needed to. At the secret door, he gave the signal he had worked out with Darren.

Mark reached up and pulled the panel back, but did not stand in the doorway. He was afraid someone might shoot him. Instead, he called out to the darkness.

"Darren, it's me, Mark."

A rush of movement startled him. Multiple voices exploded as one. Like magic, they were all right in front of him, grabbing him, hugging him, and yanking his arms to get him inside. They all talked at once. Darren hugged him hard. The reception, coupled with the relief he felt in seeing that they were alive, choked him up. Unable to speak for a moment, he scanned their elated faces and held up his hands for quiet. He couldn't help but let a smile cross his face, mirroring theirs. It was good to have that emotional connection with someone again.

His eyes met Lynn's. This time, she didn't look away. Tears welled in her eyes and he had a sudden urge to rush to her and hold her tight.

One of the girls broke the spell. "We were so worried you wouldn't come back."

"Okay, settle down and I'll fill you in on what happened. First things first, though. Darren, you need to shut off the generator for a while, at least until I figure out how to make it quieter. We don't need the noise leading them to us. We have to be very careful … they are all around us right now."

Mark walked back to the wall and made sure it was closed securely. One of the things he noticed when the door opened was how bad it smelled inside. There were entirely too many bodies in that small confined space. They would have to work on expanding the area and venting the air somehow.

"Okay, is everyone here?" He looked around and ran through a quick checklist. "Okay, good. Is anyone hurt?"

No one responded to that one. Lynn finally said. "Well, I guess Ruthie kinda twisted her ankle a bit when we were running through the woods. Other than that we're all fine. Darren has been doing a great job of taking care of us."

One of the girls said in a meek voice, "We thought you were dead."

"Well, as you can see, the reports of my demise have been greatly exaggerated."

That brought smiles. Mark went into selected details of everything that happened since he'd driven off. When he was done, he cut the questions short. "It's been a very long night and day. I'm exhausted and starved."

Lynn gasped as Mark stood up. She pointed to his leg. "You're hurt! You've been asking us if we're okay and you're the one who needs help."

The leg had a steady throb that he had been ignoring. Now that she pointed it out, it began to hurt anew. Mark dropped back to his seat as everyone crowded in close to get a look. Lynn ordered them back.

"Darren, I know you must have a first aid kit around here. Get it for me," she said. "The rest of you get back and give me some room to move." She knelt in front of him and began pulling up the leg of his jeans to get a look. Mark winced as her fingers brushed the wound.

"The pants are going to have to come off so I can see the extent of the injury. Do you know what caused it?"

"A bullet."

A collective gasp sounded and they all stared at him.

"Well, I'm not a doctor, but I was a nurse. I'll do the best I can, but you understand if the bullet's still in there it has to come out. That could be very painful. Then we're going to have to worry about infection."

Darren came back with the kit.

"Do you want me to do it or not?"

Mark sighed. "Okay, but let's do it in the basement where it won't matter if we make a mess." He stood up. "Check the kit and see what else you might need. Darren can find it for you. I'll go get set up. The rest of you need to get some sleep."

Mark hooked up the monitors. "Darren, keep an eye on the screen. If you see anything, come get us."

Mark went out to the basement. He grabbed a chair and while he waited for Lynn, studying the walls to see where he could create space for the new members of his little tribe, without making it obvious that the basement had been shortened.

He looked up as Lynn approached. She looked down at the items she had gathered for the surgery: tweezers, pliers, a utility knife, a bottle of whiskey, and towels. She'd pulled back her blonde hair and knotted it on top. Even in the dim light of the basement he found her attractive, in an understated way. As she glanced up and gave him a nervous smile, he noticed she had warm blue eyes.

"Are you ready?"

"As ready as I can be."

"You need some help getting those jeans off?"

He laughed but didn't make the reply he might have under normal circumstances. He stood up and unbuckled his pants. Just before he let them drop he said, "By the way, my name's Mark."

She laughed, "Making it official, since we're getting so personal, you mean." She knelt and helped him off with his shoes. He tried not to wince in front of her, but the pain had returned and was sharp. She pulled his jeans off the rest of the way. He held his breath. She looked up at him, her eyes now serious. "Wouldn't you prefer to lie down?"

Mark shrugged. "Would it be better for you?"

"What would be better for me would be more light and having you lying up higher."

"We could go upstairs but if someone came, we would never make it back here. We'd have to lead them away from the kids." He slid to the floor and propped his leg up on the chair.

She shone a flashlight directly into the wound and used wipes and a spray disinfectant to clean the area. Lighting a match she held it under tweezers. "This is going to hurt." She handed him a towel and he looked at her, confused.

"Bite on it." He frowned. She started to push the tweezers in then stopped. "Now," she said, then came the pain. He bit the towel.

Thirteen

MARK RESTED THE NEXT two days. The kids took turns going upstairs and watching at the windows. Lynn's children were Caleb and Ruth. Alyssa was the redhead. She and Ruth were classmates and friends. Twice they ran back with news that a car had driven past. Evidently the Horde still hunted for him.

Lynn spent time checking the stores, preparing meals, and checking on Mark's leg. Mark sat with pencil and paper, designing new living quarters. They would have to get out and scrounge more materials to build the room. The inactivity made him antsy. He tried to get up and walk, but each time the pain drove him right back down. He swallowed some prescription pain pills he'd collected and that eased the ache somewhat. Lynn also gave him some antibiotics he had in the storage room to help fight infection.

On the third day, he forced himself to move despite the pain.

"Don't try to move too much," Lynn warned. "I don't want you tearing open my handiwork."

Frustrated, Mark's tone sounded harsher than he intended. "There's too much work to be done. I can't just sit and do nothing."

Immediately, Lynn backed away and lowered her eyes, fear and pain on her face. Mark instantly regretted his words, confused by her reaction. "Lynn, it's none of my business how things were for you and your kids before, but things are different now. It's important you understand that."

Mark sat down and reached for her hand. She pulled it away.

"Hey, I'm sorry. I wasn't yelling at you. I'm just frustrated about not being able to get things done. I'm falling behind schedule and with this many mouths to feed we're going to have to step up collections. I'm not mad at you. You have a voice here. I value what you do and say. Okay?"

She nodded, but wouldn't look at him. Mark understood. It would take time for her to know and trust him. He would just have to show her that life could be different.

"We're in this together ... as a team." He turned to all of them. "We didn't create this problem, but we do have to survive it. It may not be what you want or what you're used to, but unfortunately it's what we have. The best way to do that is to help and look out for each other."

He needed to make sure Lynn was on board as a partner, not as a servant. They were strangers, thrown together in an unusual situation, but he didn't want her to feel like an outsider. "Lynn," he said her name to get her to look at him. "I'll wait until tomorrow, but then we have to go out and start hunting for what we'll need to live. Okay?"

She seemed surprised that he had asked her. She studied him for a moment then nodded.

For the rest of the day, Mark ran the generator so he could drill anchor holes in the concrete floors and walls. He could build a new wall the entire length of the back without drawing too much attention to it. The space would only be four feet wide but forty feet long. Under his supervision, the kids unloaded the metal shelves lining the basement wall and moved the units forward. He didn't have enough wood to build the walls yet, so they did what they could.

By the evening, they were exhausted. The meal Lynn prepared for them consisted of canned soup, peanut butter and jelly sandwiches, carrot strips, and fried potatoes. With six mouths to feed, the stores would be depleted soon. They would have to expand their hunting grounds. With the scavengers out there, it would be difficult to move undetected.

As they prepared for bed, Mark and Lynn discussed plans for the next day. "I'll take the two boys with me to do some hunting. What I'd really like you and the girls to do is start planting a garden. I've been collecting seed packets and there should be enough there to produce enough fresh food to see us through for a while. Can you do that?"

"Yes."

"Our second greatest concern right now is running out of food and water. We'll have to go on strict rations for a while. I'll leave that in your hands."

"All right."

He wanted her to have input and not just feel like he was dictating to her.

"If there is anything you can think of that would help or anything you want us to be looking for while we're out collecting, let me know."

She nodded again. For a moment, she looked like she wanted to say something and thought better of it.

"What? Tell me what you were gonna say."

She hesitated before blurting out, "I don't think we should be separating jobs by boy/girl. I think we all should be doing everything."

Mark looked at her for a moment, pondering what she

said. He had the feeling it took a lot of willpower to push the words out of her mouth. For that reason alone, he decided to side with her so she would know her opinions counted.

"Okay, we'll split the kids up, a boy and a girl in each group. When we get a chance, I want to teach everyone how to shoot too. You never know when that might be needed."

Lynn gave him a quick smile then averted her eyes. That was as much as Mark dared to try for the time being. They said goodnight and went to bed. Mark set up a rotating watch each night in lieu of running the generator or using up the batteries. Each person took a two-hour shift. Darren had first watch and was already on duty. They had one watch and whoever was on guard duty wore it. More watches were on the list of things to start collecting.

Mark had the third shift from two to four and was awakened by Ruth. He took the watch and his rifle upstairs. Walking a path through the rooms he checked all the windows then repeated the action from the second floor. He wouldn't allow the kids to go to the second floor, fearing they might get trapped up there if intruders hit in a sudden rush. But it gave him a better view of the streets and if he got trapped there, he could hold his own. When all seemed clear, he went back downstairs and settled in a chair by the front window.

When it was time for Mark to wake the next shift, he continued to watch. He knew he needed sleep but so did they, and a tired lookout didn't see much. He would wake the next person an hour before dawn so he could grab a couple of hours for himself. He wanted to be up and out early, figuring that would be the least likely time anyone would be out looking for them.

By seven, Darren and Ruth were in the van with Mark, ready to roll. Each carried a knife and a .22 handgun.

Lynn had compiled a list of items she wanted them to look for. With women in the house, the normal list had changed and expanded.

Mark drove out of the subdivision and into the one behind. It looked as though some of the houses had been ransacked in the first block. It was a smaller development and they wouldn't be spending time burying the dead. They needed to collect as much as possible and head back. Mark's plan was to be back to the house by noon. With three of them searching, they should be able to clear a house fast.

Within three hours, they'd cleared nearly twenty houses. The van was almost full, surprising Mark with the amount of food and drinks they found. For whatever reason, this subdivision had hardly been touched by the Horde. With two hours to go before his self-imposed deadline, Mark considered extending it. He was afraid to leave such a gold mine for fear it would be ravaged the next day.

The next hour they cleared six more houses, which Mark estimated was about a third of the development.

They were currently clearing a court that held twelve houses. Mark pulled up in the driveway of a house near the center of the circular court. They had been parking in the middle of three houses. They would clear the right, the center, then the left, before moving down to the next three. That way they could save on gas, yet still keep the van close enough in case they had to escape. As Mark pulled into the driveway to do the seventh eighth and ninth houses he announced they had an hour to go.

"We have these six houses to finish then we're done." He opened the door, stepped out, and heard something fall to the ground. A bullet whistled between the door and the van just as Mark bent to pick up the package of Ramen noodles.

"Get in the van," he screamed as more shots smacked

into the van. He had his handgun out to cover Ruth and Darren as they scrambled back inside. The shots came from the house they were parked in front of.

"Crawl to the back and keep down." He returned fire, triggering two shots towards each gunman. Reaching inside the van he inserted the key, turned it, and slid the transmission into neutral. More shots peppered the van as it rolled back. If he put the van in reverse and jumped in he would be an easy target through the windshield, so he let the van roll, using the door as cover. When it bounced into the street, Mark reached in and yanked the wheel, putting it broadside to the house.

"Go on, you dirty thieves, get out of here," a voice yelled from the house. They ceased firing when they saw the van rolling away. "Run away, you scavengers."

"Don't shoot, we're leaving. We mean you no harm," Mark called out.

"Like we're gonna trust you. Get out of here or die."

Mark jumped into the van and started the engine. These gunmen weren't from the Horde, or they would not have stopped shooting. If only they would let him get close enough to talk to them, Mark might be able to convince them to join forces. He would have to give some thought as to how best approach them. But it wouldn't be today. He drove down the block and stopped around the corner, out of sight of the house.

"Are you two all right?"

"Yeah, just scared," Darren announced. Ruth was crying.

"It's all right, Ruth, we're safe now."

"I don't think we'll ever really be safe," she said.

Mark's mouth moved to answer, but no words came out. He noticed several bullet holes in the side panels where sunlight poured through. She might be right.

"Well, let's finish up here and get back. We've got enough time to do maybe six more houses. Let me get out first."

Neither of the kids argued.

They flew through the next three houses and had just moved to the final three when shots erupted again. This time, however, the shots were not directed toward them. "I think it's back at that house that fired at us." Mark grabbed his rifle. "You two get in the van. Ruth, here's the keys. You do know how to drive, don't you?"

She nodded. "I've got my temps, but not my license."

"I don't think anyone's gonna ticket you. Get in the driver's seat and put the keys in the ignition, but don't start it. If I yell for you to leave, you go. If I'm not back in twenty minutes, you go. Darren, you know the way back, right?"

"Yeah, but where are you gonna be?" A note of panic rose in his voice.

Mark touched his arm. "I'll be fine. I'm gonna check and see if the people in that house need help."

"Why?" Ruth asked. "They tried to kill us."

"Yeah, that's true, but if people tried to come in our house, wouldn't we defend it?"

"I guess."

"I think that's all they were doing. They may be just like us. I'd like to find out."

WHILE CALEB AND ALYSSA sorted food items, Lynn dug through the storage area making an inventory of medical supplies. Her eyes fell on a gun. She didn't know much about them but picked it up. Hefting it, she was surprised at how lightweight it was. She looked at the cylinder and saw the tips of bullets. She thought about Mark; he seemed okay, but then, so had John when she first met him. An image of her husband appeared in her mind's eye. She shuddered.

He had been verbally abusive to both her and the kids.

Nothing was ever right or good enough. Despite her best efforts. Lately, his abuse had turned more physical. He had forced himself on her twice. She touched her cheek where he'd slapped her, then her bicep where the bruise from his grip was only now fading. She had planned on leaving him, before everything went crazy.

They would stay for a while, until she knew her children were safe. But no man, would ever hurt her or the kids again. She slid the gun into her waistband and covered it with her shirt.

Fourteen

THE GUN BATTLE HAD intensified. Reports from a lot more guns echoed through the court. Mark ran to the corner house and peeked around it. Three cars had pulled up in a line in front of the house. About ten men exchanged shots with the people inside. As he watched, some of the men split off and ran toward the bordering houses. Mark didn't know how many people were in the house, but he had a bad feeling there were about to be a few less.

Mark went back to the fence and jumped it. He ran from yard to yard, vaulting fences, trying to get closer without being seen. The targeted house was the fifth from the corner. When he got within sight, he moved toward the front of a neighboring house to get his bearings and find where the attackers were. Were these attackers part of the Horde? If so, the size of the gang was discouraging. They had the house surrounded. The defenders were firing from the front and the back, trying to keep the assailants at bay.

Moving cautiously, Mark went to the back yard and climbed another cedar fence. Staying close to the house as he advanced, he stopped at the rear corner. Mark had a clear view of the side and rear of the defending house. Two men in the back were firing at the house, trying to keep them occupied. Another man was attempting to get in through a side window. He had pulled off the screen and about to pry open the window. Inpatient, he took the rifle he carried and smashed the glass with the butt. If he couldn't get in, he would at least be able to shoot inside.

Mark crawled to the fence between the two houses. A gate to the front yard stood to the right. The man was outside the gate, near the back third of the house. Mark lifted the metal loop from the post. He had the 9mm out and held the rifle in his left hand. From that angle, only one of the shooters in the back could see him and possibly two from the front. The gate creaked, but the attacker was too intent on trying to get in the window to notice.

Sliding through the gate, Mark was now six feet from his target. Mark moved fast, grabbed the man's legs, and yanked him to the ground.

"Hey!" he said in surprise, before Mark brought the gun crashing down on his head. Another punch to the face and he stayed down. Taking the intruder's rifle, Mark tossed it through the broken window and went to the back corner. Putting his 9mm away, he leveled the rifle. He had a good line of sight on the first man and took the shot. The man fell back from the impact.

The second man saw his partner go down and swung toward the new threat. Mark dropped him before he could get off a shot. The back was now clear. Mark ran to where the first man fell and took his gun. Searching the dead man's pockets, he found two more magazines. As he ran toward the second man, someone from the house shot at him. He dove to the ground and crawled to the tree the second body was behind. Once again he stripped the man of his weapons. Now he just had to get to the house without being shot.

Ripping the man's bloody shirt off Mark waved it in the air, hoping it would serve as a white flag, even though it was blue and blood red.

"Don't shoot," he called. "I'm not with them."

Another shot told him they didn't believe him. He couldn't afford to be pinned down back there. The shooting out front had come to a momentary lull. The sudden quiet was eerie. A car approached at high speed and screeched to a stop. He needed to see what was happening. He was about to try the makeshift flag again when a shot rang out, followed by a scream from the house. He risked a quick peek and the person at the window was looking away. It might be the best the chance he would get to move.

Then the man left the window entirely. Mark's was sure someone inside had taken a bullet. He sprinted to the side of the house with the dead men's guns, stopping under the broken window. He rose up as high as he could reach and tried to listen.

"Oh, God, it hurts, it hurts!" The voice sounded either female or perhaps teenage.

"Watch the front," a man's voice commanded. "Keep focused or we'll all end up shot, and worse, than this."

"But we're almost out of ammunition and there are so many of them. How are we supposed to fight them all?"

Another male voice added, "Maybe we should see if they're willing to make a deal."

"Are you nuts? You know what they want – our food, our supplies, and the women. They won't make a deal with us, at least not one they'll abide by."

"But Frank, I only have one bullet left."

"I don't have any," another voice replied. "How can we win?"

"Not to mention, Mary needs medical assistance."

Frank said, "So what, you just want to give up? They'll kill us for sure. And James, in case you hadn't noticed, there *is* no medical assistance. I don't know about you guys, but I'm not giving up. If I'm gonna die, I'm going down fighting."

Mark grabbed the window sill and chinned himself up so he could see into the room. Two older men and an older woman huddled around a woman writhing on the floor. "He's right, don't give into them."

Someone screamed and several bodies jumped and pointed guns at Mark.

"Don't shoot. Here, take these guns. I took them off the guys out back." He dropped them on the floor next to the rifle they hadn't noticed yet. "I've seen what they'll do to you if you give up. The men will die and the women will be passed around. I'll help you from out here."

"They're moving out there. He might be a distraction so they can rush the house."

All eyes swung toward the front windows. Mark could see where things were headed and before they had a chance to swing back his way and shoot, he dropped down. He would have to convince them he was helping by taking out a few more attackers.

He crawled to the front corner and peered out at the street. Sure enough, they were assaulting the house. The new car had brought more men.

Two men jumped up on the porch. One of them aimed a shotgun at the door and fired into the hinges. Three others slid to a stop underneath the front windows. He couldn't tell how many, but some of the men ran to the opposite side of the house, making an end run. That left three more shooters still behind the cars. They were keeping up a constant covering fire.

Mark pulled out the handgun and leaned around the corner. The men under the windows were all crouched down, waiting for the door to swing open. The two men closest to Mark had their backs to him. The man closest to the porch faced Mark but looked at the windows above. He decided to chance it because the people in the house had run out of time.

After the third shotgun blast, the second man on the porch grabbed the door and yanked it away from the frame. A shot from inside was fired too soon, burying in the door. The two men went inside. The firing was intense. The three men under the window stood up to pour bullets through the windows. As they did, Mark opened fire. He shot the first man in the back, throwing him forward into the middle man.

The man looked at his partner's body sinking to the ground. Mark shot twice more. Bloody geysers erupted in the man's chest. He toppled over face first, leaving the third man staring right at Mark with his gun already up. Mark rolled to the side.

The man was good. He kept tracking Mark and had him lined up for the shot, but before he could pull the trigger, a gun pointed out the window above and fired straight down into the man's head.

Mark lay on his back, staring up at the man in the window, unable to believe his luck. Then shots began hitting the ground around him.

Luck could be fleeting.

He crawled around the corner until he was out of sight. Leaning against the wall, he said a quick "thank you," then went to the back of the house to see how things were there.

Two men were on the deck, firing through the broken patio door and a shattered kitchen window. They had the defenders pinned down. Mark took a deep breath and stepped around the corner, pulling the trigger non-stop. He drilled three rounds into the first man as he walked forward. When the man fell sideways, Mark continued firing toward the second man. However, that man saw Mark coming and ran for the railing of the deck. He put a hand on the deck and swung his legs up and over as Mark's rounds found their target. The man fell over the rail, hitting the ground hard.

Mark's first instinct was to follow him up to the rail, but if the guy were still alive, he could be lying there waiting for Mark to check on him. He grabbed a small flower pot off the rail nearest him and moved along the side of the deck. He pitched the pot over the rail near where he saw the man fall. Just as he suspected, the man fired in response to the crashing flower pot. Mark ran past the deck and finished his magazine at the man.

With his gun now empty, Mark took his enemy's gun. There were no extra magazines, which suggested that the attackers were probably running low too. On the porch, Mark had better luck. That man had an extra magazine and three rounds in his gun. He stripped out the mag and put the full one in. The man defending the back, thankfully, did not fire at him this time. Mark gave him a wave, then hurried off toward the front.

Another vehicle entered the court and approached the house. Mark shook his head. *Was the Horde never ending?* The battle intensified again. Mark moved to the front corner. One of the men on the porch was down, lying in a bloody heap across the threshold. The other was nowhere to be seen. The door was on the ground. The firefight inside had ceased.

Mark looked at the street. An SUV had pulled up and swung sideways about ten yards from the other cars. Four people stood behind it, shooting at the attackers. The defenders in the house renewed their efforts. The remaining attackers, realizing they were now outnumbered, tried to flee. One took off running, trying to reach the cover of the houses. Another jumped in the nearest car and tried to peel out. A third attempted to get in the passenger side. The driver didn't wait for him. He took off, leaving the man standing all alone in the middle of the street where he didn't last long.

Mark slid the rifle from his shoulder and lined up a hasty shot at the running man. He had little time to adjust, though it was not a long shot for his weapon or his skill. The man tumbled forward between the houses. Mark turned toward the escaping car as the sound of gunfire increased. The windshield and side windows shattered from multiple impacts, causing the driver to jump the curb and crash head-on into a tree. The dazed man tried to open the door but was dropped as soon as he attempted to stand.

The fight was over.

Mark stepped out and swung his weapon from side to side, making sure no more targets presented themselves. He heard the sound of running getting closer and instinct caused him to level the rifle at the advancing figures. But, a closer look at the group caused his mouth to fall open.

"I thought I told you to stay put," Mark admonished Ruth and Darren.

Ruth replied, "Then who would have come to your rescue?"

Mark started to reply, then realized he didn't have one.

Lynn came up, followed by Caleb. She seemed relieved, stopping in front of him, her face flushed. For a moment, he thought she was going to hug him. A few awkward seconds later, she lowered her head and turned away.

Mark turned to the house.

"Hello, in the house, anyone still alive in there?"

A shaky male voice responded after a slight delay. "Yes, we're still alive." It almost sounded like a question, as if he didn't believe his own words.

"Does anyone need medical attention?" Lynn asked.

"Yes," a female voice called.

"No," a harsh male voice countered. "How do we know we can trust them?"

"Maybe because we just risked our lives to save you," Mark shouted. "Look, there's a nurse out here who can help your wounded if you need it. We're not coming in unless you ask, but it sounds like you could use some help."

There was some quiet murmuring inside then the first voice called out, "Okay, but just the nurse."

Lynn turned to get her things from the SUV. Mark grabbed her arm and stopped her. "Hold on," he said. She tensed. Then to the house, "That's not happening. As much as you don't trust us, we don't know you. I'm not letting her come in unprotected. I'm coming too. Just the two of us."

"What can we do? We need the help!" the woman said.

The man continued to negotiate. "Leave your weapons outside."

"Again," Mark said, "not gonna happen. If we didn't want to help you in the first place, we could have let those animals overwhelm you. We're not a danger to you. We aren't going to be unprotected either. Now you decide, but those injured are not getting any better while we talk."

"Please," the woman cried, "just come in and help us."

Mark released Lynn's arm and nodded for her to go. She went to the SUV to collect whatever supplies she brought.

"You others," Mark said to the kids, "go round up

anything of value, especially the weapons. Hey, where's the van?"

"Back at the house," replied Darren. "When we saw the extra car coming to join the fight we thought you might need some help too. We didn't want to get the van shot up so we found the SUV with keys in it."

"Yeah, my mom got real military on us and began giving orders."

"She was really cool," commented Darren.

"Yeah, she was, wasn't she?" Ruth added.

Mark smiled at Lynn as she came back.

"What?" she asked.

"Nothing. You kids get going. We'll be out shortly."

Mark went to the destroyed front door and stepped in. He had restrung the rifle and held a handgun in a two-handed grip, ready, but aimed at the floor. He held up a hand toward Lynn to prevent her from entering. A body lay on the floor just inside the living room.

"Let's not get trigger happy here." He looked around the collection of scared people. They all held weapons pointed in various directions. He nodded at the two men who had them pointed at him. "Agreed?"

No one spoke.

"Oh, for God's sake." An older woman pushed her way from the back. "Stop being so stupid! Why God gave men testosterone is beyond me. He should have given it to women who would know how to use it properly." She grabbed the barrel of one of the rifles and pushed it up. "Mary is going to die without help, and if she does, I'm going to blame you."

She turned toward Mark. "Please, help her. She's my sister."

Mark relaxed the gun so it hung at his side and motioned for Lynn to step in. Without looking at anything else, Lynn went straight to the wounded

109

woman. While she had everyone's attention, Mark took the opportunity to do some examining of his own.

The defenders consisted of five adults, three male. If any children were on site they were not evident. They all appeared to be in their fifties by Mark's estimation. One of the men had blood leaking down his arm, but didn't seem to be aware of it.

"Looks like you got hit too," Mark said.

The man looked at it and shrugged it off. "Just a scratch."

"Still it should be cleaned and bandaged. You can't risk infection. You want me to do it?"

"No," he said. His tone was angry.

Mark shrugged. If the man didn't want help, he wasn't going to beg him.

Lynn stood up.

"It looks like she took a bullet in the side just below the rib cage. It appears to be still in there. I didn't want to probe too much without putting her under somehow. I can't tell how much damage has been done internally without getting in there and I'm not a surgeon. I have knowledge, but no practical experience. Still, I may be the best bet she has. You all discuss it and let me know what you want to do."

She walked out on the porch. Mark followed.

"Can you do it?"

"I think so. I've never done it before. I've assisted a few times and that's the extent of my expertise. Depending on where the bullet is lodged, I'm pretty sure I can get it out. The problem is if there's any internal damage I can't see or fix. We also don't have the right equipment, facilities, drugs, or tools to do it properly. I could do everything right and she still might die."

They went back in and stood over Mary, who clutched her stomach, moaning from the pain. "Please, help me," she said hoarsely.

"Mary, I'm not a doctor. I'll do the best I can. That's all I can promise."

The other woman started to cry. "Help her if you can ... she's my sister."

"I'll need some things. The men can start gathering them while you and I get her ready. We need to get her up on a solid table with as much light as possible."

Mark decided to check on the kids. He found them sitting on the tailgate of the SUV. Caleb had his arm around Ruth, who was crying.

"It's just been too much for her," he explained. "All the violence and the dead bodies, it's just been too much ... for all of us."

"Yeah, I know. It's been hard on you kids. You handled things better than I thought you might." Mark looked away for a second. He had forgotten they were just kids. Less than a month ago they'd been texting, playing sports or video games, and watching crazy stuff on TV. They never dreamed they'd be in gun battles or running for their lives. They could've gone their entire lives without seeing a dead body outside of a funeral home. How many had they seen in just a few days, including friends and family? They were doing pretty well, all things considered.

It wasn't what I would want for my own kids, but what can I do?

"I'm sorry you have to go through this. I really am. I wish it could be another way. Maybe someday it will be. But you can't get to someday if you don't survive today. You did what you needed to do. And you probably saved a few lives today, including mine."

Mark started back toward the house. It was important to keep them occupied and not let them dwell on all the death that surrounded them. "We need the gas from these cars. Why don't you guys go through some of these houses and see if you can find some gas cans and some tubing to siphon with. You remember what I showed you, I'm sure."

A shrill scream made Mark stop at the front door. He didn't want to go in; he knew what to expect. He didn't think there was much hope for the poor woman, but they had to try. To do otherwise would be inhuman and they'd seen enough of that kind of behavior. The scream came again. He swallowed hard and went inside.

Fifteen

THEY WERE ALL GATHERED around the kitchen table. Two of the men were holding the wounded woman's arms and legs down. She had a dish towel in her mouth to bite down on. The other woman assisted Lynn while the man with the injured arm and the attitude sat in a chair in the corner with his rifle in his hands and his head down. His eyes were closed and Mark couldn't decide if he was sleeping or praying.

"What can I do to help?" he asked.

Lynn handed him some latex gloves. "Take that flashlight and shine it down in the wound," she said without looking up. "I've had her swallow a sleeping pill and a large slug of cough medicine with codeine. She's feeling woozy, but the pain is still severe. I'm trying to reach the bullet without injuring her further."

Lynn probed with a metal skewer. "Ah, there it is. Okay, hold her tight. I'm going in for a closer look."

The woman moaned. It would be a blessing for all if the poor woman would pass out.

"I'll have to widen the hole to get it out. It hit the rib and is turned slightly. I was hoping to be able to pull it straight back out. I'm not sure these tweezers are wide enough or long enough to get a grip on it but it's all I've got to use."

"What are you going to use to cut her with?" Mark asked.

Lynn held up an Exact-o-knife. "I sterilized it, it should work."

Mark took the tweezers. Depending on the caliber of the slug they might need to be widened. He looked at the hole then back to the tweezers, then he bent them so the gap was wider.

"Okay, here comes the hard part. Hold her tight."

Lynn placed the razor against the torn flesh of the wound. Instantly, the woman began screaming and kicking. It was so forceful one leg broke free. Lynn looked both men in the eyes to make sure they were ready, then made her first incision. That was enough to send the tormented woman mercifully into unconsciousness. A collective sigh escaped them. Lynn worked faster now, trying to get finished before Mary woke up.

Fifteen minutes later, after multiple failed attempts, the bullet came free, clattering off the table and down to the floor. She widened the hole some more and tried to locate any internal damage. Minutes later, shaking her head, Lynn said, "I think that's it. I can't see anything else. There's too much blood and no way to clear it to see past it." Lynn used regular white thread to close the wound up after dousing it with disinfectant. Putting a bandage over the wound, Lynn stepped back and everyone relaxed.

"That's all I can do for now. You will have to watch her. The bandage will have to be changed and you will have to check for fever and redness at the stitches. Keep her feet up and keep her warm." She shrugged. "Other than that, all we can do is pray." She went into the kitchen to clean herself and the equipment using bleach and hand sanitizer.

They'd never introduced themselves. "My name's Mark, that's Lynn."

The man who had been holding the wounded woman's arms offered his hand. "I'm James and I want to thank you for all you and the lady there did for us." Mark shook it and looked at the others as James introduced them.

"That's Artie down by the feet, and Frank is the one in the corner. His wife Mary is the one on the table and my wife's the one standing. That's Maggie."

"I know you're not going to be able to move Mary yet, but this house no longer looks defensible. You may want to think about moving to a house you can secure."

"Don't you be worrying about where we're gonna be," Frank said, standing up. "We'll take care of ourselves."

His tone was defensive, making Mark bristle.

"Now, Frank, these good people helped us. There's no cause to be talking to them like that."

Frank walked to the table and looked down at his wife. "I don't think it's in our best interest to be telling anyone what our plans are."

Mark stared at Frank. "And it wasn't in our best interest to intervene in your fight. Fortunately for you, there are still some good people left in the world who are willing to stick their necks out for others." He turned back to James. "If you need any help you can find us at 5942 Eaglewood. There are plenty of houses next to us that we could help you fortify and defend. In this new world, it's good to have friends. You're welcome anytime. Lynn, we should be going."

"I'll check back with you tomorrow if you'd like," Lynn said to Maggie.

"That would be real nice, and thank you, for everything."

Lynn smiled and gave her a reassuring hug.

Loaded in the SUV, Mark asked, "What do you

think?"

She shook her head. "I just don't know. I couldn't find any internal damage but I was only guessing at what to look for. She'll be lucky to avoid infection. There are just no drugs to fight it and no blood to replace what she's lost. Depends on how strong she is. I'll know probably in about two days."

"You did real good in there. I was impressed."

Lynn looked at him searching his face. After a few seconds, she turned and mumbled, "Thanks." She brushed a strand of hair from her face and looked out the side window.

Sixteen

BACK AT THE HOUSE they unloaded the SUV and left it in the street. It might not hurt to have an extra vehicle available with the amount of people they had living there now.

They hauled the wood paneling and two-by-fours from the van. Mark had pried off a basement wall. It wasn't exactly the same as what was up already but it was close. Once they put the shelves in front of it, no one would be able to tell the difference. They spent the rest of the day constructing the women's sleeping quarters. Mark ran a line of two-by-fours along the floor from the wall he had constructed to the far basement wall and anchored them to the concrete. Using the remaining wood, he made supports that tied into the floor joists above, then nailed on the paneling. Alyssa shone a flashlight along the floor, sides, and ceiling to make sure no light penetrated. Mark used caulk to fill in where needed. He cut a section of the original paneled wall to use as a privacy door between the two rooms.

Meanwhile, Lynn supervised the setup of the space. They cleaned the walls and ceiling of any spider webs and painted the basement wall a light green. Next she had the girls put down throw rugs they had collected to add warmth. They had found one fold-up bed and placed it at the far end. Until other beds could be found, the two girls would be on sleeping bags with foam padding underneath them. Those could be rolled up and stored out of the way.

When they finished replacing the shelves and reloading them, they all collapsed on the floor of the main room, exhausted. The kids' resilience impressed Mark. If they still had any thoughts of the gun fight earlier, they carried them in silence and did not let it show.

They were discussing what to have for dinner.

"What sounds really good to me is pizza," Caleb said.

"Yeah, it does. Too bad we can't pick up the phone and order some," Darren replied.

They laughed, but as it faded away they all fell silent. They might never again be able to order pizza. Mark could see the change on their faces.

"Well, who says we can't?" he said.

"Yeah, right," Alyssa said, placing her elbows on her knees and her face in her hands. "Let's just pick up the phone and see who answers."

Mark ignored her and stood up, trying not to show how tired and sore his body was.

"Don't need a phone to make it ourselves, now, do we?" He bobbed his head from side to side in mock attitude.

They all lifted their heads and Mark could see a flicker of hope in their eyes. He walked into the storage area and came back out with a bag of flour, a small packet of dry yeast, and some seasonings.

"You want pizza? I'll make you pizza. Who's gonna help?"

No one spoke at first.

"Hey, you gonna sit around moping, crying about what you can't have, or are you gonna get up off your lazy butts and make the best damn pizza you've ever had?"

Lynn jumped up, put on a tired smile, and said, "I'm in."

"Awesome. Why don't you check and see what we've got for toppings."

"Darren, in the bottom left-hand side of the cooler there should be two bags of shredded cheese. It's not mozzarella but it'll do."

"Ruth, get me a large bowl from supplies. Alyssa, I need three bottles of water. Caleb, upstairs in the cabinet to the left of the stove you'll find two round pizza pans. One is solid, the other has a bunch of holes in it. Bring them both. And be very cautious. Look around before you start moving."

Everyone moved with a more excited step. It was amazing what something that reminded them of more normal times could do for their dispositions.

Mark went about making the dough, adding olive oil, onion powder and basil to the mix. Lynn opened a small can of tomato paste, mixed in some Italian seasoning with garlic powder, and stirred in water until the sauce was smooth. After kneading the dough, Mark covered the bowl with a towel and they all sat around impatiently, watching it rise.

Half an hour later, they were all tired and extremely hungry so, rather than let it rise to its fullest, Mark worked the dough again. He tossed it and stretched it until it was close to round, then formed it to the holed pan. He spread the sauce on then let Lynn top it with canned mushrooms and cheese. Darren turned on the gas grill in the cave. Mark placed the pan on the grill and they all stood around and anxiously watched the pizza cook. Mark had to widen the small opening in the dirt ceiling to prevent the cave from filling with smoke. The pizza to cooked quickly over the open flames.

119

Mark pulled the pan off the grill, slid the pizza onto the other pan and told someone to slice it while he stretched out a second pie and placed it on the grill. He sat down to enjoy his two slices but before he took a bite, he scanned the quiet group. They were munching happily. It made him smile. It felt like … family.

His mind wandered a moment to his own family. He looked at Lynn and felt guilty. He wasn't trying to replace his wife and son; he just needed the feeling of family.

"Okay," Alyssa admitted, "This *is* the best pizza I ever had."

Mark smiled and pushed the guilt away. It was what it was.

"I told you," he bragged.

The others agreed. They were easily done before the second pie was ready, waiting for it to bake. The second one lasted a little longer than the first, but they were all smiling and full when it was gone.

After clean up and bathroom breaks, they fell into their various sleeping accommodations. The girls having their own space made a lot more room for everyone. It also made it less stuffy. Lynn ushered the girls into their room. She stopped as her glance caught Mark's eyes. They locked for a few seconds before Lynn smiled, lowered her head, and closed their door.

LYNN LAY AWAKE LISTENING to the soft, steady breaths of the girls. The day had been exciting, to say the least. The gunfight had terrified her, but shooting was certainly better than being shot at. She thought about Mary and said a prayer. Then her thoughts turned to Mark. He seemed okay, but she'd been deceived before. Regardless, she wasn't about to let her guard down. Touching the gun under her pillow she closed her eyes.

Seventeen

MARK LET THEM SLEEP in longer than usual the next morning. Lord knew he needed sleep too, but letting them get some much-needed rest would go a long way to getting more work out of them today. It would be good for their mental state, as well. He had hooked up the battery to the monitors so he could keep watch without having to be upstairs or waking anyone else to do it. While they slept, he jotted down chores that needed to be done. With six of them working, it should go quickly.

It was nearly eight when Lynn appeared. She carried her shoes and had a look on her face that was a cross between perplexed and worried.

"What happened?" she whispered, as she closed the door behind her. The two boys were snoring, so Mark got up and motioned for Lynn to follow. He led her upstairs. They sat at the kitchen table and focused their eyes outside. In normal times, it would have been a pleasant view. Now they were more concerned with anyone seeing them.

"Why didn't you wake us?" she asked as she bent over to tie her shoes.

"I just thought everyone could use the rest."

"Including you." She sat up and pulled her hair back

in a ponytail. As she did, she caught a whiff of her underarms. "Dear Lord, do I smell that bad?"

Mark laughed. "Not that I noticed. But then, we're all in the same boat."

"It would be awesome if we could figure out a way to shower. I know we can't spare the water but it sure would be nice to feel clean, even once in a while."

"Let me work on that idea for a bit. I may be able to rig something up. The problem is making sure we never run out of drinking water. It could eventually become a commodity that's worth more than oil ever was."

They fell silent and glanced around uncomfortably. Mark looked at Lynn as she stared outside. Her face had several small imperfections that he realized were scars. He could only speculate where they came from; he wasn't about to ask, but some her reactions to being touched led him to believe her marriage might have been less than peaceful. She didn't smile much, but when she did, it warmed him in a way that made him feel that everything still had a chance to be all right.

She caught him looking at her and her cheeks flushed. She looked away and said, "Well, maybe we should be getting the kids up. I'm sure you have lots for us to do."

"There's no rush. Let them sleep. You don't mind sitting with me, do you?"

"No, I don't mind." Yet clearly she was uncomfortable.

"What do you think happened?" Lynn asked.

A question he had tried to answer many times.

"I really don't know. There are so many possibilities. What I don't understand is why us? I mean, what's so special or different about us that we survived and so many others didn't? Do we have some special trait that whatever this is had no effect on us? Or is it just ... random survival?"

"You mean luck?"

"I guess. We'll probably never know for sure."

"Maybe it's God's plan." She looked at him as though she thought he would yell at her for voicing her opinion.

"After everything I've seen in the past few weeks I'm not sure I believe in God anymore. If He exists, then He's given up on us; that's for sure."

Lynn took a breath as if to say something more, then thought better of it. It bothered Mark.

"Lynn, look, I don't know what you were used to before, and it's none of my business, but if you have something to say you have a right to say it. I may not agree, but that doesn't mean you can't have a different opinion. I'm not going to be mad or yell at you. We need to get used to each other and the best way to do that is to communicate. We each have to have an equal voice here. The kids depend on us to make the decisions. It's the only way it'll work, okay?"

She nodded. "Okay." She hesitated. "I just think with the world as screwed up as it is, that maybe this is God's way of cleaning house and starting over. Maybe we were chosen for a reason."

"There must be a reason, I'll agree to that, but I'm not going to give God credit. Sorry. It's just my personal opinion. No one will be able to convince me that my wife and son needed *cleansing.*" He realized his voice had turned bitter. He calmed himself. "But if you're right, and there is some plan, I wish He would make it known to us. And real soon would be nice."

"I understand. You think God took your loved ones away. Maybe He took them because He didn't want them to suffer through what comes next. I know it sounds trite but there has to be a reason. I have to believe that or I won't be able to face the day. If ever we needed God, it is now. I believe He'll be there for us when we need Him."

"I hope for all of our sakes you're right."

"Look," she said, pointing out the window. "It's a blue

123

jay."

A blue bird had landed on the deck railing. Its head danced around, searching for food, as if nothing had changed. "I think God just sent us a sign."

Mark smiled but didn't speak. It was what he saw when he looked past the bird that had his attention.

Where he'd buried his wife and son.

Eighteen

THEY SAT UNTIL THE blue jay flew off, taking that as a signal that it was time to start the day. Downstairs, the boys were up and the girls were stirring. While they ate breakfast, Mark explained the jobs he had lined up for them. He wanted them to feel part of building their new home. It was also important that everyone pull their fair share.

"Lynn, do you have anything to add or anything you want added to the list?"

She thought, then offered several things, including finding large clean plastic barrels to begin catching rain water. They split up the chores and went to work. Mark was impressed by the fact there was minimal complaining.

Today, Caleb and Alyssa got to go on the hunt. Mark did a mental head slap to remind himself that he needed to teach the kids how to handle guns. They had been a big help the day before but hadn't really hit anyone. They had served as a great distraction, but other than that, they'd just wasted bullets. It might be a good idea to make sure they all knew how to drive.

Taking the back road out of the subdivision, Mark retraced the route he'd taken the day before. With all the recent hostile activity in the area, he drove with extreme caution. They were getting a much later start than usual but he first wanted to look in on their new friends and make sure they were all right. He approached the street, inching to the corner. At the entrance to the court, he stopped and peered down the road. Most of the cars were still there, but someone had moved the bodies. Not seeing anything suspicious or threatening, Mark turned down the street then stopped.

Putting the van in reverse he pulled around the block and parked behind Frank's house.

"Caleb, get in the driver's seat. If you hear any gunshots, you drive around the corner, out of sight, and wait for me there. You understand?"

"Yes, sir."

Mark climbed out with his gun in hand, looking at the rear of the house. Something felt wrong. He couldn't put his finger on it, but something was making the hairs at the back of his neck stand up. He approached from behind and one house to the side. He stopped twice but nothing moved or made a sound. Making his way to the front porch he hesitated. Remembering Frank's itchy trigger finger, he decided to announce his presence. He called out.

"Hello in the house. Anyone awake?"

Only silence greeted him.

He climbed the steps.

"Frank? James? Maggie?"

Still no reply.

Maybe they had taken his advice and moved to another house. He wanted to look but didn't want to get shot if he startled them from their sleep. He stepped past the threshold, stopping in the living room. There he called out to them again.

His gun was up and ready now. He entered as if he were clearing a house in a combat zone. In the kitchen the story unfolded. Frank lay on the floor with multiple gunshot wounds. Someone had taken a shotgun and blown away his face. Mark prayed he had already been dead at the time. Artie was on the kitchen floor. The back of his head was gone as if he had been shot execution style, but with something big. Mary had never had a chance. She was still on the table but was naked. They had used her. He could only hope she was still unconscious when they came. Her throat had been cut. James and Maggie were nowhere to be seen. Could they have been taken? Judging from the condition of the others, that wasn't very likely. Someone had been very angry. Perhaps it was retaliation for losing so many of their own men.

As Mark looked at the ruined bodies, the first thought he had was they had been taken by surprise. He had been wrong; he wasn't too numb to feel. He thought about burying them, but things were different now. It was too dangerous to be in one place for too long. Taking a quick look around the house and not finding the other two, he left.

"Are they okay?" Caleb asked as he climbed back to his seat.

"Yeah, they've moved on to a better place," Mark lied.

Nineteen

THEY NEEDED SOME DISTANCE from the subdivisions, so Mark turned down the road that ran between the two subdivisions and headed west. He wanted to avoid main roads if possible, but the road he was on dead ended into Walden Road and he was forced to take it. He drove south for a half mile before turning west again. Five miles out, they were in farm country. The houses were spread out and looked untouched.

They came to a line of large pine trees on the right, set back about ten yards from the road. They acted as a barrier, preventing anyone from seeing what was beyond. Curious to see what they protected, Mark turned right at the next road. A large farmhouse stood at the end of a long dirt and gravel driveway. A garage and a barn stood behind and to the left of the house, as well as a series of greenhouses. Cornfields surrounded the back and left of the buildings stretching on for a great distance. Across the street were three two-story houses, but other than those only the rooftop could be seen of the next closest neighbor.

Staring at the sea of green stalks, Mark had visions of fresh vegetables. He drove up the driveway, thinking how perfect the farm looked, how perfect it would be to live there.

Stepping out of the van, Mark held his hands up high so if anyone was watching they could see he wasn't a threat.

"Is anyone home?" he called out in a loud voice.

He walked closer to the house and opened up a dialog with it, since no human was answering.

"We would like to trade for some of your corn. If you're interested, come out and talk to me. If you want us to go, you're going to have to tell me that too, because if I don't hear anything we're going to come exploring."

He stopped about twenty feet from the stone front porch.

"Last chance. We aren't here to hurt anyone." Nothing. "Okay, we're coming in."

He thudded his feet loudly on the wooden steps. At the front door, he peered through the windows into an immaculate home. It was decorated in country style and well cared for.

The door knob turned when he tried it, so he pushed the door open and slid out his gun. Advancing through the rooms, Mark had the feeling it had been long ago abandoned. There was a thin coat of dust built up, but other than that the house was as spotless as it had appeared from the window. Also important was the absence of the smell of decaying bodies. After searching each room, Mark went back to the porch and motioned the others forward. Caleb put the van in gear and drove. Mark signaled for him to park on the side of the house, out of sight from the road.

He stood at the door and waited for Caleb and Alyssa to come around the corner. When they did, he thought they were holding hands until they saw him looking. They were too obvious when they stepped away from each other. Mark looked away, pretending he hadn't noticed, but he would have to give some thought as to whether he should say something, either to them or to Lynn. Could it really do any harm? If anything, it was nice to see that some things never changed. Regardless of the situation, life and love still went on.

"You two take the house. You know what to look for, and split up so it goes faster." He gave them each a look. "I'll search the outbuildings."

He walked to the garage, stopping at the van to pick up two five-gallon gas containers. The garage, like the house, was unlocked and just as neat and organized. The people who'd lived there took great care of their things. Mark was willing to bet it was an older couple with some well-raised children. The garage was huge. He found a large storage tank for gas against the back wall. A fifty-five-gallon drum of oil, with a pump, stood next to the tank. Various farm equipment stood lined up inside. A huge work bench covered one side wall and a portion of the back. All sorts of power tools were stored on shelves below the workbench. Stairs led up to a floored attic used for storage of smaller less-used items.

An older model Buick took up one parking slot while an immaculate vintage pickup truck filled the other. A snowplow blade and a riding lawn mower stood against the back wall. Mark stood there, marveling at how well ordered everything was. He couldn't bring himself to touch anything. He filled up the two gas cans from the tank then set them down outside and closed the door.

Next he headed for the barn. The noise caught his attention first. Mark slowed his step and followed the sound and then the smell hit him. He found three adult-sized carcasses scattered along the side of the barn. You couldn't call them corpses any longer because what remained was only recognizable by the bones and shreds of clothing. They appeared to have been ripped apart. Mark's immediate thought was of the pack of wild dogs that had attacked him. A chill ran up his spine. They must have been caught in the open and taken down before they had a chance. The maggots and buzzing flies had taken care of what was left. He backed up and moved to the next building.

The barn held all the larger pieces of farm equipment,

including a tractor, a large wagon, a harvester, a Bobcat loader with a backhoe attachment, and several pieces that Mark recognized, but did not know the name for. The barn, to Mark's surprise, had a dirt floor but was none the worse for it. A rear wall had been repaired as there were signs of new wood in a few different areas. A loft covered both left and right sides, leaving the center open to the rafters.

He found a shovel hanging from a wall-mounted organizer. Behind the barn, he started digging graves. About fifteen minutes later, Alyssa and Caleb came out with their arms full of treasures and loaded the van. Several more trips finished their task and brought them to Mark's side.

"Caleb, I need you to continue digging here." Mark handed him the shovel. "Alyssa, go back in the house and find three sheets."

"Off the beds?"

"It doesn't matter."

Mark walked back to the garage and found another shovel. Normally he wouldn't have bothered, but these people deserved the respect of being buried.

It took them a little more than an hour to dig three graves. They didn't need to be very big or deep. Mark wrapped the remains after finding work gloves in the garage. He wanted to show respect but he really didn't want to touch them. Sliding the bodies in the holes he covered them. Leaning his chin on the shovel he offered up a silent prayer for their souls, just in case God really did exist.

After cleaning the shovels and putting them back where they belonged, Mark gathered the rifle and the handguns, as well as a shotgun the kids found in the house. He then collected string from a kitchen drawer and some plastic and glass bottles from the recycling bin in the house. Leading Caleb and Alyssa to the edge of a small apple orchard between the cornfield and the barn, he hung the bottles from the branches. Mark talked the two kids through proper loading and firing procedures. After making sure they understood and could demonstrate the proper grip and stance, he had them dry fire a few times to get used to squeezing the trigger rather than pulling or jerking it. Then he had them load the guns and take shots at the hanging targets.

He let them empty a magazine each then had them try a few rounds each with the rifle. They ended by firing the shotgun once each. The recoil knocked Caleb back and dropped Alyssa on her butt. They showed some promise with the handguns, although both needed more practice than Mark was willing to waste bullets on. The way they had been going through them, Mark was afraid of running out. He knew they understood how to shoot now. Whether or not they could pull the trigger with intent to kill was another story. Even though they had shot at the attackers the day before, both admitted they doubted they hit anyone.

Mark had them fill pillow cases with fresh corn even though the corn wasn't fully ripened yet. The apples weren't ready to be picked. The greenhouses netted them green beans and tomatoes. They would have to come back and pick more. It would be a shame to waste fresh produce. They searched the three more houses across from the farmhouse before heading home. To Mark, it had been a productive but sad day.

LYNN PACKED SUPPLIES FOOD and water in a backpack and hid it under a pile of blankets in the storage room. She had no immediate plans but wanted to be prepared, just in case. She reloaded her gun. Patting her pocket she felt the keys to the SUV parked out front. Maybe it wouldn't hurt to store a few items inside the vehicle too.

The talk in the morning with Mark had unsettled her. Not that anything he said had been threatening, in fact, it was just the opposite. Her fear had been that she found his words had relaxed her caution. She couldn't afford to let down her wall. When it was time to leave, she didn't want to hesitate.

She stopped and pictured him. The day he rescued them, the way he'd handled the people yesterday. She thought of him making the pizzas last night and most of all she remembered his eyes. The tension faded from her. Then just as quick, she forced her resolve to stiffen. No, she would not be lulled and allow herself or the children to fall into another bad situation.

The past few days had given her new courage. She'd discovered an inner strength she had thought long dead. Lynn knew she could take care of herself if need be and no one would ever control her again.

Taking the box of remaining bullets, she dug out the pack and slammed them angrily inside.

Twenty

AFTER A LIGHT LUNCH, the entire group dove into the projects Mark had on his list. The list included putting the finishing touches on the girls' bedroom for comfort and security, and completing the underground cavern, including putting in a metal vent with slats in the ceiling that could be opened when needed and wide enough that it could be used as an escape hatch in an emergency. There would only be a little more than eighteen inches clearance in some places, between the ground and the heavy support beams under the deck, so they would have to crawl, but at least they had an option now in case they were trapped.

The vent in place, Mark gave some thought to digging the cavern out farther so there was room enough for all of them to fit inside comfortably. Right now, the room was full of propane tanks and generators. The more stuff they collected for their survival, the more space they needed for storage. Mark stacked the tanks more efficiently to make more room, but expanding the cave would have to wait for another day. It was dinner time and this night was for enjoying fresh food.

Lynn had decided to grill the ears of corn and green beans. She brushed them with olive oil and wrapped them in foil, placing them on the grill in the cave. Mark opened the vent and they all sat and waited eagerly for their treat.

Mark passed around a bag of beef jerky with teriyaki flavoring and opened two cans of sliced peaches. When the corn was done, the room filled with the sound of crunching. The ears were a little pale, not quite fully ripened, but it made no difference to the group; they ate and asked for more. The green beans had blackened slightly but tasted wonderful. It may not have been what any of them would have chosen for a meal a month ago, but, today, it was a banquet.

They were in the process of cleaning up when Caleb's ears perked up. "Shh, I think someone's in the house."

Out of habit, they all stopped and ducked.

Mark whispered. "If you have something in your hand, set it down on the floor away from your feet as quiet as you can." He didn't want anyone to inadvertently drop or bump something that would give away their presence. He walked to the stacked car batteries and hooked his security cameras up to one of them. It took a moment for the monitor to come to life. He was angry with himself for being lax. Not only had he allowed the meal to distract him from his normal security routine, but he had failed to hook up the monitors. He hoped his incompetence wouldn't cost them their lives.

With it dark outside, the images were very difficult to see in detail. They all watched as the screen flicked from one view to another.

It was hard to see anything out of the ordinary until Lynn said, "There."

Mark moved closer to the screen and saw a large dark shadow move toward one of the cameras. The screen darkened then cleared as the body moved past. A second later another form passed by. The second one appeared smaller than the first. The floorboards above them creaked ever-so-slightly. The intruders were in the family room. How had the intruders gotten in without being heard? There had been no sound of glass breaking. They had all been too focused on their food.

After the monitor cycled through one more time and no other forms came into view, Mark froze the picture on the family room. They watched as the two undefined forms turned around and started back the way they came. The footsteps made it easy to figure out where they were. They moved to the kitchen and Mark hit another button until he had the right camera angle. At that moment, a sudden flash of light illuminated the couple. It allowed them to see that it was a man and a woman, but they could not make out their faces.

"One of them has a flashlight," Mark announced. He heard the basement door creak open. "Caleb, turn out the lights. Lynn, take the girls and Darren inside the cave and get ready to close it like I showed you."

Mark moved to the wooden dividing wall as everyone moved. He turned his head and placed his ear against the wall to try to hear what was happening on the other side.

"No one's here," he heard a woman say. "Maybe they were attacked too."

"Could be, but I'd think their bodies would still be lying around. Or at least there would be a lot of blood."

"Maybe they just packed up and left, fearing someone would come looking for them."

"Most like. Well, at any rate, they ain't here. Look, there's some sleeping bags. Maybe we should just stay here for tonight."

"It's as good a place as any, I guess. I'll go upstairs and lock the doors."

Mark had to make a decision. He had a feeling the two intruders were James and Maggie. He couldn't be sure from the dark images on the screen. He was afraid to risk their hiding place in case he was wrong so decided to wait until morning.

In the cave he said, "Two people are camping out in our basement. We're going to have to be very quiet until the morning. Lynn, let's wait for about half an hour then get the beds ready. If anyone has to go to the bathroom, use that bucket over there in the corner. We must be as quiet as possible so we don't give ourselves away."

A short time later, Mark and Lynn went to the girls' room and set up the bedding. One at a time, the girls settled in. When they were done, Mark and Darren set up the boy's room. Mark let Caleb use the cot because he planned on staying awake to keep watch. He told them he might wake them to take a turn on watch if he couldn't keep his eyes open. He also told them not to snore, or he'd wake them too.

His head started bouncing off his chest about three a.m. He shook himself and stood to stretch. He was about to wake Caleb to take his place when movement on the screen caught his eye. He kept the monitor running, depleting one battery already. When the picture flicked from the inside to the outside view, he thought he saw something. He waited for it to cycle through again, but when it did, there was nothing there.

Before he could take one more step, glass shattered. From the sound, it came from the back of the house. He watched the monitor closer now, tired eyes no longer a problem. Both boys sat up, looking around. Mark hit the button and froze the picture. Three men came through the patio door window.

The men separated and ran through the house. Their footsteps thundered above him. By the way they were moving it was obvious they weren't there to ransack. Instead, they were looking for someone. If they came downstairs, they would easily find the two people there. Finding them, they would most likely give up the search.

Mark could sacrifice them to save Lynn and the kids.

In his heart, however, he knew he couldn't do it. He wasn't built that way. He had played God once. He could not decide who would live and who would be sacrificed for the greater good.

The boys, wide awake, looked frightened. "Darren, go get the girls. Caleb, get the guns. And be very quiet."

He went to the wall and pushed it open just enough for him to slip out. He stood out of sight next to the metal racks, scanning the basement. The two people were whispering and trying to be quiet as they looked for someplace to hide, already aware of the danger they were in. Mark crouched, duck-walking toward them. They were in front of him, using the two sleeping bags to cover them. Evidently their plan was to hope they wouldn't be seen. Mark crept up behind them. Knowing they would jump and make noise if he startled them, he wrapped an arm around each one and clamped his hands over their mouths.

"Shh! If you want to live, follow me. Hurry, before they get down here." Mark released them and started back to the opening. He stopped and motioned for them to hurry. The hunters were in the kitchen now. As the man came forward, Mark grabbed his arm and all but flung him through the doorway. The woman was too slow. Mark reached out and grabbed her shirt, snagging her bra in the handful, and hauled her forward as the basement door was swung open. Mark followed, almost falling on her. Running steps tramped down the wooden stairs. Mark was just able to pull the panel shut, but it had made noise. The only thing he could hope for was that it had been lost in the intruder's thundering footsteps.

"I know I heard something down here. Tear the place apart."

"Don't worry, if they're down here, we'll find them."

A third voice said, "You sure this is the house you saw

them come in?"

"Absolutely sure. I marked the spot I was standing in. You saw it. It was this house. Two people, a man and a woman. I think they were older by the way they walked."

The sound of things being thrown around the basement came through the thin dividing wall.

"I think they were here. Look, there's two sleeping bags here that look like they been used. I don't see them, though. They must have skated when you came and got us."

"Maybe, but I'm telling you it seemed like they were looking for this house, like they expected someone else to be here. One of them even said, 'Is this the right house?'"

"Huh, we'll have to keep it staked out then and see if anyone shows up."

Mark closed his eyes and cursed to himself. They could very well be trapped down there for a while.

"Yeah, let's go. Ain't no one here now."

In the safe room, Mark could hear the trio plod back upstairs. The large dark blobs moved past the camera and out the rear door. He reset the monitor to go back to roaming. Another camera picked the men up again, outside, as they moved toward the wooded area at the back of the lot. They would have to be very cautious when leaving from now on.

Twenty-One

THE NEW COUPLE WAS indeed James and Maggie. After getting everyone settled back down, Lynn brought the two of them some water then made them peanut butter sandwiches. They scarfed the sandwiches down, so Lynn made two more.

"God, it's good to see you," James said. "We haven't eaten in longer than I can remember."

"What happened?" Mark asked. "I went back to check up on you and found the others dead." He was aware of all eyes turning toward him when he made that announcement. Earlier, he had lied about what he found there.

"You never told us that!" exclaimed Alyssa.

"Did more show up?" Mark asked, without responding to Alyssa.

"The others were responsible for packing. Our job was to move the bodies and the cars. Then we were finding a new place to live," James explained. "Maggie and I piled the bodies into the largest cars and drove them away. After unloading the bodies, we drove back. As we came to our street, we noticed two new cars out front. We continued past, driving around the block. Coming through the backyard of the house behind ours, we stopped when we heard the shots. About fifteen minutes later, the cars drove off. When we went inside, well, you know what was there." His voice faltered; Maggie cried.

"They had taken much of what was packed. We gathered what we could carry and left, thinking they would be back for the rest of the stuff. We hid what we were carrying then wandered around a bit before coming here. When we didn't find you, we thought you'd packed up and moved off yourselves. Didn't realize there were so many of you."

Lynn hugged Maggie. "I'm so sorry, Maggie." When they broke apart, her eyes were moist too.

"I don't understand," Maggie said. "Haven't we all suffered enough? There are so few of us left in the world. Why do these animals have to kill us? It doesn't make any sense."

James hugged his wife, her crying muffled against his chest. "So where do we go from here?"

Mark said, looking at Lynn, "I wasn't going to bring it up until tomorrow, but I think it's time we moved out of this neighborhood. In fact, I think I've found just the place for us." He started relaying details of the farmhouse.

When he was done, Lynn shooed the girls back to their room. "Let's discuss it in the morning.

Maggie, why don't you take the cot?"

Mark said, "Caleb, you've got the next watch. Wake Darren to relieve you in two hours. Wake me immediately if you see anything out there. James, pull up some floor and make yourself comfortable."

"Will do." He kissed his wife good night and curled up on the floor next to her.

Mark was down and out in minutes. The next thing he knew, Lynn shook him awake, wearing a weary smile.

"Sorry. I know you're tired, but I didn't think you'd want to sleep the morning away."

"No, you're right. Thank you." He rubbed his face. When he lowered his hands, he was looking at a cup of coffee. Lynn wore a bigger smile. "Thought this might help you get started." He smiled back and accepted the cup. Again, Lynn turned her head rather than face him. It would take some time. Still, it had been a nice moment.

Mark stood and took a long sip of the hot drink. It wasn't the best coffee he'd ever tasted, but under these circumstances, it hit the right spots. His coffee finished, everyone gathered around in the cramped room, waiting for him to explain his plan. After laying it all out and answering questions, Mark told them to begin packing. Before they made any kind of move outside, Mark first wanted to sneak upstairs with his binoculars. He wanted to scan the woods and streets to determine if anyone was watching them.

He opened the basement door, alert in case someone had hidden out of sight. Nothing happened, so he crawled through the kitchen, into the dining room, and around to the staircase to the second floor. Once upstairs, Mark moved to the small bedroom at the back of the house. He slipped the binoculars between the drapes and took a long close look at the woods. Ten minutes later, as sure as he could be that no one was watching, he moved to the front bedroom to have a look at the streets.

Nothing obvious, or out of the ordinary appeared on the street, no cars or trucks that hadn't been there before. Two houses sat directly across from his that offered a good view for anyone staking out his place. It was difficult to see inside either house. Mark spent a lot of time trying to catch any movement through the windows. He was about to go look at the back once more when he thought he saw the curtain move in the living room window of the house to the left.

Focusing the binoculars on that window, he made out a finger poking through the drapes holding them to one side. At least one person was in that house. Mark backed away from the window and gave it some thought. Then he walked to the back bedroom again. There was still no obvious sign of a watcher back there, but it stood to reason that if they were watching the front, someone was hidden there too. He would have to go out and look for himself.

Back in the basement he said, "Lynn, what did you do with the keys from the car you parked in the senior center parking lot?"

"Um, I just left them in the ignition, I think. Why?"

"I'm thinking of taking a test run to see who's watching. I'm certain there's someone in the house across the street. But there doesn't seem to be anyone out back. At least I didn't see anyone. The way I figure it, if I couldn't see them they couldn't see me. They would have to be near the edge for me to see anything. I'm gonna go take a closer look."

"But what if someone's out there?" Ruth asked with great concern.

"I guess I'll have to deal with him," he said trying to sound casual and reassuring about it.

"They'll see you coming. You won't stand a chance," said Caleb. "What if I stand watch at the back door in case you need help?"

Mark thought it over. It was a good suggestion. "Okay, but what I want you to do is stay by the kitchen window and watch for my signal. If no one is there, I want to move some of you out of here. I think it's time to relocate. We'll have to do it quick and quiet and be very organized. It will take a lot of runs to move everything."

Lynn moved forward and looked him straight in the eyes. "I know you need to do this, but we would all be lost without you. Please be careful. Don't take any unnecessary risks."

He met her gaze. "I won't. I promise."

Mark gathered up what he thought he might need. At the kitchen window, he took one last look at the woods, nodded to Caleb. "I'll be back in a few minutes."

As soon as he was ready to move, Mark crept as close to the shattered patio door as he could get without being seen. In one long stride, he ducked under the hanging bits of glass and ran down the deck steps. Without hesitating, Mark sprinted for the tree line, stopping midway through and dropping to one knee. The shotgun he carried was up, sweeping from side to side. Nothing moved. He couldn't believe whoever was watching for them was so incompetent as to leave them an exit route. Waiting another minute to be sure he was clear, he bolted for the parking lot.

The car was where Lynn left it and apparently had escaped notice. The keys dangled from the ignition. Lynn and the kids had emptied it of their belongings. Mark wasted little time cranking it up and driving off. His eyes flicked from one mirror to another, anticipating someone bursting from the trees after him.

He stopped the car next to a building about forty feet from the road. There, he got out and moved along the wall until he was able to focus the binoculars down the street in both directions. The roadblock had gone. Nothing moved or waited for him. If someone was in hiding, he was doing a good job.

Back in the car, he reversed until he was back where he started. Leaving the car running, Mark made his way to the edge of the tree line and waved to Caleb. Several minutes later, James, Maggie, and Alyssa left the house, their arms laden with whatever they could carry.

Mark raised the shotgun and covered them as they entered the woods. "Keep moving. The car is straight through there." He waited until they had enough time to reach the car before following them. They were piling in as he arrived. Mark shut Maggie's door then slid in next to Alyssa.

He knew the route but purposely went a different way in case they picked up a tail. It took twenty minutes before he felt it was safe enough to continue to their destination. At the farmhouse, Mark drove around back and parked. Maggie nodded her approval. "Now that's what I'm talking about," she said.

They unloaded the car and Mark left them there to head back and start the transfer process. It would be a long, arduous process unless he could somehow rid them of their watchers.

Back at the house, Mark found that Lynn and the remaining kids had made huge headway with the packing. The van was at least halfway full and some of the backup generators were in the bed of the pickup truck. Even with all that transportation, it would take several trips to move everything. The problem would be getting the trucks out of the garage without tipping their hand to the watchers. As Mark loaded the car for a second run, he plotted how best to make that happen.

The second trip, he took Ruth back with him. As the others unloaded the car, Mark went to the garage. He had been concerned about how to get the remaining generators and other large items out of the house. Once the van and pickup were out of the garage, there would be no going back. The next problem would be hauling the generators across the backyard and through the woods. The remedy for that was to take James back to his house. Mark drove the pickup and had James drive the car for extra hauling space. Mark hated leaving the women unprotected, but, with everything they'd been through over the past month, they should be capable of defending themselves. After a few defensive suggestions and words of caution, James and Mark returned to the house.

The third trip took a long time with the two of them

hauling the last three generators, two propane fueled salamanders, and the two folding cots. It was while carrying a jammed-full extra-large cooler between the two men that they hit their first snag. As they emerged from the woods a man walked toward them, with his head down. He was unaware of them until they stepped into the open. Mark could have kicked himself for getting complacent and not checking before emerging from cover.

For several seconds they all stood, staring at each other. Mark was about to try and talk to the man when he reached behind him for his gun. Mark dropped his side of the cooler and ran for the woods while trying to pull out his gun. James had been slower. The cooler flopped down at an angle catching him across the ankle, tripping him. As he hit the ground, he kicked his way free of the cooler and made a desperate attempt to crawl for cover.

The man pulled his gun free, first swinging it toward Mark. When he saw there was no chance of a shot there, he turned toward James. Lining up his shot he pulled the trigger a fraction after Mark's bullet ripped through him, throwing his shot up into the trees. Mark ran out of the woods toward the dying man. Kicking the gun clear, he looked down at the man. He was in severe pain and losing blood. He wouldn't last long. Mark closed his eyes to push aside his natural urge to help him, then turned to James.

"Quick, we have to get out of here. Someone was sure to have heard those shots."

They picked up the cooler and ran with it the best they could. Hefting it up they tossed it on top of the generators. It wasn't well balanced, but it would have to do.

"Go, and don't come back. I need to go warn Lynn and Caleb."

146

Without waiting for a reply, Mark turned back toward the house. On the way, he grabbed the now dead man and dragged him into the woods. Taking a quick look to make sure the coast was clear this time, he dashed for the house. Once inside, he ran to the garage where Lynn and Caleb still loaded boxes and bags of food into whatever empty spaces were still left.

"Trouble," Mark exclaimed. "Where's Darren?"

"In the basement," Caleb answered.

"What's happening?" Lynn asked.

"People might be coming. Hide in the van. When you hear a commotion outside, lift the doors and drive off as fast as you can. Caleb, you remember where the farmhouse is?"

"I-I think so."

"But there's still a lot left to pack," Lynn complained.

"It will have to be left behind. Maybe we can sneak back later and get it. It's too dangerous right now. Drive off and don't get separated. Hide now."

With that he spun around and ran. He caught movement outside and heard someone say, "There."

He raced for the basement door, shutting it loudly behind him. "Darren. Darren, where are you?"

The boy poked his head out the safe room opening. "Here."

"Get back in there. Hurry."

There was no mistaking he had been seen. Multiple running footsteps pounded the floor above him. He jumped through the doorway and pulled the panel shut. His pursuit came down the steps in a hurry. Mark placed a finger to his lips for Darren's benefit. He wondered about the wisdom of trying to ambush them and decided that opening the panel would give him away before he could get off a shot. He motioned Darren to the cave. He was working on removing the vent when he heard an automatic weapon spray the basement. As he looked

147

back into the safe room, bullet holes had punched through the paneling in a chest-high line. If they looked close at them or thought about why the bullets weren't ricocheting off the walls, they would discover the room. He pulled the cave door shut. The only light came in from the louvers of the vent, making it difficult to see what he was doing. The vent was just wedged in place for quick removal. Still it was a tight fit and had to be done without making noise. Mark worked on lifting one corner at a time a few inches each. Finally, it lifted free.

"I think someone's in the room," Darren whispered.

Mark had to be careful not to strike the underside of the deck with the metal frame. He tried to move the vent to one side but from below it was a difficult task. Putting the vent there as an escape route had been a brilliant idea – he just wished he had thought to practice removing it a few times. It scraped the deck before he was able to set it down. More automatic fire riddled the walls. Since the door to the cave was concrete, nothing came through but he knew that at any moment they could be discovered.

He lifted Darren, who snaked through the hole and wiggled to the edge of the deck. Mark jumped up, grabbed the vent's framework and with maximum effort hoisted himself through the opening. Because of the low clearance he couldn't leverage himself straight up. Instead, he had to bend and pull himself clear, digging his hands into the ground and pulling hand over hand. He slid the vent back in place then crawled to the edge of the deck. The bottom of the deck was covered by lattice. He had a moment's panic, berating himself for not having tested and prepared the escape route. The small panels were stapled to the support beams. Mark had to push and wiggle one section to break it free. They crawled from underneath and Mark replaced the lattice. He took a quick peek, making sure it was clear and they bolted for the trees.

Inside the woods, Mark shoved Darren to the ground and stood behind a tree as a short burst of bullets tore through the branches. Mark returned fire then hauled Darren to his feet and they were off running again. They sprinted from the back end of the trees without looking. This time, however, they were alone. Behind them, voices signaled the sound of pursuit. He eyed the car.

This would be close.

Mark jammed the keys into the ignition, started it, and peeled out as the two gunmen emerged from the trees. They opened fire on the fleeing car. Bullets pelted the trunk. Seconds later, buildings blocked the line of sight and no more shots chased them.

An angry rolling lump formed in his stomach as he thought about Lynn and Caleb. He had to get back to them before they were discovered. Panic released as bile at the back of his throat. He had to hurry. He couldn't fail them. Mark wanted to scream his fear. He couldn't lose another family. Fighting for control he swallowed hard, hoping all emotion would go with it.

Twenty-Two

MARK RIPPED THE WHEEL turning north on Walden Road and jammed the pedal to the floor. At Erie he turned right, barely slowing, then right again into the subdivision. He needed to draw the gunmen away from Lynn and Caleb so they could make their getaway. .

He rounded the corner of his street and slowed down, not wanting to run headlong into the shooters. All he wanted them to do was catch sight of him and begin pursuit. Up ahead the two men had climbed into a car. Mark floored it, not so much for the speed, but to rev the engine and draw their attention. They had an immediate reaction within the car. The driver, without thinking, opened his door to get out and shoot. Mark veered toward the open door, slamming it shut and just missing the man's leg.

Mark blasted his horn three times as he drove away, hoping that would be enough signal for Lynn and Caleb to move. Mark checked his mirrors. The car made a U-turn in the street and took up the chase. He was around the next corner before he could see if Lynn and Caleb made their escape.

The subdivision had some short streets and several curved roads that kept them out of view of the pursuing car. Leaving the development in a sharp, uncontrolled turn, Mark accelerated down the back road until he hit Walden again. There, he made a sharp left. A quarter mile farther was the turn for the farmhouse. He hadn't planned on taking it but when he looked back, there was no sign of pursuit. Making a last-second decision, Mark pulled the wheel right. As far as he could tell they were in the clear, which should have made him relax. But something nagged at him. He shook his head and swore under his breath. They shouldn't have been able to lose them that easy. The chasing car was just too close to them for that. So either Mark had done more damage to the shooter's car then he thought ... or Lynn and Caleb had been discovered.

The more he thought about it, the more afraid for their safety he became. An internal battle waged within him. He had Darren's safety to consider too. Mark decided to go to the farmhouse. While there he could change vehicles and gather whatever weapons he might need to go back and try to rescue them.

He stopped short of the farmhouse and looked behind him to make sure no one was hanging back. Seeing the road empty, he made the turn, pulling up the driveway and around back where the others were waiting for him. The pickup truck had already been unloaded.

Mark hopped out and ran for the house. He went through the assorted weapons laid out on the living room floor. He grabbed a box of 9mm shells for his pistol, a box of shotgun shells and ten rounds for the rifle. He already had the survival knife at his belt. He turned, snatching the binoculars and two bottles of water off the kitchen table, and ran back out.

Darren had already explained what happened. The group stood around and waited for Mark to tell them what he needed them to do.

"I'm taking the truck and going back to see what

happened to Lynn and Caleb. It may be nothing, but I need to make sure. The rest of you …"

Just then, a white van raced toward them from the opposite direction Mark had come. Every member of the group scattered and had a gun of some sort, pulled and aimed at the approaching vehicle.

The van barreled closer. It looked out of control, but Caleb was driving it. "Hold your fire!" Mark cautioned.

Caleb swerved around the corner, swinging back equally as hard to turn into the driveway. For a brief instant, it appeared as though the van would flip on its side. Caleb fought the wheel for control. He braked to a skidding stop less than a foot from the back of the car, sending the others scurrying for safety.

Caleb was out the door almost before the van stopped.

"They've got her! They've got my mom!" His voice frantic, he turned to Mark. "Please, we have to save her."

Caleb was in a panic. His words were jumbled. Mark shook him. "Settle down. Caleb," he shouted, starting to feel the same panic. "Calm down and tell me what happened."

"We-we heard the horn and figured that was the signal. I opened both doors and we drove down the driveway. I turned left and my mom followed, but by the time we got to the main road, a car was following us. I tried to go fast and make sharp turns, but we couldn't shake them. One of them leaned out the window and started shooting at Mom. I don't know what happened, but she just stopped and I heard this huge crash. The truck was pushed off the road and the car was locked up underneath it. I saw the guy who was shooting go flying out the window. He rolled and rolled. I didn't see if he got up.

"I stopped to see if I could help Mom, but she jumped out of the truck and started running. I saw her waving her arms at me to go, but I didn't want to leave her. I didn't understand why she was running toward a house instead of toward me. Then I saw another car was coming.

"I thought she was going to try to hide until I could get here and get help. I started driving, but I watched in the mirror. The driver got out and chased her while the other car stopped to help. When I turned the corner, I stopped. I saw the man tackle her."

Caleb began crying hard. "He was sitting on her and she was fighting him. I stopped. I wanted to go back, but the man motioned for the other guy to come after me, so I drove away." He fell to the ground and Ruth dropped to hold him. They were both crying.

"She did it on purpose, didn't she?" he said between sobs. "She let them hit her so I could get away."

Mark knew it was most likely true. What parent wouldn't sacrifice himself for their child? But she wasn't dead yet. Bad things would happen to her, things he didn't want to think about, but they wouldn't kill her – at least, not right away. He clenched his jaw, knowing what had to be done and where he would have to go to find her.

Just then, their heads lifted as the sound of another vehicle approached. It came from the same direction as Caleb had and moved slowly, as if searching for something.

"That's the car!" Caleb shouted, pointing at it.

The driver braked; they'd been spotted. Mark could not let this car get away. The driver would come back with a swarm of others. Mark was angry and tired of running. This man had to die.

The car accelerated. Mark, with 9mm in hand, ran around the back of the house heading toward the pine-tree-lined street. He had to cut off this man before he got out of range. Mark broke through the prickly branches, level with the car. His gun was up already and he just pulled the trigger.

Both driver side windows exploded and the car lurched to the side of the road, throwing up gravel from the sloping shoulder. Several rocks hit Mark as he continued to run after the car, keeping up a constant barrage. The driver attempted to right himself as he slipped farther into the drainage ditch that ran along that side of the road. The tail end swerved toward the bottom even as the front tires dug for purchase and began to pull the car out.

Mark closed the distance down to thirty feet. The car was broadside to him as it struggled to rise. He stopped shooting, hoping for a better target. The driver was trying to keep his head down below the level of the door. He stretched a gun out the window and fired several times in Mark's direction, all the while keeping his foot pinned to the accelerator.

As the car climbed back to the road, Mark stopped ten feet away, put two hands on his gun, and sighted as best he could, praying the man would give him even the tiniest of targets.

The front wheels grabbed the road and lurched forward. The driver was smart enough not to lift his head above the door frame. Mark wasn't going to get a better chance so he fired into the door until he heard a cry of pain from inside. The man's body jerked upright, giving Mark a shot at his head. Mark fired twice. The car jumped forward, crossed the road, and then crashed into a pine tree. The wheels continued to spin as Mark advanced on the car. He wasn't sure how many shots he had left, but couldn't afford to take his eyes off the man to check.

The far door opened and the man tried to climb out. Mark ran to get around the car before the man could set himself to take a shot. At the trunk, he stopped to use it for cover. The driver crawled out and fell in the sloping grass facing him. His head and face were covered in blood. He struggled to lift the gun to bring it on target. He had blood streaking into his eyes.

He saw Mark and fired into the ground, unable to lift the barrel higher. Mark drew a bead on the man's head and pulled the trigger. Nothing happened. Empty.

The driver looked from side to side. Painful grunts escaped him as he spun. Mark dropped his gun, pulled the knife and advanced. He plunged the knife into the man, piercing his heart.

Mark peeled the gun from the dead man's hands and stood up. He had to move the car and the body, but there was no time. Lynn's safety, and possibly her life, depended on how fast he could get to her. The others would have to see to cleaning up the mess. He raced back to the house, horrible memories of Summer assaulting him.

Twenty-Three

FIFTEEN MINUTES LATER, with Caleb directing him, he went searching for Lynn. Mark didn't want to take the young man. Caleb, however, was determined to help save his mother. He felt responsible for her capture. He climbed in the van and refused to get out.

"Do you understand what we are going to do? Do you know what might happen to us? Are you sure you want to find your mother and know what they might have done to her? You better think real hard about this. I can't afford to have you freeze up on me out there. It could get us both killed."

But in the end, the boy could not be dissuaded. His mother had sacrificed herself for him. How could he not do the same? Mark understood and secretly applauded the boy's intentions, but he would have to emotionally detach himself once they started whatever it was they were going to do. Otherwise, Caleb's inexperience could get Mark killed.

While they'd argued, the others emptied the van completely, placing the AK-47 in the back with his rifle and a second shotgun. Caleb already carried a handgun. Before they left, Mark made sure James knew to hide the car and body as far from the house as possible and to keep everyone inside until they came back. He didn't have to say *if we come back*. He assumed they all understood that.

They found the crash site. The pickup truck was still there, the contents hadn't been removed. Once they had Lynn, they'd never bothered to check it. Mark was sure they would be back for the items later.

He tried not to think about what Lynn was going through. He couldn't afford to be distracted. He hoped she could survive her ordeal, both physically and mentally. The one thought he allowed to run through his mind was that they would pay for hurting her. Even if it cost him his life, they would pay.

The downtown area of the small city was only a few blocks long. Mark took back roads until he came to Main Street. They approached from the south where the street was on a slight decline. It offered a full-length view down the street. What he saw surprised him; the streets were free of debris. What surprised him more was there was no sign of any bodies. Someone had cleaned up the street. His thoughts went immediately to the large man he had seen at Summer's. Could he have somehow forced the insanity to stop? No sign of life showed anywhere. Maybe he just killed everyone off whom he couldn't control.

The thought of one person capable of doing that was scary. If he were that organized and wielded that much power, he would be difficult to take down.

Mark got out of the van and walked up the steps of St. Joseph's Church. It gave him a different angle. There, he discovered where the Horde was sheltered: in what had once been an upscale chain hotel. It stood eight stories high. Mark speculated that the top floor housed suites. If he was the man in charge, that's where he'd be.

What he didn't know was how many members of the Horde there were. Mark had no way of knowing how many of the people he'd seen during his previous visit had survived. It appeared as though quite a few had, but they had taken some significant casualties in the past week.

Could there be that many more of the Horde left?

They sure didn't seem to be interested in recruiting any new members. The Horde would rather kill than recruit. Mark remembered an old Stephen King novel that had an equal number of good and bad people at the end.

Where are all the good people hiding?

A concrete bridge crossed a small creek at the bottom of the hill. Just beyond that on the right was the hotel, less than a hundred yards from where he stood. Mark climbed back in the van and pulled across the street into the church parking lot. They were now on the same side as the hotel. Trees along the creek and the higher level of the lot hid them from view from the hotel.

Mark got out and walked to the edge of the embankment that ran down to the creek. He stopped near the tree line and used the binoculars to scan the hotel grounds. Little of the parking lot showed. Most of it was on the far side of the hotel, blocked from view. However, a steady flow of vehicles pulled in and out of the lot. That didn't bode well for making an undetected rescue attempt. He noticed men and a few women walking around carrying guns. Most of them had rifles or shotguns over their shoulders.

Mark tried to see in the windows, but most had the curtains drawn. He scanned the entire height of the building, stopping at the penthouse suites. The question was: would the men who'd captured Lynn take her to the leader or would they keep her for themselves in their own room somewhere? Having to check every room would make the task more difficult.

Mark pulled the glasses from his face and squeezed

the bridge of his nose hard. He needed the pain to refocus. This was no time for emotions; that would do neither of them any good. This was time to put on his killing face.

A face he had worn too much of late. A face he feared had become permanent.

Mark raised the binoculars again and angled them to ground level. He studied the men to see if they had any kind of uniform, dress, or symbol that identified them with the others. It didn't appear so. They were all dressed differently. He watched the one door he could see and noticed there were no guards or anyone checking ID. Unless someone was stationed on the inside checking, it should be easy enough to get in. The hard part would be getting back out.

Below, he caught movement in the woods on the far side of the creek. A man was leading a teenage girl along the bank of the creek. She wasn't fighting him, but he was all but dragging her. The man stopped abruptly and spun on the girl. He slapped her, knocking the girl to the ground. She screamed and covered her head expecting more blows to land.

Anger shot through Mark. A red flash clouded his eyes, but he couldn't allow himself to be distracted. Fighting to control his initial response to run across the creek and throttle the man, Mark went back to the van, trying to calm down. He couldn't afford to feel. He just needed to react. He put the glasses back and picked up the shotgun. Everything had been reloaded. With one deep breath, he felt himself change like a man with two personalities.

"Stay in the back and keep the doors locked. Do not leave this van." His tone was harsh. Mark barely recognized his own voice. "I will knock on the outside five times fast to let you know it's me. If I'm coming on the run, I will scream your name. If that happens, unlock

159

the back doors and start the engine. As soon as I'm inside, you move. You got that?"

"Shouldn't I go with you? After all, she is my mom."

Mark softened his voice. The boy was hurting too. "I respect that you want to help with this, I really do. But you are not experienced at all and you will only get in my way. You can help me, and hopefully your mother, best by being our getaway driver. If we're not back by morning, we won't be coming back. Get out of here fast. Tell me you understand and can do what I asked."

"Okay, but you have to come back." His voice cracked.

Mark said, "Control yourself or you will be of no use when we need you."

Caleb nodded and dried his eyes. "Okay. Just please bring her back."

Mark smiled but there was no humor in it. "I intend to." He slipped a ball cap on and turned to leave, thought for a second, then added. "I might be sending a teenage girl up to you. If she comes, it will be in the next five minutes. Be watching for her. Let her in if she wants, otherwise let her go her own way and lock back up." He jogged off.

Mark tried not to hurry to save the girl from her ordeal. He had to remind himself not to react blindly and give himself away. Rescuing Lynn was still the mission and he couldn't accomplish that by drawing attention to himself. He kept his head down and walked across the bridge. Once on the other side, he stepped off the sidewalk and down along the ridge of the bank.

Mark spied them through the trees. He slid down the slope of the bank, watching the man pull the girl through the trees. Mark had made a decision. He couldn't let this brute abuse the girl. Up ahead the man stopped. He flung the girl in front of him. "You wanted to be outside, we're outside. Now get that dress off."

Tears streaming, she offered no protest. Her fingers

160

fumbled down the buttons of her dress. Her abuser stood watching, so absorbed in his victim's progress he was unaware of Mark's advance.

With the dress open, hanging from her shoulders, the man stepped forward to fondle her small breasts. The young girl looked over the stocky man's shoulder, his way, but Mark wasn't sure she really saw him.

Mark hoped to be able to sneak up and drive his knife into the man, but when he got about ten feet away, the man turned his head.

"What the fuck do you want?" he bellowed.

Mark tried to sound calm. "To see if I can have seconds."

"Fuck you. Get out of here and find your own woman." He never stopped thrusting.

"Had one. I just brought her in, but they took her from me." Mark stepped closer. The girl's eyes flicked to him then away. There was a spark still there, he thought.

"Ain't that a shame? You know all the new women gotta be cleared by the boss before they get divvied up. Go complain to him. Now leave me the fuck alone."

"Sure, man, I'm going." Mark backed away. As his target swung back to the girl, Mark stepped forward, his knife down along his right leg. A snapping twig under Mark's foot turned the man to protest again. Mark lunged and drove the blade deep into the man's gut. He slapped his left hand over the man's mouth and allowing all his fury to release, drove him backward, lifting the blade to the man's sternum. Mark pushed him up against a tree and held him there as the life drained from him. He let the body slump to the ground.

The girl never moved, as Mark stepped toward her. Her eyes changed from wide-eyed shock, back to a glossed over blank stare. She shivered visibly then, perhaps thinking she was now Mark's property, dropped the dress from her shoulders to the ground.

"I'm not here for that," he said, looking at the hotel to see if the killing had been witnessed. "If you want to be free from all of this madness, cross the creek and climb to the top of the hill. There's a boy in a van there. Get in and wait. No one will hurt you or try to do what that man was doing. Do you understand me?"

Her nod was slow as if only doing it because she was asked to. Fear shone in her eyes, the kind of fear you get when you dare hope for something only to find out it's a different sort of hell.

"Get dressed and cross the water – don't use the bridge. If you don't want to get in the van then just keep going. Find someplace to hide." He tried to sound like a father instead of the cold-blooded predator who had just killed a man in front of her.

As she dressed, Mark rolled the dead man's body down the bank into some long grass near the creek. The girl stood there waiting. "It's okay, you're free to go."

She started to sway, trying to get up enough courage to take the first step.

Just as she did, Mark said, "Wait." She deflated, as if any hope had been snatched from her. "Can you tell me how they get into the hotel?"

Tears ran down her face. Her body began to shake.

"I'm sorry, you're free to go. I just need to know how to get in. There's someone inside I need to rescue. Can you tell me anything that would help?"

The girl's lips trembled, attempting to form words, but nothing would come.

"It's okay, go now. And whatever you decide, good luck." With that, he turned and headed for the hotel. He didn't want her to think it was a trick, so he didn't look back. Then he heard, "There's a key."

He stopped and looked at her. She pointed to the dead man. "He *owned* me and has a key ... for his room." She covered her face and sobbed. Her whole body convulsed.

Mark wanted to go to her, to hug her and comfort her, but he decided that after what she had been through, touching her might not be the best thing.

"He can't hurt you anymore."

Mark slid down the bank and searched the man's pockets, finding a key ring with three keys on it. One looked like a car key; a second one looked too small to be a room key. He held up the third one and the girl nodded.

"Do you know what room?"

"428."

"Thank you." He turned to climb the slope towards the hotel.

"Did you really mean what you said?" He stopped again. "About being free?"

"Yes. But there are others like me and you are welcome to join us. You will be expected to do your share of the chores, but you will never be owned by anyone. It's up to you. If you don't like it, you'll be free to leave at any time." He gave her what he hoped looked like a reassuring smile. "Go."

She took two steps toward the water and stopped. "She has to go upstairs," she said. "Your friend, she has to go to Buster first, before whoever brought her in can have her. He will ... he will do things to her ... then give her away. If she hasn't been here long, then she will be there." She sidestepped carefully down the side of the bank. Before stepping into the water, she looked up at Mark.

He nodded and turned. Mark hoped she would take his offer and go to the van. He hoped he would be alive to know if she had.

Twenty-Four

WHILE HE APPROACHED THE hotel, he reviewed what he'd seen from above. He estimated seeing about twenty people come and go from the building and parking lot, although he had no way of knowing how many were inside. He'd also seen a few women moving among the men. They looked like they were part of the gang and not just property.

Mark kept his head down and his eyes up and moving, analyzing the changing scenario before him. As he drew nearer the side door, he wondered if the key would open that too. Most hotels used a key or key card to open any door other than the main one. He doubted any electronics were still working, so key cards were out. However, hotels wouldn't use a key rather than a key card. Someone must have retooled the doors to take keys. If he had a choice, he much preferred going in the side door rather than walking around the building and entering the front.

Ten feet from the door, two men came out. They paid him no attention, turning toward the parking lot. Mark jogged a few steps and managed to catch the door before it closed. He stepped through and let it shut behind him. He stood there, taking in the surroundings. Stairs ran up to his right. A heavy fire door stood in front of him with a small window giving him a view down the length of the first-floor hall.

Several people moved to and from rooms. He tested the door to see if it would open from his side. It did. Mark hoped that meant the ones above him would open as well.

He looked up the stairs to make sure they were clear then started up. At each floor, he peered through the window. He saw very few people, which made him think maybe there weren't as many enemies as he'd feared. Above him, Mark heard a door open, Footsteps descended. He hesitated. Looking through the fourth-floor window he saw one man walking toward him. Mark was hoping to get to room 428 without being seen.

The man coming down the stairs was only one flight away. The man on the floor stopped at the second door down from the fire door. He slid a key into a padlock attached to the door. Mark could now see how the rooms had been altered. A hasp had been screwed into the door above the knob with a corresponding hook on the frame. Making a snap decision, he drew his knife and pushed through the fire door looking down at the key in his hand. He had to time his attack right.

He could feel the man look up as the lock snapped open. Mark dropped his key and bent to pick it up as the man pushed his door open. As soon as he saw the door ajar, Mark sprang at the man, crashing him into the door, slamming it hard against the inner wall. He brought the knife up. The blade dug the man's belly, but he was both quick and strong. His powerful hands wrapped around Mark's wrist preventing him from pushing the blade any deeper.

Fearing the man on the stairs would hear, Mark went into a frenzy of motion. He head-butted the man, brought a knee to his groin, and then kicked him on the side of his knee. As soon as he felt his opponent begin to tip in that direction, Mark pushed hard, toppling him into the room with Mark landing on top of him. The momentum and force of Mark's weight jammed the knife into the man's stomach, causing a cry of pain that Mark could not prevent. The man's legs

165

thrashed and Mark used every ounce of strength to push the knife in deeper.

Keeping one hand on the knife, he covered the man's mouth with the other. As the man weakened, Mark reached a foot back and kicked the door closed just as he heard the fire door open. Mark pressed his weight down, trying to control the man's efforts to dislodge him. Muffled cries seeped out as the man threw his head from side to side. Mark had to let go of the knife so he could use both hands. He held him down for several minutes until the man stopped moving.

Rolling off the body, he lay on his back to catch his breath. After a minute, he stood and searched the man's room for a shirt to replace his bloody one. Finding an old Harley T-shirt he slipped it on then grabbed the man's key. Peeking into the hallway he saw that it was clear. Mark went out, locked the door, and pocketed the key.

The window in the fire door showed the landing was empty, so he stepped out and started up the stairs again. However, the higher he climbed, the more populated the floors seemed to be. Even if he did manage to get to Lynn, it would be impossible to get back out again if the alarm went up.

Mark reached the top floor and paused to catch his breath. Glancing through the window, he saw several men down the hall. There appeared to be only six rooms on this floor. Two of the men were guarding a door. Two other men were in the hall farther down. One sat on the floor while the other paced in front of him. Mark couldn't be positive, but the man pacing looked familiar.

Mark leaned against the wall and tried to think of a plan that would not get him killed. He was falling short of ideas. In his mind, he went through the motions of an assault. *Walk through the door at a quick pace, shotgun in my hand pointing down at the floor in a casual, non-threatening manner. I'll head straight for the guards until they react, hoping I can get close*

166

enough to blast them before they can move.

In his vision of how things would go, he'd pump two rounds at the guards, swing toward the other two, and fire two more shots. He would then turn the barrel to the door and blow it open. Whoever was inside would be prepared by then, so he would kick the door open but stay back. Dropping the empty shotgun, he would pull out the 9mm. He would toss one guard's body through the door first to draw fire, then follow it in.

From there, without knowing the layout of the room or how many people were in there, things got sketchy. Regardless, even if he were successful, the shots would alert everyone else in the vicinity, making the trip back down suicide. There just wasn't any way for that charging scenario to play out with both Lynn and him walking away. He had to find another way.

He thought about just going to the guards and offering to buy Lynn back. Maybe he could pretend to need to talk to the big boss, to gain entrance to the room and go from there, but neither idea had any real chance of success. In the end, he'd have to shoot it out with somebody. He supposed he could go with the first plan and just barricade them in the room. They would live longer; but, eventually, the result would be the same.

Unable to come up with anything that would give them good odds of surviving, Mark decided to go with plan number one. At least he would be doing something. The thought of Lynn in the hands of those animals was enough to make him want to kill them all. He wished he'd brought more bullets.

Mark looked down the hallway, took several fast breaths, and reached for the door. Then he stopped. The door between the two guards opened and a large man came out, wearing bibs with the straps hanging down past his waist. Mark recognized him: the man from Summer's house. He had forgotten how big the man was. The guards were not small by any means, but the guy was taller by four or five inches.

He said something to one of the guards, then stepped back into the room. The guard walked down the hall and spoke to the pacing man. The other man stood while the pacing man walked into the room.

Several minutes later, the door opened and the pacing man came back out, dragging Lynn behind him. She didn't resist and looked battered. Her shirt was torn and her hair was disheveled. The man leaning against the wall fell in behind them as they headed for the stairs.

Twenty-Five

MARK'S HEART POUNDED FASTER. *She was alive!* His breath caught and something seemed to lodge in his throat making swallowing difficult. It was all he could do to keep from running down the hall and grabbing her.

But with the guards behind them and eight flights of stairs to descend, starting a gunfight now would be suicide. He strangled his emotions and looked around for someplace to hide. He ran back downstairs two flights and waited for the door to open. When it did, the group burst out and started plodding down the stairs.

"So what did Buster say?"

"The bastard said he liked her and was tempted to keep her for himself. He liked the way she fought. He said I could take her, but he might want me to bring her back a few more times before all the fight goes out of her."

Mark retreated down the next flight as the men continued down.

"She's ours now. He shouldn't be able to take her back whenever he wants to. He gets enough women, he doesn't need ours."

"That's what I'm saying. I think we should change rooms, so he doesn't know where to find us. If we stall him long enough, he'll find another woman."

"Sounds good to me, but I want her a few times before we go."

"You horny bastard. Yeah, but I get her first."

"That's cool, just don't beat her so much she won't respond for me."

Mark's jaw clenched. He moved and hid twice more before the group went through the fifth-floor fire door. He ran back upstairs, taking them two at a time. He had to get to them before they disappeared into a room. At the door, he peered through the window and watched as the lead man unlocked a door about four rooms down the hall. Lynn stood there with her head down, trying to push the other man away as he attempted to kiss her.

The assailant slapped Lynn and fire flashed behind Mark's eyes. He heard her cry out through the door. In a flash, she whipped around and slapped him back, surprising him. Her attacker said, "You fucking bitch!" and hit her. All the plans left his mind.

He slid the shotgun off his shoulder and pulled the fire door open. His gaze bored a hole through Lynn's molester. The first man opened the room door and looked up to see Mark coming at them. He grabbed Lynn and, pulling her from his partner's grasp, dragged her through the door.

The second man had been so busy trying to grab Lynn's breasts that he was slow to notice Mark's aggressive approach. He started to follow them inside the room but with Lynn out of the way, he no longer had any cover. Too enraged to care about the noise, Mark leveled the gun and pulled the trigger. At that range, the pellets splattered blood and flesh over the hallway.

In the room, the remaining captor was trying to close the door, draw his gun, and hold onto Lynn at the same time. Lynn must have realized whatever was happening might be her last chance of breaking free. She attacked

170

her captor in a frenzy of kicks and wild swinging fists. Snarls and growls escaped her as she fought in desperation.

Mark kicked open the door and the gunman turned his full attention on him. He tried to aim his gun at Mark, but Lynn sank her teeth into his arm. Mark let the shotgun sag toward the floor and pulled out the 9mm. He stepped forward, placed the barrel against his target's forehead and pulled the trigger. The force propelled the man backward, leaving Lynn standing there in shock. She turned to face Mark. With a shriek, she hurled herself at him.

"Lynn, Lynn! It's me – Mark."

He tried to fend off her wild blows. She connected several times before he was able to wrap her arms up in his hands. Mark pulled her forward wrapping his arms around her ending her thrashing.

In a softer voice, he tried again. "Lynn, It's Mark. It's all right. You're safe."

She looked up at him, her battered face already showing the bruises. Her lip, cut and now swollen, as was her right eye. He eased his grip to allow her to move; but when he did, she threw herself back into his arms and cried in long, hard sobs.

With his foot, Mark reached back and kicked the door shut. They wouldn't have much time, but he had to let her compose herself. He needed her alert and responsive if they were to have any chance of getting out of there.

Mark stroked her hair, wanting to comfort and protect her. He had a good idea of what they'd done to her, but he would help her recover and move past it. He only hoped she was capable of doing that.

"We have to get out of here before anyone else comes. Someone had to hear the shots." Her body trembled against his. "Can you run? Are you okay?"

She pulled back and wiped her eyes. "Yes, get me the

171

hell out of here." She bent down and picked up the dead man's gun, aimed it at his head. Shaking with barely contained rage, she pulled it back and stomped on his crotch with all the force she could muster. "I wish he were still alive to feel that."

Twenty-Six

MARK OPENED THE DOOR and peeked out. From the far end of the hall, two men advanced toward the body. They held handguns. He closed the door and waited, not sure if they saw him or not.

"Sweet Jesus, look at that mess."

"Whoever did it is in that room."

"Should will call for help or see who it is?"

"Let's see who it is first."

They couldn't prevent them from opening the door. Mark pushed Lynn forward and ripped the gun from her hands. The beds were recessed behind the bathroom wall. The bathroom was next to the door on the left. Mark pressed himself against that wall, next to the first bed. He extended the gun along the wall and waited. Lynn was shocked and about to say something when the door pushed open. No one was there at first then a head peeked in from the right. When the lead attacker saw her standing there with a body behind her, he stepped in with his gun pointed at her. A second man followed close behind.

"What the hell did you do, bitch? They're gonna execute you for this."

Lynn backed up two steps until her heels hit the body.

"Hey, Joe, she's not bad looking. Maybe we should just keep her for ourselves."

"No way. Look what she did to them. You want to try and sleep at night knowing what this crazy bitch could do to you? Not me, man. She needs to be put down."

She backed up again and tripped over the body. Mark couldn't tell if it had been on purpose or not. One of her small breasts bounced past a tear in her shirt. Mark watched and waited for the men to pass the wall where he would have a shot.

Lynn began to crab walk backward. The arm and gun of the first man were now in line with Mark.

"You gonna do it or are we gonna take her to Buster?"

"I guess it depends on whether she puts up a fight. What about it crazy bitch? You gonna come along peaceful or do I have to shoot you right here?"

Her back hit the wall-mounted heater. Her face looked panicked. She held up her hands and said, "Please, can't you just let me go?"

The first man was level with Mark. He was afraid to move for fear the man's peripheral vision would pick him up. He needed his prey to go farther to enable him to get a shot at the second man.

"Hey, Joe, maybe we could let her go if she does us both first."

"Man, are you that horny? You want to do her so bad, go ahead. Just make sure she ain't got a knife or something she can cut your nuts off with."

"I ain't worried," the second man said, moving forward. "I'll beat the shit out of her if she tries anything."

The first man turned to let his partner pass and was now face to face with Mark and his gun. Mark didn't wait, he blew the man's face all over his partner, then slid forward and shot him too before he could utter a sound. The two bodies collapsed next to the other one.

Mark raced to the door and looked out. No one else was on the floor yet, so he dragged the body from the hall into the room. Feeling he might need the extra weapons, he picked up the extra guns, sliding one in his belt and giving the other two to Lynn.

"We need to get out of here fast. We're gonna leave the room and walk casually down the stairs. When we exit the building, you follow me like you're my pet. Try not to look around too much. Keep your head down, but your eyes alert. Oh, and hold the guns under your shirt. Ready?"

She looked at him tight-lipped, like she was working hard to hold it together.

His tone softened. "Are you okay? Can you do this or do you want me to carry you?"

She shook her head then covered her face to fight back the emotions.

"Lynn, I know what they did. I know it's hard to deal with, but you can get past it. I need you to push it aside until we're out of here. Your kids need you. They need to see you're still as strong as always." He paused. "And I need you, too."

She uncovered her face and looked at him, but the tears continued to roll.

"I do. And not just to help get us out of here. I need you to help me remember that there is still some good worth fighting for in this mad world. That there might still be hope for a future. Caleb is waiting for us. Can you hold it together long enough for us to get to safety?"

"Yes."

He nodded and turned. She grabbed his arm to turn him back.

"I prayed you'd come. I-I knew you would."

He smiled grimly. "We're not out of here yet."

In the hall, he picked up the shotgun and closed the door. The hall was still empty. They started toward the fire door. As they reached it, the fire door at the far end of the hall opened and two more men came into view. Mark glanced back but kept moving. As the door closed behind them, he started running down the stairs.

At the ground floor, he stopped. No one followed them yet. He pushed through the outside door and turned left. They walked across the grass, Lynn several paces behind, almost running to keep up. There was activity behind them, but no one paid any attention to them.

When they passed the building, he heard someone yell, "Hey! Hey, you two, stop."

"Don't look back," Mark instructed Lynn. "Just keep moving."

"If you don't stop right now I'm gonna shoot."

That made Mark glance over his right shoulder, but no one was there.

The shot hit in front of his foot as he neared the creek. He jumped from surprise. He turned and swept his gun up. A man with a handgun was hanging out the window of the room they had left the bodies in. He fired again but, at that distance and angle, the shot went wide.

Not wanting to draw too much attention, Mark didn't return fire. He started running, sliding down the bank to the creek where they had more cover than crossing the bridge. They both slid on their sides, righting themselves when they hit the bottom. As they splashed across the shallow water, more shots ripped into the trees, but none close to them.

They climbed the other side and started up to the church parking lot. It was higher and steeper on that side. Mark hoped he would still see the van when he got to the top. Before they crested the slope, he saw the van's roof and new hope bloomed. He risked a turn to look for pursuit and was dismayed at the number of people racing after them.

He grabbed Lynn's hand and pulled her up the remaining few feet and yelled, "Run for the van!"

Mark wished he had his rifle just then. He could put an instant stop to the pursuit. Nearly twenty people were coming after them. Closer to the van, he began yelling for Caleb. Caleb's head appeared through the driver's window. His first instinct when he saw his mother, was to jump out and run to her. Mark screamed at him, "Start the engine! Start the damn engine!" It took one look over Mark's shoulders at the pursuit for Caleb to jump back in. The motor turned over as Lynn reached the side door.

Lynn swept it open and froze in place as a strange face peered fearfully back at her. Mark had no time for introductions or explanations. He grabbed Lynn around the waist with both hands and pushed her inside. He dove in after her, yelling, "Go! Go! Go!"

He pulled the door shut as Caleb started driving. The posse started firing at them. Some of the shots were finding their range, boring holes through the van's thin metal panels. Mark snatched up the rifle and ordered the two women to lie down.

Caleb accelerated and Mark opened one of the rear doors. Lying down he took a hurried aim and squeezed off three successive shots into the crowd. He hadn't really targeted anyone. He was more interested in stopping them from returning fire. The first shot missed everyone but the next two found targets. It was enough to stop the pursuit. The others scattered or dropped to the ground for cover. Mark was about to fire once more, but Caleb bounced the van over the curb, lifting Mark off the floor. He grabbed the door to prevent being thrown out. Scooting forward, he managed to snag the door and pull it closed.

Through the window, Mark watched the posse turn around and run back to the hotel.

"More speed Caleb; we're gonna have company

soon."

Caleb was not used to driving fast. His fingers were white on the wheel. Mark had to make a choice, either drive or try and stop the chase cars. He could already see vehicles leaving the parking lot behind them. He thought about what would give them the best chance of escaping.

"Caleb, turn right at the next street then pull over."

"What?" he said. "Why?"

Mark didn't have time for lengthy discussions. "Do as I tell you!"

Caleb was startled by the tone but did as commanded. The tires screeched as he made the turn. He hit the brakes hard, throwing all of them forward.

Lynn grabbed Mark's arm as he reached for the AK-47. "What are you doing?" she asked, her voice fearful.

"What I have to." There wasn't time for this. He pulled his arm away and lifted the gun.

"No, they'll kill you."

"I need to slow them down."

Lynn shook her head and her eyes welled up. "No."

"I have to. I'll get back to you when I can. Now go!"

He opened the sliding door and slid out, slinging the rifle. With a sudden burst of movement, Lynn grabbed Mark's face and kissed him hard. "You'd better come back."

Mark was shocked, but there was no time for this either. "Go."

He pulled the AK out, shut the door, and slapped the side. Caleb spun out and disappeared around the next corner.

Mark ran to the corner of Main Street and propped the AK on top of a mailbox, which gave him solid cover and a good view down the road. Balancing the weapon on top he unslung his rifle. He didn't have long to wait.

The sound of multiple engines raced toward him. The sun reflected off the lead car's windshield as it crested the rise in the road. It looked like a Grand Prix race with that many cars following.

Mark adjusted the sight, took careful aim, and fired into the windshield of the first car. The car veered off the road and slammed into a phone pole, lifting the tail-end off the ground. The pole snapped clean from its base hanging by the wires.

The next car swerved to the right, making it more difficult for Mark to line up a shot. He fired into the driver's side window but didn't think it was a hit. Still, the car bounced up over the curb and braked to a stop on the front lawn of a house.

The following cars were getting too close, but Mark tried one more shot. It was hurried and spider-webbed the glass, but the car kept coming. He threw the rifle over his shoulder and went for the AK. With the cars bearing down, he opened fire, strafing a line from one car to the next.

The first turned sideways and rolled, flipping over several times. The second car rammed into the first at full speed, causing an explosion that rocked the ground beneath Mark's feet. His next shots created a series of crashes that ended any pursuit by car. Mark ejected the magazine and rammed in another. He fired until it too was empty.

As men climbed from the wreckage, Mark knew it was time to run. He hoisted the AK and ran to his left down the side street. He slapped in the final magazine while he was running. As his pursuers took up the chase on foot, Mark fired the remaining rounds into them, dropping several and sending the rest scurrying for cover. So far he had been very lucky and no shots yet followed his retreat.

Twenty-Seven

MARK MADE IT TO the end of the short block and turned the corner to his right. The pursuit was more cautious now, fearing the AK. Sucking in huge gulps of air to catch his breath, Mark waited until there were enough targets to make it worthwhile using up the final magazine. He depressed the trigger and hosed down the entire street. He knew he'd done some damage but not enough to prevent them from advancing.

He tossed the AK into some bushes in front of a house, slid the rifle from his shoulder, and took cover. He hated to lose the automatic weapon but empty it would be a hindrance to carry. He quickly reloaded the five shot magazine of the rifle as he watched the men gather confidence and begin to follow him once more.

Mark sighted the lead man, wanting the others to see him go down. He hoped they would scamper for cover once more, giving him time to get some distance. It was an easy shot and the man dropped. Just as he planned, the remaining pursuit scattered. He counted a dozen men and added three more for any he couldn't see. As soon as the men took cover, Mark broke to his left and ran as hard as he could. He crossed the street and turned the corner at the far end of the block.

Ahead of him the street stretched on beyond sight. To the right was a high fence that separated the back of a line of stores from the neighborhood. He could scale it but it would be a long run in the open before he could reach cover. His best bet was the houses to the left.

He stayed on the sidewalk and ran for all he was worth. Allowing himself two minutes of open running, Mark kept track in his head before he sought cover. From then on he would run through yards, hopping fences and trying not to get seen or flanked.

Mark took stock of his weapons. He had the rifle and one more refill of bullets. His 9mm and two extra magazines, the handgun he'd picked up in the room with an unknown amount of rounds, and his knife.

Huh. Fifteen to one. No problem.

Mark ran on. At the end of the block, he cut left. The time he would have in the open was limited. For the moment, he wanted to get some distance to enable him to find a place to hide until his pursuers went past. Then he could double back. Mark ran down residential streets. There were plenty of places to hide. The question was to what extent would the Horde be willing to search for him?

After three blocks, Mark could no longer keep up the pace. His lungs burned. He gasped for air.

He needed to stop and find someplace to hide. Turning up the next street Mark ducked between the fourth and fifth houses on the block. There he slowed his speed. It took great effort to control the loud sucking sound he made trying to draw in air.

Forcing his body to continue running Mark entered the backyard and hopped the rear fence. Exiting on the next block Mark glanced to his left. Seeing the road was still clear he continued across the street and repeated the process for the next few blocks like some bizarre form of steeplechase.

Then everything changed. At the far end of the block, he spotted movement.

He dove to the ground in a backyard and waited for any sign that he'd been noticed. Two men ran down the side street at the far end of the block. He risked a glance, lifting his head high enough to see, but they were now out of sight. As yet, no one appeared to the right, but they would be there soon. It was time to seek shelter.

Staying low, he crawled back toward the house. Maybe if he waited long enough, the pursuit would pass him. Stopping at a small deck he scrambled up the steps to try the door. It was locked. He couldn't afford to make any noise breaking the glass, so he hurdled the railing. Using the butt of the rifle, he dug a trench deep enough to slide under the deck.

He just started wiggling his way underneath when he heard a voice. "Nothing here." It had come from his left. He froze. Panic flared ripping the air from his lungs. Then he jerked, knocking his head on the underside of the deck, as another voice replied, "Nothing here either."

A line of gunmen was methodically clearing the houses yard by yard. Someone with some brains had organized the search.

"I still think we should be checking the houses too," the man to the left said.

The searcher in front of Mark looked in the direction of the back of the house. "Nah, only if it's obvious someone has broken in. There are others behind us checking the houses. Our job is to check if he's in the open and flush him into the ones waiting in front. The cars that went up ahead will trap him between us."

The two men climbed over the fence and moved through the yards. When they disappeared between the houses of the next block, Mark breathed again. Processing what he'd heard, Mark knew a second wave of searchers would be coming through soon. That they'd sent men ahead to cut him off was good to know, but what he'd anticipated. He hadn't planned on continuing forward. As long as whoever was running the pursuit thought that was his plan he should be able to escape. He just needed to be patient. He slid further under the deck.

Mark snaked his hands back out and tried leveling off the dirt he had dug away. If discovered, he would be trapped. His only hope was to escape without having to shoot his way out.

He placed the rifle on the ground in front of him, pulled out the 9mm and the knife, and settled down to wait. About ten minutes later, the patio door opened and footsteps padded on the wood above him. He hadn't been prepared for that. He was on his belly, thinking whoever would come would be in front of him. As he thought about it now, it only made sense they would come in from the front of the house, otherwise if he had been hiding inside he could just run out the other way unnoticed. But now, he couldn't see above him to find out if his life was in jeopardy. Trying to flip over was too risky with the man so close. He was defenseless. The only thing he could do was close his eyes and wait ... and pray.

The man stood there for an eternity. Finally, he walked down the steps and into the backyard. There he stopped and waited. Mark couldn't understand what he was doing until a voice from farther down yelled. "Count off!"

"One."

"Two."

"Three."

They stopped at eight.

"Move right!"

The searcher in front of Mark moved to the right and climbed the fence. He heard the searcher's partner, two houses to the left, do the same thing, entering the house next door. A chill crept up his spine as he realized how well orchestrated the search was.

They must want me real bad to go through that much trouble.

He had to reassess his idea of what their setup was. If they were going in one house from the front, then one from the back, they must have someone out on the street to prevent him from doubling back. This was likely to take longer than he'd hoped.

Five minutes later, the searchers were back in the yards and the countdown repeated. The voice in charge yelled, "Forward," and the eight men climbed the rear fence and smashed their way into the houses in front of them.

Mark could do nothing but wait them out. The worst might be behind him. Another fifteen minutes and the command issued to move on. Mark breathed a sigh of relief. It was too soon to crawl back out, but for the first time he felt he had a chance. The first wave had to be two blocks away by then.

He listened as the calls were given, each one fading as they moved farther. They crossed the next street. Maybe he'd been wrong about the follow-up men. They should've come into view by then if they were there. Pushing the piled dirt aside, he began crawling out from his hiding place. He pushed the rifle out ahead of him then pulled himself forward. A sound froze him.

Another man walked out from the side of the house, moving toward the fence. His head swiveled back and forth, his rifle hung downward in his left hand.

Mark was half out from under the deck. Afraid to move in either direction for fear of making a sound, he kept the 9mm trained on the man's back. Mark tensed as the gunman was about to turn around when someone down the line called, "Got something?"

He stopped his turn and replied, "No, just a feeling.

184

Maybe he's close. Or maybe we've been doing this too long."

"Yeah, I hear ya. Let's move. We're falling behind. Don't want to be blamed if he slips between us."

"I hear that."

He went to the fence, leaned an assault rifle up against it and lit a cigarette. This man was quite tall. He lifted a leg and basically stepped over the fence straddling it. As he reached down for his weapon, he jiggled the fence, causing the rifle to slide down to the ground.

"Shit," he said, reaching back over the fence to retrieve the gun. He raised his head and looked directly at Mark. Mark fired instinctively, hitting the split-rail fence underneath the man. He tried to fall to the other side but his foot caught on the metal wiring.

Mark slid out and jumped to his feet. He fired twice more through the fencing, snatched up the rifle, and ran around the house without knowing if he'd hit the man.

Voices shouted behind him relayed the message he'd been found.

"He's here! Back this way!"

"Stay in your lanes. Flush him forward."

"Don't let him turn!"

And just like that, all hope faded.

Twenty-Eight

MARK WAS ACROSS THE street and into another backyard before anyone saw him. As he crossed the next street, however, he spotted a Jeep parked facing him on the wrong side of the road. It was down at the end of the block to his right with two men in it. The command vehicle. It gave him an idea.

In the backyard, he ran right and hopped the side fence. Working his way down the street he got behind the Jeep. If he could take them by surprise, he could take the Jeep and make his escape, since everyone else was on foot. If that didn't work, he would get to the side street where he would attempt to find a car.

Granted, it wasn't much, but it was a plan.

Reaching the yard of the house just past where the Jeep was parked Mark turned toward the street. The men in the Jeep were the only ones to see where he'd crossed the street. As soon as the pursuit arrived, the people in the Jeep would direct them. But going sideways instead of away from the chasers ate up his lead. He questioned the intelligence of turning back rather than fleeing, but it would be just a matter of time before they caught him. He couldn't hope to beat them all.

His hopes relied on getting to that Jeep before anyone

saw him.

As he moved from the cover of the house on the east side, the first pursuer emerged from between two houses about midway down the block on the west side. Mark was in the middle of the street racing for the Jeep. The passenger in the Jeep opened his door to signal to the approaching gunman, unaware that Mark was closing on him. He was dressed in army camouflage like he was running a military operation. Before he could turn around in response to the approaching gunman's waving arms, Mark shot him in the back.

The gunman stopped, knelt, and fired at Mark. Using the open door for cover, Mark kept low and ran toward the Jeep. The driver spun wildly in each direction looking over his shoulders. The shooter in the street advanced. Mark popped up and fired twice at him, missing both times. The man ducked and fired back.

The driver started the motor, but before he could put it in gear, Mark reached the door and fired inside once. The man squealed as the bullet ripped into his leg.

The advancing man kept shooting at the Jeep's door, trying to keep Mark pinned down.

Mark popped up in the space between the door and the frame and squeezed off two more rounds. This time the bullets spun the shooter around and down.

At least six more men were running toward the Jeep from behind the downed shooter. He needed to move now, or it would be too late. The man in the driver's seat pulled a pistol. Mark dove for the ground as the shot shattered the window. Reaching his arm back through the door Mark fired several times. The man slumped over the wheel. Reaching in, Mark hauled him out of the Jeep as more shots landed around him. Dumping the body to the ground, Mark tossed in the rifle and scrambled into the driver's seat. Keeping his head down, he shifted into reverse and floored it.

Bullets peppered the vehicle like hail. Several rounds punched through the windshield. When he reached what he thought was the end of the street, he spun the wheel hard. His estimation was wrong. The rear tires bumped up the curb. He crashed into a small tree, slamming him into the wheel. He was broadside to the approaching squad. Mark risked a look. Just as his head came up, a man's face appeared in the window. Mark lifted the 9mm and shot him. Men were closing in around him from all directions. Bullets tore into the Jeep's interior. He threw the shift into drive and shoved the pedal to the floor. The car leaped forward as bullets struck the side. A bullet punched through the door and creased the top of his thigh.

One man jumped on the hood while another hopped on the rear bumper. For fear others might catch him, Mark didn't want to risk slamming on the brakes to dislodge them. Instead, he continued accelerating and fired through the windshield. This time, however, the window spider-webbed from the bullet's impact, distorting Mark's view of the road ahead. Seeing the gun aimed at him, the rider on the hood let go and attempted to roll off. However, Mark's next shot found him, causing the man to roll over the front bumper. The Jeep bounced over the human speed bump, causing Mark to lose his grip on the wheel. He swore, fought to regain control, but the Jeep lurched sideways and hit a curb, almost toppling on its side.

Mark dropped the gun on the passenger's seat to turn the wheel with both hands. With great relief, he managed to swing the Jeep back onto the road. The near miss took his mind from the second man clinging to the Jeep until he heard him on the roof. Mark reached for the gun on the seat as the first bullet hit the console right next to him. He swerved the vehicle back and forth, forcing his unwanted passenger to hold on with both hands or be tossed to the road.

In the mirror, he could see men still pursuing him, shooting at the Jeep in spite of their comrade on top. He had just found the butt of the pistol when one of the rear tires blew. The Jeep was thrown to the right, driving at an angle. The rider on the roof slid to that side, his legs dangling over the edge as he hung on to the cargo rack. With both hands steadying the wheel, Mark risked a glance at the gun.

It was no longer on the seat. It had bounced to the floor.

"Damn!"

Mark dared not take his foot off the gas pedal. He knew the drag of the blown tire would slow him down. The men in the mirror looked smaller as Mark pulled away. He had to keep going. A bullet destroyed the side mirror. Another whizzed past his ear.

The attacker hanging from the luggage rack began to kick the side of the Jeep, trying to get enough traction to climb back on top. Mark watched as one leg disappeared.

Mark looked down at the gun agonizingly out of reach. It was only a matter of time before shots began raining down upon him again. He doubted he'd be as lucky this time. There had to be something he could do.

Then he remembered the second gun he had picked up and stashed at the small of his back. He leaned forward and pulled the gun free, just as a gun snaked through the shattered passenger window. The first shot passed behind Mark's head, burying in the seat; a second whizzed past his head.

Mark pointed the gun toward the roof and fired several times. He was rewarded with a scream and a body flying from the vehicle.

Mark was just thinking he might make it when the other rear tire blew. The Jeep swerved again while he put a death grip on the wheel to keep the vehicle moving. He

189

saved it from crashing, but much of his speed had been bled off. He looked in the rearview mirror. The pursuit, which had stopped because he was pulling away, started again when they heard the tire give way.

Mark wasn't going to get anywhere like that. He had a block and a half lead. He turned at the next corner, drove far enough so as not to be seen, and abandoned the Jeep. Grabbing the rifle and both handguns, he sprinted for his life down once-desirable suburban streets.

Twenty-Nine

HE TOOK OFF AT a fast jog. At the first street he came to, he went left, running the length of the street before turning right again. Exhausted and bleeding in places where he hadn't realized he was injured, he could taste the expended gasses from the guns. Desperate for water and rest, Mark knew he couldn't stop. As he ran, he reevaluated his position and options. He was about two miles from his old house. There would be shelter and the only two men who were aware of the secret room were dead. He was also certain there was still a case or two of food and water in the cavern.

With his destination now set, he settled into an easy jog to save what little energy reserves he had left. His breathing became more ragged and his heart pounded as though trying to escape his chest. Every muscle in his body felt on fire. He lost track of how far he had gone. Several times, he stopped to look behind him, thinking he heard cars approaching. Each time, he was wrong. It was his imagination or his paranoia.

With the sun low, leaving only an hour or so of daylight, Mark finally did hear cars. But, in the exhausted state he was in, he didn't hear them soon enough and didn't react in time when he did. He was still on the street, staggering from his exertion, when a blue Chevy and a green Ford came to the intersection fifty yards behind him.

He dashed for the cover of a small white birch and pulled the rifle from his shoulder. The cars hesitated, then swung toward him side-by-side, revving their engines as if getting ready to drag race. Then as one, they exploded forward.

Mark wiped the sweat from his eyes and lined up the shot. They were barreling at him, speed increasing by the second. He squeezed the trigger and the driver of the Chevy rocked backward and fell forward on the wheel. The car bumped the Ford, sending it careening up and over the curb on the far side.

The Chevy, after bouncing off the Ford, changed course and now bore down on his tree again. Mark dashed toward the corner house seconds before the car crashed head-on into the tree. The tree bent over, splintering at the point of impact. The car rode up on the trunk and stopped as if impaled.

The driver of the Ford did a squealing one-eighty turn on the road, facing Mark only twenty yards away. There were two men inside. Both side windows rolled down. The driver stuck a gun out the window. The passenger climbed out the window and sat on the door frame, aiming a gun, then fired.

Mark was in the open. He raised the rifle hurriedly and fired back. The bullet ricocheted off the roof inches to the right of the shooter. Then Mark turned and ran.

The car raced toward him jumping the curb. It would be on him in seconds. Mark dove and rolled as the car sped past. The driver braked and spun another one-eighty. Mark got to his feet, ran the other direction, and hid behind the wrecked car just as the bullets would have reached him. The driver braked hard, sliding past the wreck. Mark dropped the rifle, pulled out both handguns, and like some old-time western sheriff, advanced on the car with both guns blazing. He hit the driver several times before switching both barrels at the passenger. The passenger ducked back inside for better cover and tried firing out the window, past the body of the driver.

Fire erupted in his right side; he'd been hit again. Still, he continued. The nonstop shooting kept the man's head down. Mark jumped on the hood and emptied both guns through the windshield. If the man wasn't dead, Mark was now an easy target and out of bullets. But after a moment, no shot came.

Mark slumped on the hood and stared at the sky. His body was so drained it would have been easy to close his eyes right there. He was tired – tired of fighting, tired of being shot at, tired of killing and damned tired of running. This senseless killing had to end. But the only way he could see that happening would involve more fighting and killing, and if he didn't succeed, definitely more running.

Mark dragged up enough energy to slide off the car and stand on rubbery legs. Sliding the 9mm in his belt, he dropped the other one and grabbed both of the dead men's guns. After examining them, he found they were of different calibers and both only had two bullets left. He retrieved his rifle and found only one round left there. It was time to run again because, with only five shots, he wouldn't be doing much fighting.

With the sun beginning to set, Mark started a slow easy jog. He cupped one hand over the wound in his side and made for his house and a long night.

Thirty

BY THE TIME MARK made it back to his street, darkness was complete. He hid in the overgrown bushes of the corner house and scanned the area, wishing he had thought to carry the binoculars with him. No unfamiliar cars had parked on the street or in any driveways. Mark made his way to the house the watchers had used, across from his. Once there, he ran around the back and checked the doors. The one behind the garage was open. Mark glanced in, then entered. He was in a small utility room that led into the main house.

He stood listening for anything that disturbed the quiet. When nothing did, he moved into the house. It was empty. Mark rummaged through his neighbor's drawers until he found a clean white T-shirt. Using the knife, he cut a long strip, then two wider ones. Folding the wider ones, he placed them over the two bullet holes, front and back, in his side. The longer strip he tied around his body to hold the bandages in place. It would have to do for now.

From the front windows, Mark checked the street. Seeing it was clear, he bolted out the front door. He sprinted across the street toward the open garage doors of his house. It was then that he heard the tires squealing from around the corner of the next block. Someone was coming in a hurry.

Time was once again running out. Mark had a decision to make: either go inside and hide in the safe room, or keep going into the woods behind the house and try to make it to the farmhouse. With his energy depleted and bleeding from multiple wounds he wouldn't make the five-mile trek to the new house. Opting for his old house, he hoped the safe room was still safe. If he was going to continue, he needed rest.

Mark pulled the garage door shut. Once inside the house, he went to the curtained living room windows just as three cars came to a stop outside the house. "Oh, shit!" He turned and ran for the basement steps. Mark had just made it inside the hidden room when, once again, the main floor was full of activity. It sounded as though an army had just invaded.

He decided not to take the chance that whoever was up there didn't know about the room. He went into the cave and looked around before closing the door. It was dark with the door closed.

Feeling his way to the far side of the cave, he found the two stacks of food and water cases. Pulling a water bottle loose, he sat on top of the cases. He tried to force himself to drink slowly. Even so, he chugged it too fast, pulled a second one free, and started on it.

Through the walls came the sound of things being moved. Something crashed. The intruders were searching for him. He froze and listened. As far as he could tell, no one had discovered the safe room yet. He was in for a long wait.

An hour later, Mark could still hear the invaders moving around. The sounds of the night came through the vent. It was peaceful. In spite of the danger that surrounded him, he was overcome by his exhaustion and nodded off. He awoke, startled, not knowing how long he'd been asleep. Finishing the second water, he relieved himself inside the two empty bottles and sealed them closed with the caps. Even though he knew he would probably never come back to this house, he couldn't bring himself to urinate in the corner.

His stomach growled. Mark hadn't eaten anything since early morning. He pulled out a can of something and jammed the blade of his survival knife straight down into the lid, working it like a small hand saw. He was half way around when he felt the pull tab on top. He tipped the can to his mouth and poured out cold mini ravioli. The filling was meat and cheese. It was something he'd never had in his house, but now, it tasted like gourmet Italian.

When Mark finished, he stood and stretched. A sharp pain tore through his body. The bullet wounds had become a dull ache forgotten until he tried to move. Touching the makeshift bandage his fingers came away wet.

Pressing his ear to the cement wall, Mark could not tell from the lack of sound if it was safe to leave the cave. He nudged the door open enough to poke his head out. The hidden room had not been discovered. Leaving the cave, he debated leaving the door open or closed. One way kept the room secret, the other saved a few seconds if he was on the run. He left it open.

Again Mark listened, his ear against the much thinner paneling. The basement seemed empty. He waited another twenty minutes before venturing from the safe room, into the basement. Nothing set off an alarm so he continued on to the stairs, climbing with caution. With each step, he moved farther away from safety. The basement door stood open like an ominously beckoning portal to a different dimension. Sharp pain stabbed his side with each step he climbed. He fought to keep his breathing even. Mark stopped two steps from the top. Placing his hands on the floor he leaned his body forward and peered into the darkness of the kitchen. He couldn't see much other than the large shapes of the island in front of him and the cabinets and refrigerator to his right. He would have to rely on his hearing, something Sandra had always said was not very good.

He crawled up the remaining steps and across the kitchen floor to the row of cabinets that divided the cooking area from the eating space. The patio door was ten feet to his left. Mark waited there, unmoving for several minutes. Although he hadn't heard anything to make him think otherwise, his internal alarms were going off. The hair on the back of his neck stood at attention. Thinking he was being too paranoid, he finally moved from his cramped position, making a small sound. Then, beyond the dining space, someone said, "It's him!" and then, "Shoot!"

The house erupted into a war-zone as bullets whined all around him, slamming into cabinets, appliances, and walls. No one could see where they were shooting; they just shot. In a lull, Mark scampered backward to the head of the stairs. Someone from the family room made a move toward him. Mark fired at the sound and a body skidded to a stop a few feet from him.

He slid down the stairs, waiting at the bottom. From different areas of the house, footsteps pounded the floorboards as the ambush closed on his position. The first man in the doorway made the mistake of thinking Mark was on the run. He thumped down the steps then fell the rest of the way as Mark drilled two shots into him. He dove to the side and a barrage of bullets began chipping away at the concrete wall behind where he had been. They had too many guns to stand and fight. He ran to the safe room and closed himself in. The shooting continued, the entire basement sprayed with a wild barrage of bullets. Some of the rounds found their way through the wood paneling of the safe room, making Mark duck back. Finally, the shooting ceased.

"Where'd he go?"

"I don't know, but he's down here somewhere."

"We searched. There isn't any place for him to hide."

"Each of you take a corner."

The search was over fast with everyone reporting back that no one was there.

"We all heard him come down here. Hell, he shot Eddie from down here. He has to be here. We need lots of flashlights. He's hiding here someplace."

"Fuck this, let's burn his ass out."

"Hell, yeah."

"Start piling up stuff that'll burn."

Mark ran for the cave as soon as they mentioned fire. With the door closed and the cave outside the actual house, he might stand a chance of surviving a fire. His only concern was that the smoke might get in and drive him out, right into their waiting guns. He went to the vent and worked it free. Hoisting himself out of the hole, Mark belly crawled out from under the deck. He started to run for the woods then thought of something else. He crept back inside the house through the patio door, being careful not to kick any of the broken glass. Mark tiptoed to the basement door and listened.

"That's got it," one man said.

The dancing glow of the fire played across the basement wall. He inched the basement door shut then dragged the body of the man he had shot earlier out of the way. Grabbing the refrigerator, he wiggled it forward. He wouldn't have much time before they reacted because the refrigerator made noise as he rolled it away from the wall. The men below responded instantly. Mark moved the refrigerator in front of the basement door as footsteps thundered up the stairs. He tipped it so that it wedged between the basement door and the island cabinet.

The men pushed against the door but the barrier held. Then, apparently thinking that he was holding it shut, they fired into the door. Someone else threw his weight against wood. The door bounced in its frame. Mark fired several times into the door to back them up. Someone yelled about putting out the fire. A lot of noise, confusion and chaos came from behind the door. It was time for him to leave. Mark ran into the family room, grabbed an armful of family pictures, and sprinted outside. They were still attempting to break down the door when he left the house. He had no idea if his barricade would hold up for long.

He ran into the woods and buried his mementos under some loose dirt and leaves. Looking back, one long wisp of smoke escaped out the vent under the deck. He sighed.

Years of memories about to go up in flames.

Looking down at the two graves, he said, "I'm sorry, Sandra."

Then he left. He had a long way to go.

Thirty-One

IN THE DARKNESS, it was safer and easier staying on the streets. Mark would see any headlights before they could see him. He stayed toward the side of the road, so if he had to seek cover, he wouldn't have far to run. Once, he tried to look back at the sky to see if there was a glow from the fire, but too many trees stood in the way.

Besides, if the house was burning, he really didn't want to know. The memories there were all he had left of his previous, normal life.

He kept jogging and exhaustion once more took hold of his body. He forced himself to focus on something happy. His mind took him to thoughts of Sandra and his children. It made the distance pass easier.

He thought about Lynn and the guilt he felt about his growing feelings for her. He again apologized to his wife and asked for forgiveness. Before he realized, he was past the farmhouse. He changed course and went toward the house from a different direction than he had intended.

Staying in the shadows, Mark observed the peacefulness that surrounded their new home. Nothing appeared to be wrong, yet still he waited. He wanted to make sure all was as it appeared to be and he wasn't inadvertently leading the wolves to the chicken coop. He also wanted a moment to calm down. When he went inside, Mark wanted to appear strong and not look like the wounded, emotional wreck that he was.

From a side glance of the tree-lined street to the right of the house, Mark thought he saw a shadow move within the others. He watched more intently and saw the darker shape move again. Only starlight lit the night, but it was enough to show someone was outside, perhaps getting ready to attack the house. He advanced with caution. Where there was one, there might be others.

He perked up from another boost of adrenaline and again slid into the role of killer; or perhaps it was protector. It was more difficult to differentiate between them now. Not sure if he could survive another prolonged fight, Mark would have to put whoever it was down fast and silently to have a chance.

Crossing the street in front of the house Mark slid the knife from its sheath. Mark put the rifle down, hiding it under the bushes by the porch. From there, he peered around the corner and focused on the area where he had seen the shadow. Now that he was closer, he could make out the outline of a man crouching between two pine trees. The man was watching the road in the opposite direction, as if looking for reinforcements to arrive.

Mark crept from his cover and made his way to the pine trees. One tree at a time, he moved until he was only one tree away from the man. His heart pounded and he fought to control his breathing. Taking a man down from a distance with a rifle was one thing, but up close, hand-to-hand, was an entirely different matter. If the man were waiting for others to come, Mark hoped that meant he was alone.

Time stopped. The night stilled; no breeze, no insect noises, nothing, as if the two men were isolated. Mark moved around the branches of the last tree, trying to use it for cover without touching it and giving himself away. He crept to within four feet when the man stiffened and began to rise. Mark chose that moment to lunge at the man before he could turn around. He snaked his left hand around the man's mouth, bringing the blade up to his throat. The man let out a startled high-pitched cry, muffled by Mark's determined hand. A fraction of a second from slicing the watcher's throat to the bone, Mark realized that that this was no fully grown man, more like a teenager.

Caleb?

Mark gasped and released the boy, who slumped to the ground.

"Oh God, Caleb, I didn't know it was you. Oh Lord, if You truly exist, please let him be all right!" He bent to the boy who squirmed away in panic. The sounds escaping his throat were unintelligible, like an animal.

"Caleb, it's me, Mark. Let me see how badly you're cut."

Just then, the rear door slammed open and Lynn ran out on the back porch, carrying a gun. "Caleb!"

"Lynn, it's me, Mark. Caleb's here. He needs help."

"Mark? Oh God, Mark, is it really you?" She ran down the stairs. The rest of the family followed carrying guns.

Lynn ran toward Mark. As she drew near he pointed toward a tree. "I think Caleb needs you. I-I thought he was one of them. I almost killed him."

She went to Caleb, who had crawled under the wide, low hanging branches of the pine tree. His eyes were wide with fear, his hands pressed to his neck. When she coaxed him out, his hands were wet with blood. Mark was relieved to see Caleb standing and the blood wasn't squirting. He hadn't hit an artery.

Lynn tensed when she saw the blood. She hurried her son into the house where they used a flashlight to examine the wound. A shallow two-inch cut showed on the left side of his neck. The boy was more frightened than hurt.

Mark collapsed into a chair and wrapped his hands around his face. He'd almost killed the boy. *What kind of a blood-thirsty animal have I become?* He had become so numb to taking life he never considered the watcher might be a friend instead of a foe. He saw a target and decided to take it out. Where had the old Mark gone?

Mark watched Lynn work. Her face went through several emotional changes. Tension tightened around her like a clamp. How much more could she take? How much more could any of them endure?

"It shouldn't need stitches because the cut is fortunately not that deep," she reported, her voice even, yet strained. She struggled to get the words out. Her body shook, her lips trembled. Lynn blotted, cleaned and applied an ointment along its length, placing butterfly bandages across the width, and a gauze pad over the top. She led Caleb to the living room and had him lie down on a couch.

"I'm so sorry, Lynn. I never even thought it might be one of you. I just reacted like some psycho killer."

"Don't think that way, Mark." James tried to console him. "How could you have known?"

Caleb still shivered. He closed his eyes. Lynn snapped off the flashlight. "Let's leave to him rest." She left the living room and the others followed.

THE RAGE INSIDE HER had reached bursting point. When they were in the kitchen, the fury released. Rounding on Mark she shoved him hard with both hands. "What the hell were you thinking?" She shoved him again. "How could you have mistaken my son for one of those animals?"

Lynn pushed him again then punched him in the chest. She slapped his face hard, the contact held in the air like a gunshot. A vision of the large, brutal man who had assaulted her transforming Mark's face. He became the target for all her pain, anguish and hatred. Unleashing a flurry of punches, Lynn battered her foe, a steady onslaught of curses accompanying the attack.

After one vicious punch to the stomach. Mark winced and doubled over.

"Stop!" Darren shouted. He ran between Mark and Lynn crying. "Don't you hit him. He's hurt."

Seeing the blood soaking his shirt Lynn's hands flew to her face.

"Oh, Mark, I'm—"

He held up his hands to stop her.

"I'm sorry. I'm glad Caleb's not hurt seriously." His voice was distant. He backed away from the group and walked to the back door.

"Mark ..." Lynn tried to grab his arm and stop him, but he shook her off.

How fast the emotions had changed between them. She reached a tentative hand toward him.

"But you're hurt. Please let me help you. I'm sorry.

Mark turned to leave, but Darren wrapped his arms around him and held tight. "No, I won't let you go.

"Darren, bring him here," James said.

Darren pulled on Mark, who resisted at first. But when he looked into the boy's tear streaked face gave in.

Lynn started to touch Mark, hesitated then lifted his shirt. The bloody bandage hung loose, away from the wound. "I'm sorry," she said again, wiping the welling tears from her eyes. She checked the wounds and started giving orders to the group for the items she would need. In a flurry of movement, they fell about their assignments.

"You need to lie down," Lynn said. She led him to the bedroom. "Lie down." Mark did as ordered. With everything Lynn had asked for gathered, she told Maggie to stay and chased everyone else away closing the door.

Swallowing all emotion Lynn turned to her work.

Thirty-Two

WHEN THE NOISE FROM the barn door woke him, Mark was still so spent that, had it been one of the Horde, he wouldn't have been able to defend himself. But it wasn't an enemy; it was James.

"Rise and shine, Mark. I let you sleep in. The others are up and doing chores already."

Mark grunted, but even though his brain sent signals, his body was on strike.

James sat down next to him. "You all right?"

Mark grunted again. "I'll survive." After Lynn had finished mending him, she left the room without saying a word. Mark went outside and made a bed of straw in the barn. The words she hit him with had hurt far worse than any physical blows she dealt. The look of pure hatred in her eyes had pierced him through to his soul.

"Yeah, there's no doubt, physically, but I'm not so sure, mentally. You've done a lot in the past few weeks. I don't need to tell you these are not normal times. There isn't anyone in that house who thinks you're one of the bad guys. You've done what you needed to do. There isn't one person here whose life you haven't saved at least once, so you keep that in mind. I know you feel bad about last night, but in the end, no one was seriously hurt, and lessons were learned. Don't let the emotional scars make you incapable of doing what needs to be done. We're a long way from being safe. We need you to be strong, for all of us.

"Your lady friend feels bad. Last night was more frazzled nerves than any real anger at you. She knows that, believe me. Give her a chance." James stood up and brushed the hay from his pants. "Anyway, enough lectures from an old man. Time to get up. There's a lot still to be done." He walked to the door.

"Thank you."

James smiled. "No problem. Now get your lazy ass up." He left, closing the door part way behind him.

Mark stood up but stopped. His body hurt so bad he couldn't move any farther. As slowly as he could, Mark went through a series of stretches.

"I-I thought you might like some coffee."

He jumped. He hadn't heard Lynn slip in. She stood there, looking at him, her eyes welling up.

He took in the details of her face. Beyond the cuts, bruises, and swelling, her eyes were puffy, her nose red, and her cheeks streaked. He cared about this woman. *Sandra, forgive me.* He didn't really know her, but he cared enough never to want to hurt her like she had been hurt in the past, like yesterday and like last night. She stood not six feet away with a cup of coffee as a peace offering, sloshing it a little over her shaking hands.

He smiled and stepped forward to relieve her of the cup. As soon as he took control of it, she rushed into his arms, spilling most of the coffee on the ground. Her head rested on his chest. He placed one tentative arm loosely around her back. Neither of them spoke as she cried.

When she regained control, she couldn't raise her eyes to look at him.

"I'm sorry. I should never have hit you or said those things, especially after you came to rescue me. I can't

206

even begin to explain what was going through my mind. Please forgive me."

"There's nothing to forgive."

"No," she said, her voice angry. "There is. My God, you came after me knowing you could be killed! You are the most decent man I've ever known. I ... like you. I want you to know that. But that's all I can give right now. After what happened yesterday with ... those men ... it may be all I'm ever able to offer you."

Mark put his hand under her chin and lifted it so he could look into her eyes. "You just have to keep being you. Don't let those animals steal you away. That would be sad, because ... I like you too. I like you the way you are."

Her body shook. "I can't get it out of my head."

"Hopefully, with time ... I know that's lame, but know this – I will always be here for you, to help you whenever you need me."

James came to the door and called in. "Okay, you two, you've had your break. We need to make plans for the day and it's getting harder for me to keep the kids out of here. The nosy little buggers want to see what's going on."

"We all right now?" he asked.

"Yes."

"Okay, let's go do our share."

After a busy morning, of newly assigned chores, from which Mark was excluded, the entire family sat down to a midday meal of boiled corn, peanut butter sandwiches, potato chips, and canned pears. The girl from the hotel was with them. Her name was Mallory and she'd cleaned up well. Alyssa was sitting on one side of Caleb and Mallory on the other. Mark sensed trouble in the future, but he'd let Lynn worry about that.

Mark eyed Caleb, but no animosity displayed on the young man's face. The bandage had been changed and a tiny drop of blood dotted the new one.

"I'm sorry, Caleb."

"No, don't be. I'm mad at myself for being so easy to sneak up on and for being so afraid."

"There's nothing wrong with being afraid. It's not like you were raised to be in combat."

"You never seem to be afraid."

"That doesn't mean I'm not. I just don't allow it to paralyze me. If you do that, you're as good as dead. Maybe what we all need is a little training."

Lynn said, "It can't hurt any of us to be better prepared."

"Well," said James, "that's something we should discuss while everyone is here. We should make some plans on how to best defend this place. It's a lot more wide open out here than the house was."

"We're farther from the city out here; but, it stands to reason, eventually someone will come out this far." Mark looked around the table, from face to face. "The more things we can prepare for, the better we'll be. There is strength in numbers and maybe we'll find some others to join us out here."

Over their meal, they made plans. They tried to allow for any type of situation, but that was next to impossible. With the basic outlines done, it was just a matter of implementing them. But, that brought them to the final topic broached by James.

"You know, it's not over between them and us, right? If we relax for a moment, they could show up and destroy whatever we try to build."

That changed the mood.

"Say it, James," Mark said. He knew what was coming and had planned to bring it up himself.

"Well, it's just that this is never going to be over until one of us is destroyed."

"And?"

"Well, I've been thinking that maybe it would be better to take the fight to them rather than wait until they come for us. It takes away their surprise and gives us an advantage."

"I'm not saying I agree," replied Mark, "but did you have anything in mind?"

"I think we take it to where they live and burn the place down."

Total silence descended over the group for the better part of a minute. In truth, Mark had come to the same conclusion. It was the only way to prevent their new family from having to look over their shoulders for the rest of their lives. They could build something special out here, but would never really live in peace until the threat from the Horde was dealt with.

"Why don't we give that some thought and talk about it later. In the meantime, we have lots to do. We need to send some of you out to start collecting again. We can't sit back with this many mouths to feed and expect the food and water to hold out. I'm going to make a side trip to talk to an old farmer I met. I want to learn how to build a windmill. The rest of you will be assigned watch and defense-building duties. James, why don't you handle that?"

So Caleb, Alyssa and Lynn went collecting while Mark went to see Jarrod.

Thirty-Three

MARK TOOK THE PICKUP truck from the garage and drove to Jarrod's house. When no one answered the door, Mark had a bad feeling. There were no obvious signs of forced entry, no signs of bullet holes or a struggle. With the house empty, Mark walked to examine the outbuildings. He drew his gun as he headed toward the first, a large steel construction which housed farm equipment. With that vacant as well, Mark moved on to the old wooden barn. Several wire-mesh-covered pens were attached to the structure.

From somewhere in the distance, a cow bellowed. As Mark moved closer to the barn, the sound of chickens cackling reached him. He went in that direction. Rounding the building, he spied Jarrod standing in the middle of a small army of chickens, scattering feed. He put his gun away as Jarrod noticed him and waved.

"Well, I see you made it to wherever it was you were going," he said with a smile. He finished his task and walked over to the fence. He had on overalls, a straw hat, and rubber boots. He leaned against the fence, sucking on a long blade of grass.

"Yeah, I made it. It was quite a trip. How've you been here?"

"Oh, can't complain. Got all my friends here to keep me company."

"No one's been around to bother you?"

"Nah, did see a coupla cars go buy the main drag down there a day or so back, but no one's come to bother me."

"We had to move from our previous location. We were attacked. That puts the bad guys only about three or four miles from you. Sooner or later, they'll make it out this far. Did you ever go find anymore shotgun shells?"

"Nah, I haven't thought about it much since you were here."

Mark reached in his pocket and pulled out two shells. "Here, I brought you a reload."

Jarrod reached out and took them. "Well, that's right nice of you. I appreciate it. I hope I don't ever have to use 'em, but it'll be good knowing I got some backups. Want a beer?"

"I was hoping you'd ask."

Jarrod went through the barn and peeled off his rubber boots. The two men walked back to the house. Once inside with a cold beer in front of them, Jarrod asked, "So what brings you out this far? I know it's not just to bring me some shells."

"No, it's not. As I said, we were forced to move to a larger, safer location. We settled in a farm about three miles south of here. Our numbers have grown, and like you, we'd like to make it permanent. To do that, we need to find a source of electricity and I thought of your windmill. I'm here to get information on how to build one."

Jarrod took a long pull on his bottle and then set it down as he thought. "Well, I'll tell you, I understand the workings okay and can probably help you build one, but in truth, I paid a fella to hook it up so it worked right. Now, of course, being a man who hates to pay others to do the work, I watched him close. That way, in case there was a problem, I could do it myself. It's been a few years and my memory ain't quite what it once was, but I think I could get it

211

working if you want to try it."

Mark smiled, "Jarrod, that would be great. If you can give me a list of materials, I can start trying to find them."

"Well, I think I got an idea about that too. There's an old boy down the road a spell that's got hisself three of them. Two of those modern turbine types, like I got, and an old wooden one. I don't know for sure he's alive, but if there's nobody home we might be able to dismantle the whole kit-and-caboodle right there. Save you a lot of running around, that's for sure."

"Okay, that sounds good. Can you give me directions?"

"You sure are one anxious son-of-a-gun, ain't you? Tell me, you think you can take it down by yourself? You got the tools to do it? Or how about a truck big enough to haul it?"

"Ah, no, but I'll figure out something."

"Well, let me figure it out for you, 'cause obviously you ain't got a clue as to what you're getting into. I got everything you need right here. Now, you want my help or not?"

Mark smiled. "Absolutely."

"Okay, now we're getting somewhere. I got just one request though. I want a nice home-cooked meal and be able to sit at a table with other people to talk to. Deal?" He stuck out his long fingers.

"No deal," said Mark firmly and Jarrod's eyebrows went up. "Friends don't need deals. You can come to dinner anytime." Mark took the man's hand and Jarrod smiled.

"Since you seem to be in a hurry, let's finish our beers and then I can gather up what we'll need."

A little more than an hour later, they were on the road, with Jarrod driving an over-sized pickup truck with dual wheels for hauling heavy loads and towing a long flatbed trailer. In the back seat of the cab was an assortment of tools, including wrenches that could easily fit around Mark's thigh.

The drive took less than ten minutes and they had no sign

of any other vehicles on the road. Jarrod pulled into the long driveway of a large commercial farm. An empty fresh produce market stood near the road. Behind it was a row of greenhouses. Beyond that was a very large updated farmhouse that looked big enough for ten people. Assorted outbuildings followed, all surrounded by a sea of corn and soybeans. Smaller patches held green beans, peppers, tomatoes, and melons. Between the outbuildings and the fields was a row of three windmills: two large three propeller wind turbines, like Jarrod had, and an older shorter wooden one, with eighteen blades that looked like an over-sized ceiling fan.

"There they are. The taller ones run all the electricity. The shorter one runs the water pumps."

Jarrod knocked on the door, but got no answer. He tried the knob and finding it open, the two men entered. Mark kept his hand close to the gun just in case.

"Hullo," shouted Jarrod. "Anyone at home?"

They waited, but no answer came. In the kitchen, they found a sheep dog lying on the floor, breathing rapidly with shallow breaths, too weak to move, barely able to lift its head. As Jarrod got closer, a very faint whine escaped the animal. The tip of its tail started up, but dropped before it rose far. Signs of a frantic search for food were evident. The large bin that held dog food had been upended and emptied, the water dish overturned. Piles of dog poop lined the floor in front of the back door. It had been trapped in the kitchen and no one had been able to come for it. It was a miracle the dog had survived.

Jarrod knelt next to the creature. "Poor fella. Don't expect there's much hope of you recovering. Still, hope is hope. See if you can find something for this boy to eat."

Mark searched the cupboards finding a variety of canned goods while Jarrod got some water. "Now, see the advantage of a windmill. It kept the power up so's the well could pump water." He set the bowl down and lifted the dog's muzzle above the water. The dog flicked its tongue down and lapped what it could.

"Try that cabinet there," Jarrod pointed, "the one with all the scratches on it."

Mark opened the door and found a bag of dry dog food. He pulled it out and opened it.

"See how smart this boy is? He knew there was food in there he just couldn't get to it. Put some water on the food to soften it up a bit. Make it easier to chew and digest."

Mark did as instructed, setting the bowl down by Jarrod. Jarrod took one piece at a time and tried to feed it to the dog. It wanted to eat but had little energy to chew.

"Why don't you search the rest of the house while I take care of him?"

The smell told him what he would find. Mark found two little girls on the floor in what looked like a playroom. The father was dead on the bathroom floor, the mother was still in bed. Two young adults were dead in separate rooms. Once again Mark pondered on the random death toll. Why did an entire family get wiped out and yet Lynn's whole family survived? It was a mystery and somewhere a smarter man than he was hopefully trying solve it.

Mark didn't search the rooms. He just closed the doors and went back downstairs.

In the kitchen, the dog had taken some food and had found its voice. It was whining.

"We'll check back on him later. I'll open the outside door and maybe he'll get up enough strength to follow us out." He went to the rear door and began cleaning up the piles. "What'd you find upstairs?'

"All dead."

Jarrod paused. "That's a real shame. They was good people." He opened the door and walked out.

Thirty-Four

THEY STARTED ON THE smaller wooden windmill. They had no way of getting up high enough to work on the other two. There were rungs, but climbing that high to work wasn't practical or safe. The wooden one could be climbed from any direction and was less than half the height. Still it was difficult work, being so far off the ground. It took their combined strength to take the center hub apart. When Mark's wound began to bleed again, he let Jarrod do most of the work as far as disconnecting any wires and important parts. Using the winch on Jarrod's truck, they lowered the eighteen blade fan, the gearbox, and the tail vane to the flatbed. After disconnecting all the important parts, they worked down the four sides, detaching all the supporting cross beams and the pump rod. The work took most of the day. Finally, as the sun was setting, they called it quits. They still needed something to cut the four main legs from the cement they stood in, but that would have to wait.

The two men loaded what they had on the flatbed. After Mark had gathered an assortment of fresh produce, they hauled everything to the new house. No one came out to greet them when they pulled up the driveway.

"Ah, you didn't make up these people just to get my help, did you?"

Mark laughed. "No, they're probably hiding because they didn't recognize the truck. I'd better show myself before they start shooting."

"Well, there's a good idea."

Mark opened the door and stood so the others could see him. The back door flew open and the mob rushed out.

"Hey, everyone, meet Jarrod."

"Damn, you wasn't kidding.'

Mark let them introduce themselves and went to unload the truck. Over a simple dinner, they made plans to meet the next day to finish taking down the windmill. Jarrod left deep into the darkness of night.

The morning came too early for Mark. His body ached even more than the day before. This time he dragged Caleb with him so they could retrieve the pickup truck Mark had left at Jarrod's. Jarrod collected several bags of cement mix and two post-hole diggers. They followed him back to the farm. Jarrod checked on the dog and informed them that he was still alive. The food was half gone and the water needed refilling, so the animal was at least eating and drinking.

Assigning Mark to cut the posts, Jarrod gave Caleb the task of digging up the cable and unhooking the batteries. Jarrod started up a front loader and scooped up the batteries, depositing them on the flat bed. He then helped Caleb dig. After the four posts were down, they loaded them. Jarrod filled several large buckets with water to use for cement. They traveled in a caravan back to the house.

Jarrod showed them where the windmill needed to be erected. Most of the day was spent taking turns digging holes deep enough to support the poles. After seating the posts, they poured the cement. Then, before it could set, Mark and Jarrod attached the crossbeams to hold the poles together in the proper positions. After each one was bolted in place, they climbed it and placed the next one above it. Halfway up, they called it a day. Everyone was exhausted. They would have to wait until the next day to finish the job.

Lynn and Maggie had planned a feast in Jarrod's honor. They made a pot of vegetable soup, corn-on-the-cob, tuna casserole, canned chicken and gravy over rice, and fresh baked bread, all cooked over grills and the firepit. The gathered family was excited by the prospect of fresh food. Jarrod led the way with his boisterous voice and endless stories. Everyone forgot about the troubles, if only for a short time, and everyone was smiling as the night ended.

Jarrod promised to be back the next day to finish the windmill. When he had gone, everyone dragged themselves to their rooms. It had been another long day. They were so tired, they forgot to set a watch for the night.

The next morning, as promised, Jarrod arrived bringing with him two nice surprises. The first was his new friend Buddy, the dog. He carted Buddy in an old red wagon filled with blankets. The dog seemed to have more strength and was able to keep his head up. When the kids saw him, they made a fuss. Buddy attempted several times to get to his feet but didn't quite have the strength yet. He had enough, though, to keep his tail wagging.

The second surprise was a butchered pig with a long pole through the center. He pointed to the fire pit behind the house and instructed Maggie and Lynn on how to do a pig roast. He jammed two metal poles with tines on one end into the ground. Mark and Jarrod hoisted the pig up by the spit and set each end in the tines. Leaving Lynn and Maggie to figure things out from there, Jarrod went back to his truck for his tools.

Screwing the remaining cross bars onto the main poles of the windmill tower filled the morning. With the four sides secured, Jarrod scampered to the top. Again, using the winch, they hoisted the blade assembly to the top where Jarrod seated it. From there, it was all Jarrod's fine-tuning of the project.

Placing the batteries in the garage, they hooked up the wires to them and the pump. Jarrod tied into the pipes connecting to the well.

"Okay, that's all I can do for today," Jarrod announced. "I'll come back tomorrow and finish the connections. I still need to attach a filtering system. Now you'll need some wind."

"Sounds great," Mark responded. "It'll be nice having running water again."

"Ha, who you kidding? It'll be lucky if the darn thing works at all. If it does, you're still not gonna be able to do too much. This one will meet your water needs unless there's no wind. You're gonna have to build a couple more of these if you want electricity. One may not generate enough power."

"Well, it's a start. We couldn't have done it without you. I can never thank you enough."

"Sure you can … just feed me."

They laughed and went to see what Maggie and Lynn had put together.

Lynn and Maggie had collected two picnic tables from neighboring houses. Jarrod, having thought of everything, turned on a battery-powered radio. The only cassette tape Jarrod owned, however, was bluegrass music. He also pulled out a cooler that held six bottles of cold beer, six cans of pop, and a bottle of white wine.

The pig turned out a little charred on the outside, but no one complained. It had been a long time since any of them tasted fresh meat. It became the newest best meal they'd ever had. Jarrod again was the life of the party, telling tall tales and jokes. They laughed and danced, and at the end of the night, life seemed normal.

Jarrod wanted to leave the remaining pig which would be enough for another ten meals. But after Maggie explained they had nowhere cold enough to store it, Jarrod packed it into coolers and took it home. He promised to bring it back when they had refrigeration.

"After all," he said, "I gotta come back to make sure the windmill works, anyways."

He drove off with Buddy and once more the night became quiet.

As they cleaned up, Mark noticed a flicker of light from down the road. He looked at the others, still on a high from their meal. No one else had noticed. Not wanting to ruin their mood or cause them to worry, he excused himself, saying he had to use the crude outhouse they had constructed behind the barn.

Once there, he raced through the cornfields, estimating the distance he needed to go to be past where he saw the light. The light hadn't been bright or large enough to have been a headlight ... more like a flashlight. Mark moved toward the street, stopping at the pine tree line. Catching the light flicker on and off again farther to his right, he bolted across the road, dropping into the drainage ditch. From there, he crawled along the ridge to the where he'd last seen the light. He was about fifty yards from the house and across the street. Behind him was a large bare field that stretched on a long way, the open ground bordered along the road by overgrown weeds.

Mark crawled along the edge of the weeds, trying not to rustle anything. When he peered through them, the light flashed once more. Whoever the person was twenty yards away, intended moving toward the house. His thoughts went back to Caleb and the near tragedy.

But this was not Caleb. The person was shorter and Mark had been standing next to Caleb when he first saw the flicker of light.

Staying low, Mark walked thirty feet away from the intruder, into the open field. When he was in line with the creeper, he moved toward him. Mark was in the open, but would make less noise coming through the field then along the trees and brush. He could also advance quicker and have a better shot should the need arise.

The figure slowed, then turned around to look behind him. Mark froze. Any movement would give him away. He wanted to be closer before he took the intruder down.

After a few seconds, the man started moving again. Mark waited a bit, then followed. The spy stopped at the edge of the tree, even with the dining room window.

Mark eased between the branches. He held his breath. The peeper was in front of him, holding binoculars against his face trying to see through the windows.

Mark leveled the gun and walked forward. At that distance, it no longer mattered if he were heard.

"Freeze!" Mark called, still moving forward.

Of course, the intruder did the opposite. As he turned and reached for what Mark assumed was a gun, Mark brought his 9mm down on his head, dropping him to the ground. He searched the body, found a gun, and slid it into his belt. Mark pocketed a knife and the flashlight and slung the binoculars around his neck by their strap. Reaching down, Mark hauled the unconscious man up and put him in a fireman's carry. He crossed the yard and made for the barn.

Once inside with the door closed, Mark tossed the man on some hay bundles. Groaning, he rolled until he fell off the bundle onto the floor. The fall seemed to revive him. He sat up with a start, fear on his face. Spotting Mark standing over him, a gun visible in the beam of the flashlight and both pointed at his face, he gasped.

"Why were you watching us?"

Mark looked at his prisoner. He was just a boy, probably no older than Caleb and too shaken to speak.

"You don't need to be afraid if you answer me. Why are you here? Are you reporting our position back to someone else?"

Still the boy didn't respond. Mark could see the boy was scared. Keeping his gun trained on him, Mark went to the workbench and pulled down some rope.

"Roll over on your stomach."

The boy tried to crawl away from Mark.

"You're gonna make me hurt you, aren't you? Last

chance. Either roll over or I shoot you in the leg. It's your choice." Mark lifted the gun and took aim. The boy rolled over.

Mark pulled the boy's arms back hard, causing him to cry out. He tied the boy's hands and feet. Then he tied those together with the boy's knees bent. Pulling out the knife he'd recovered, Mark opened it and placed it against the side of the boy's face.

"Please d-don't," he begged.

"Well, son, you're the only one who can stop me."

"A bunch of us were sent out to search for you. I'm supposed to report back to Buster. He wants to find you and *kill* you for what you did."

"Why would you want him to kill us? What have we ever done to you?"

"You're the enemy and this is war. Buster said so."

"Do you know what he did to my friend? If somebody hurt one of your friends, wouldn't you try to help them?"

"You attacked our home and killed our people."

"*Your* people are the ones raping and killing. The people *here* are just trying to survive. You destroy everything you come in contact with. We're just trying to build a life that's something halfway normal. Hasn't there been enough death already?"

"You're just trying to brainwash me. I know the truth about you."

"Tell me, boy, what did you see when you were watching us? Did you see a family having fun together? Are you afraid of those girls that were out there? We're just trying to stay alive. The difference is we would rather not kill anyone to do it."

Mark backed away and stared at the boy. The kid was right about one thing. He was brainwashed, only it was by this Buster.

"Why do you want to be like them? Wouldn't you want to live in peace? Have you forgotten what it's like to have a

221

family? Why don't you stay with us? You won't have anything to fear."

"Yes, I will. I'll have the worst thing to fear."

"What's that?"

"Buster's revenge when he catches me."

Mark tried a different tack. "Do you know how many men he has?"

"A lot more than you do," he said with defiance. Since Mark hadn't hurt him, the boy seemed braver now.

"Do they know where we are?"

"They will when I tell them," he blurted without thinking. Then he tried to edit his statement. "Yeah, they know, and they're on their way right now."

Mark smiled. He stepped forward and squatted in front of him. The boy tried to wiggle away, afraid Mark was going to cut him.

"Liar. It's too bad you don't want to join us. I guess that makes you the enemy."

He turned and left the barn, hoping his words might sink in.

Thirty-Five

"**WHERE'D YOU DISAPPEAR** to?" asked Lynn. She was still happy and relaxed after the family's wonderful evening. Of course, the two glasses of wine helped. It was nice to see her smile again.

Shame he was going to have to ruin the mood.

"Found a kid outside watching us. He claims he was scouting us out to go back and lead the Horde here."

As he expected, her face took on a harder look. The happy glow from the wine dissipated like smoke. "And for some reason, you think otherwise?"

"I think he had plenty of time to report where we were. Instead, he was watching us through binoculars." He took them off and set them down on the table. "He's about Caleb's age. I think he saw us as a family and got a little homesick. It'd be nice if we could bring him around, but maybe he's been living with the others too long. Regardless, we can't let him go until we're sure what we're doing."

"I'll sit with him a while," she said, her tone sharp. She started for the door.

Mark grabbed her arm and she responded by pulling away and raising her hand as if to strike him. She stopped and looked at her hand as if unsure why it was up there.

"He is not the one who hurt you," Mark said. Her eyes fell, apparently ashamed that he had read her intent. "Give him a chance. Maybe if we can't turn him, we can at least gather information from him."

"Mark, I'm—"

"It's okay. Go to him and see if you can work your motherly charms on him. Lynn, he's just a scared boy."

Mark walked away and the kitchen door opened and closed. He pulled out a chair in the dining room and sat down. Lynn was working very hard at being strong for all of them, but her ordeal was so fresh it had to be taking an emotional toll. He would have to watch her closely.

Mark was deep in thought when James sat down across from him.

"Problem?"

Mark told him about the captured boy.

"Hmm."

"We're running out of time already. If we're gonna make a move, it should be tomorrow."

"Looks that way."

"I've got the workings of a plan, but we're not ready. We don't have the numbers and we're relying largely on kids. The biggest problem is that I can't be everywhere at once. Whoever we use as bait to lure them away has to be an experienced driver who won't be afraid to do what's necessary to get away. The attack itself I can do, but it really needs two people. The ambush needs to work perfectly to have a chance for escape. That's where I need you. We just don't have enough experience or enough people to pull this off. It would be nice to know how many we're dealing with."

"Then we go with what we have because to do nothing will be certain death. Our only advantage is surprise."

"I don't know. It's too risky."

"Mark, staying here is too risky. Sooner or later someone will find us and tell the Horde. And in case you haven't noticed, we've been running on risk for the past month. Nowhere is safe anymore."

Mark shook his head.

"What are you really afraid of?"

"That some of these kids won't survive. They're so young and they deserve a chance at life."

"Maybe this is the best chance they'll get." He stood up. "Whatever you decide, we're all you have. And you already know, if we don't act now, we may never get the chance. If this kid found us, how long before someone more competent does? We either move again or fight."

He went into his room and closed the door, leaving Mark to sort things out. After a while, with no answers coming, he flopped on a couch where sleep fought his mind for control of his body.

Thirty-Six

A LOUD VOICE YELLING down at him woke Mark. "You're wasting the best part of the day, son. Get your lazy butt up and let's get to work."

Jarrod stood over him with a mug of coffee in his hand. Mark wiped the sleep from his eyes and looked around. The house was bustling with movement as the kids set the table and Lynn and Maggie put out breakfast. They really had become like an old-fashioned extended country family. The kids no longer complained about getting up early or doing their chores. They found comfort in the routine.

"What time is it?"

"Huh, it's just about time to go to sleep, you've been lying there so long." He reached a long arm down and helped Mark up.

They sat at the table and Mark caught Lynn's eye. "How's our guest?"

"Still there, but not very talkative. I'll go out and feed him in a minute."

"What new guest?" asked Ruth.

Mark ignored her. "Don't untie him. You'll have to feed him."

"Who's here and why does he have to be tied?" Alyssa

asked.

"I hadn't planned on it," said Lynn. "I'm not stupid you know."

"Is someone going to answer us?" Ruth said.

"I never said you were."

Lynn left the house with a plate of food.

"Why's she mad at you?" asked Caleb.

"Isn't this a great morning?" Jarrod said exuberantly. "Let's eat."

While the food was passed around Mark explained. "We had a visitor last night. A boy was spying on us." The plates stopped being passed. All eyes turned toward Mark. "I have him tied up in the barn. I want everyone to stay clear of there today."

They continued with their meal. A few minutes later, Lynn came back in. "He says he has to go to the bathroom. I fed him, but the bathroom's your job."

Mark shoveled another forkful of fried pork and potatoes into his mouth and went to do his job. In the barn, the boy was trying to work his hands free. He stopped when Mark entered.

"You gotta go?"

"No, I'm good."

"Well you better decide because this is gonna be your only chance."

"Where am I supposed to go?"

"Got a place out back."

"I'm gonna need my hands free."

"Don't think so." Mark lifted the boy up, untied his feet and led him around back to the outhouse.

BACK IN THE HOUSE, with the table now clear, Mark found some paper and a pencil and called everyone around him. He sketched out a map of the roads east of them. As he was finishing, Jarrod came in, wanting to

227

know what the holdup was.

"Jarrod, I'm sorry, but we've got some important planning to do. I don't think we're gonna have time to finish the windmill today."

"What's so all-fired important?"

"We need to deal with some people before they find us.

"Those same one's who was chasing you before?"

"Yeah."

"Huh. Whatcha got planned?"

"My friend, I appreciate all you've done for us, but this isn't your fight. If we don't take care of this now, we won't have any need for a windmill."

The older man stood there, moving his jaw from side to side. "Oh, I see. I'm a good enough friend to do the hard work, but when it comes to the easy stuff you don't want me around."

Mark smiled. "You sure you want in on this?"

"Friends don't let friends face trouble alone. They'd eventually come after me anyway. Might as well deal with this now. Besides, who would I talk to if you all were gone?"

"Okay, we could use another hand, but this will be dangerous. People will die."

The kids scooted over to make room for Jarrod.

"Okay, here's what I've got. There are three teams. We can divide those up later. I'll head up one and use Caleb as my driver. Lynn, you and James will be the other leaders." Mark looked at Caleb. "Caleb will drive past the hotel and fire blindly at the building. We need you to draw as many horde members away as possible. You will keep going and turn on this road here." Mark pointed at his map. "That's Church Street. It's important you lead the cars chasing you down this street.

Here we need something big to block the road. Cars, trucks, whatever we can find. You need to leave just enough room for Caleb to get through."

Mark switched to James and Lynn. "You will park your vehicles on the side street, then set up in these two yards. When the cars chase Caleb down this street, you will have a killing field. Keep shooting and don't let up. Take out as many as you can then run. Don't go straight back to the farm. Find someplace to hide and wait there for a while. Everyone got that?"

No one spoke. All eyes were focused on the map.

"I think Maggie and Darren should stay here to protect the farm."

"What will you be doing?" asked Lynn.

"Once Caleb draws the Horde away from the hotel I'm going to slip inside and burn it down."

James said, "All by yourself?"

"No, I'll go with him," said Jarrod. "But I'm gonna need some more shells."

Mark smiled. "That's not a problem You help yourself to any weapons you need. Are you sure you want to do this?"

"Yeah, I'm in. I'll leave Buddy here to help watch the house."

We all have some preparations to make. We'll go tonight. Anyone have any other questions?"

Maggie said, "Wouldn't it be easier to pick up and move farther away? This is madness."

Mark answered, "Yes, it would, and that's still an option. We don't have to go through with this. Maybe we can go far enough where no one will ever bother us again, or maybe we'll always just be delaying the inevitable. This is not a dictatorship. Everyone has a vote. But let's decide right now because time is running out."

"Well, I vote we leave," said Maggie.

Caleb, Ruth and Alyssa voted with Maggie.

Mallory, with pure hatred in her voice, said, "I vote to fight."

Darren fidgeted. Mark could see he wanted to say something. "It's all right, Darren, you have a voice here."

"I-I'm sorry Mark. I don't want to fight anymore."

"It's okay, none of us does."

James voted to stand and fight

"Of course you would, you old fool," Maggie said.

"Maggie, we won't be safe until this is over."

Mark looked at Jarrod. He shrugged. "If you decide to fight, I'll join you. If you decide to move, I guess I'll miss you."

When it came to Lynn's vote, her voice shook with rage. "I want them dead. I want them all dead. I'll go alone if I have to."

For a moment, all eyes were on her and no one spoke. Then, Caleb said, "I change my vote. Let's kill them all."

"Hell, yeah!" Mallory added.

Thirty-Seven

WITH THE PLAN LAID out everyone went about gathering what they would need. Two hours later Caleb walked outside carrying bottled water for his mother and sister. He handed out the bottles and wiped the sweat from his eyes with his sleeve. As he did, Caleb noticed a path had been trampled through the cornstalks past the barn. Caleb backed up the steps to get a higher view. Following the path he spotted a figure running away from the house.

"Look," he shouted. "Over there, in the cornfield." Caleb pointed.

His mother and sister looked up. Mark trotted over to where they stood. "Damn! Caleb, go check the barn. See if that boy is still there. Hurry."

Mark already knew what Caleb would find. The boy was almost clear of the field. Mark ran for the car. He had to catch the boy before he could escape and take word of their location back to the Horde. Mark started the car and raced out to the street. Tires squealed as he made the turn around the corner.

Pressing the pedal hard, the car shot down the road. At the end of the block Mark braked, the car skidding to a stop in the middle of the intersection. Putting the car in park he opened the door and took a quick look around. Not finding his prey Mark climbed on the roof to get a look into the corn field. The trampled stalks came right to the edge of the field. The boy had already exited. Where could he have gone?

Mark looked down both streets but did not see a figure or car anywhere. Jumping to the ground Mark got back into the car. He had a choice left or straight. Choosing straight Mark drove at a speed that enabled him to scan the area.

Fifteen minutes later he pounded the wheel and returned to the farmhouse. The family members joined him as he got out of the car. There was obvious concern on their faces.

"He must have had a car nearby. There's no way he walked all the way out here. I should've thought of that before. We need to go now. We can't wait for it to get dark. They could be here in less than an hour."

Everyone ran back inside and gathered whatever they were going to need. Maggie, Darren, and Buddy were staying behind to watch the house, mostly because Darren was a liability. Things would be moving too fast out there for him.

Jarrod and Mark climbed inside Jarrod's pickup and started out first. They had to get some equipment from Jarrod's house. Caleb would leave in the van by himself giving everyone fifteen minutes to get in place. Lynn and Mallory left in one pickup while Ruth, Alyssa, and James rode in the other.

Mark and Jarrod drove toward the hotel. Jarrod stopped at Church Street, off Main and turned the flatbed sideways, blocking the road halfway down the block. He then drove the John Deere 9410 combine off the ramp to complete the barricade, leaving just enough room for the van to squeeze through. Jarrod unhooked the pickup, then Mark and he drove off.

The pickups were parked out of sight on the first street past the barricade. Each team took up their assigned stations in the backyards of the two corner houses on either side of the blockade. Lynn and Mallory were on the left side while the others took the right. They assembled the equipment they had brought and waited.

Jarrod drove to a dead-end street two blocks farther down. Each man carried a five-gallon gas container and a pry bar. Jarrod had his shotgun and the remaining box of shells Mark had collected. Mark had the rifle over his shoulder and two handguns with two spare magazines for each. The five rounds in the magazine of the rifle were all he had left for it.

They stepped down the slope of the creek that ran behind the hotel. The sun was beginning to set, but there was still plenty of light. It would not be dark enough to cover their approach as they had planned. Sloshing through the shallow creek, they ducked under one overpass and continued through to the other side.

The Catholic Church loomed above them to the right. As Mark dredged past it, he whispered, "If You exist, I ask that You spare my friends. I ask nothing for myself."

They stopped at the Main Street bridge. On the other side, to the left, was the hotel. The original plan called for Jarrod to keep following the creek until he was at the far end of the hotel. But with it still being light, that was no longer a safe option. He would have to wait until the Horde was drawn off to make his approach. Mark had to stay there to cover Caleb.

Jarrod stooped under the bridge and walked through the tunnel to the far side. Mark was afraid he would keep going, but the farmer squatted down and waited. An eternity later, a vehicle approached at high speed. Mark climbed the bank to the side of the bridge and risked a glance above street level. A car exited the parking lot as the van got close. Caleb honked the horn, then began firing indiscriminate shots at the parked cars and the hotel, trying to draw as much attention as possible.

The car continued out in the street until Caleb rammed it, sending it spinning back up the driveway. However, the impact sent the van skidding to the right, jumping the curb and heading straight for the concrete bridge abutment that Mark was hiding behind. Caleb's face was panicked as he fought for control of the wheel. He turned it too hard to the left. That would have sent the van over on its side except the rear bumper clipped the end of the bridge, helping Caleb right the vehicle and bring it bouncing back to the street. Mark slid down the bank, fearing the van would roll over on top of him. A shower of stone chips fell around him.

Mark scrambled back up the opposite bank in time to see at least a dozen men running to the edge of the street, firing at the fleeing van. Others ran for their cars. As soon as the van was out of effective range, the shooters went for their cars. An assortment of vehicles made a mad dash for the street, crowding the exit, some jumping the curb. More men poured out of the hotel to give pursuit. In all, at least twenty vehicles with perhaps thirty men and women took up the chase.

Mark hoped no one would be left outside to see what he was doing, but two men stood around the crushed car helping the driver out. He couldn't do anything about them. He had to protect Caleb. Mark set the rifle on the edge of the opposite bank and took aim at a car in the back third of the pack. It was about a one-hundred-yard shot. The bullet struck the back windshield. Whether he hit the driver or not, he never knew, but the bullet had the desired effect. The car careened off the road, plowing into an apartment building. The next car swerved to the right to avoid hitting that car but smacked into another one, causing a chain reaction of minor collisions.

This time, Mark aimed at a driver who turned

broadside, braking before he crashed into the others. He made a good target, and Mark wasted no time splattering his brains all over the interior. A traffic jam ensued. The cars had to slow down and take turns maneuvering through the wrecks, allowing Caleb more time to escape.

The next shot missed, but the driver was shocked enough when his window shattered that he slammed on his brakes, causing the car behind to slam into him. The following car managed to avoid them, but the car behind that one smashed into him broadside as he tried to veer away. Only half the cars made it through, still in pursuit.

Across the street, the three men, having heard the rifle reports, had identified Mark's position and ran toward him. A shotgun began firing, taking all three men down. Jarrod had come through.

Mark looked for other targets as the cars caught behind the wrecks tried to maneuver themselves clear. One driver got out, waving his hands at the drivers in front. Mark took aim and blew a hole in the back of his head. The others looked in surprise as the man dropped, then all began searching for cover. Mark fired his final round, dropping a short, stocky woman.

Time to move.

He left the empty rifle inside the tunnel and ran through. Jarrod was nowhere to be seen. Mark figured the man had moved on to do his next job. Mark hauled the gas container up the bank, carrying his 9mm in the other hand. As he approached the hotel, a man pushed open the side door. Mark shot him and kept moving.

Mark went around the back of the hotel, setting the plastic jug down. Moving from room to room, he busted out the windows with the pry bar. The rooms appeared unoccupied and no one shot at him, so the job went easy. After breaking windows in the first three rooms, he ran back for the gas. He poured some in each room then went to the side door. Another man was exiting as Mark rounded the corner. Both men were surprised, but Mark had his gun ready, firing two rounds into the man who fell on top of the body already there.

Mark dragged both inside, leaving them under the stairs. He splashed some gasoline on the carpeting inside the first-floor door but did not go down the hall. On the second floor landing, he set the gas can down and went through the fire door. Using the pry bar, he rapped on doors on both sides of the hall and yelled fire. No one emerged. Now came the hard part. He began prying the locks off each door to make sure no one was trapped inside. His actions would take a long time, but if anyone was being held against their will, he had to make sure they had the chance to get free.

Mark thought of the other family members and prayed things were going well for them.

"I HEAR CARS," Mallory said.

"Everyone get ready," Lynn said. "Don't do anything until I say." Then, almost as an afterthought, added, "and when I say run – run." In spite of her resolve, she couldn't tamp down the fear. But each time Lynn thought she might give in to her fright, she remembered the large man and what he'd done to her and any doubts melted away, replaced by anger.

The van's tires screamed as Caleb whipped the speeding vehicle around the corner. Relief swept over Lynn. Her son was safe, for now. Through the windshield, her son's face was an almost unrecognizable mask of fear. For a moment, she didn't think the wheels would hold the road.

Caleb slowed the van down, bumped up over the curb, then worked the wheel hard, hand-over-hand, to bring the vehicle back to the road. Aiming toward the narrow opening Jarrod had left him, Caleb stopped with the rear end even with the combine. Leaving the motor running, Caleb climbed through the back and opened one of the rear doors. Jarrod had piled a few bags of cement there for Caleb to take cover behind. He raised the shotgun like Mark had taught him and waited. He looked toward Lynn and gave a quick wave, her return smile a mix of angst and pride.

It didn't take long for the first car to tear around the corner. When the driver saw the combine blocking the road, he braked hard, setting off a chain reaction of rear-end collisions. Six cars were jammed together with others still trying to make the turn.

"Now!" Lynn said.

At that moment, the sky was lit bright on both sides of the street, as flaming Molotov cocktails arced up and descended on the cars, smashing into an inferno of splashing gasoline, engulfing eight cars within seconds. Men screamed as they tried to free themselves from the flaming vehicles. Fire licked at the remaining cars as they rammed each other, attempting to get clear.

Lynn, Caleb and James open fired as the chasers jumped from their inflamed vehicles. In the mayhem, bodies piled up fast. Most fled the chaos without firing back. Ruth, Alyssa, and Mallory continued tossing the remaining bombs until gone. Then Ruth and Alyssa ran to the get-away cars while Mallory picked up her gun to add to the carnage.

The heat warmed Lynn's face. She slid another magazine into the gun and chambered a round like Mark had taught her. The ambush had worked better than they had imagined, with only sporadic return fire. Many of the animals had fallen to their barrage.

The fire spread to the next row of cars. Then, some of the men who had escaped the blaze began returning fire. Just then, one of the cars exploded. Lynn took that as a good time to leave. She shouted for Mallory to go, but the girl stood pulling the trigger wildly, loosing a maniacal scream with each shot. When her gun ran dry, Lynn grabbed the girl's arm and pulled her along. A quick glance across the road showed James was already on the move. Hopefully, they had created enough chaos that pursuit would be severely hampered. Even though they had whittled the numbers down, they were still outnumbered and outgunned.

Caleb covered the withdrawal, giving everyone time to reach the trucks. Once in the vehicle, Ruth punched the pedal and the truck lurched forward. Lynn glanced through the back window, her chest tight with fear until she saw Caleb pull behind them.

Ruth was hyperventilating. "Ruthie, relax and slow down or you'll get us killed." She touched the girl's arm and tried to sound calm. "We're all right, breathe. That's better. Now turn here."

The petrified girl made the turn. Lynn blew a breath out. They had done it, so far, though they still had a few miles to go to reach the safe house. The chosen house was hidden down a long winding driveway surrounded by trees. If they could get up the driveway quick enough no one would be able to see them from the road. Now, it was a matter of how long it would take for any pursuit to organize and how long they would have to stay hidden.

Her thoughts turned to Mark. "Please God ..." she didn't finish. God knew what she wanted.

Thirty-Eight

MARK FOUND THE SECOND floor easy going. There were only two rooms with locks on them. They ripped away from the thin wood framework with very little effort. Both rooms were empty. He brought the gas container in and poured a trail along the carpeted hallway floor.

Mark skipped the third floor; Jarrod was taking the odd-numbered ones. He glanced through the fire door window on the way up. The tall farmer was walking toward the far door. He was still alive. Two bodies were in the middle of the hall.

Knowing the army chasing Caleb could come back at any time, Mark increased his pace, taking the stairs two at a time. On the fourth floor, Mark repeated his actions. This time he had an immediate response. Two doors opened within seconds of his shouted, "Fire!"

On the fourth floor, two doors were open. Both occupants stood in their doorways holding guns, talking to each other. Mark guessed they must have heard the shots. Mark tried to decide the best approach. Before he could decide, one of the guys went back into his room leaving the door open. The other turned his back to Mark. Mark wouldn't get a better chance. Yanking the fire door open Mark fired. His target turned as both shots drilled into his gut, dropping him to his knees.

Mark kept walking, staying close to the wall with his gun leveled. He waited for the second man to poke his head out. Mark came to the wounded man and fired one round into his head. The door shut. Mark pressed against the wall and slid to the door. There he stopped and listened.

Something scratched at the door. Mark envisioned that gunman leaning against the door listening for his approach. Stepping in front of the door Mark fired a square pattern into the wood. A thud followed. The lock dangled from the hasp. Mark clipped it in place, securing the man, at least for the moment, inside.

Farther down the hall, someone pounded inside a locked room.

"Who are you?" he asked, not knowing what else to say.

If they were locked inside, they obviously had no way of getting out. It suddenly dawned on Mark why there was no one on the lower floors. If the captors were trying to keep someone locked inside, it would be a long drop to the ground from the upper rooms.

"Help me, please." A woman's voice said.

Mark slid the pry bar between the door frame and the hasp and tore it away. Before opening the door, he stepped back and readied his gun. Turning the knob he pushed the door open, but no one came out.

"You can come out now, it's safe."

"But if I leave the room and he comes back, he'll hurt me," the voice whimpered.

"Lady, in a few minutes there won't be a room to come back to. I'm gonna set this whole place on fire. This is your chance to escape. Leave here and follow the creek outside to the west." He pointed. "Go now before it's too late."

She stepped out timidly. She was slim with wild dark hair. Her dress was filthy and torn in several places. Her nervous gaze flitted down the hall.

"Go," Mark shouted. "No, wait. Are there others here that need to be freed?"

"Yes, but I don't know where. We're seldom let out of our rooms and never allowed to talk to anyone else. I have seen others, though."

"Okay, thanks."

Mark broke open the next door, but it was empty. When he came back out the woman was gone. By the time he finished the fourth floor, he had found two more women, in similar condition to the first. They were desperate to get out and held hands, following Mark wherever he went. When he got back to the stairwell to retrieve the gas he told them to stay there, which made one of them moan in fear. "You'll be safer here and you won't be in my way if more shooting starts. I promise I'll get you on the way out." They huddled together in fear but stayed.

Finishing pouring gas on the fourth he climbed to the sixth floor. The two women followed. Almost every room had a lock on it. There were forty rooms per floor. Since they were all locked from the outside, it wasn't necessary to call fire, no one could come out anyway. Mark had the two women go down the floor and call out to anyone inside while he started with the first two rooms. Finding them empty, he moved to the rooms where the women got a response.

Mark went down the hall, tearing the locks off and letting the women check the rooms. It saved a lot of time. He now had a dozen women in the hallway, whispering to each other. Some were concerned their owners would return before they could get away. Others were afraid it was just a raid by a warring faction and they were leaving one type of hell for another.

"Look, ladies, you are free to leave. You should go now before anyone comes back. I plan on burning this place to the ground. If you follow the creek in that direction, you will come to a truck. You can wait there for us to take you to safety, or you can keep on going. Either way you're free. But, you have to go now."

They talked it over. A group of more than half moved toward the door. Still others were too afraid to leave, knowing the severity of the punishment for attempted escape.

"You have to at least go to the stairwell so you're out of my way." He herded the remaining five women to the end of the hall and made them stay there. He had one more floor to go and he didn't want them clinging to him. To emphasize their need to move, Mark splashed more gas on the carpet.

At the seventh floor door, Mark heard a shotgun blast. Jarrod was on the far end of the hall firing from a doorway at two men in rooms across the hall from each other. Mark opened the door and crept down the hall to the first open doorway. The two men were five rooms away. Mark tried to decide the best way to approach when, from down the hall, he heard a "Wahoo!" Jarrod charged the shooters. He had his shotgun leveled at waist height, firing one barrel then the other. His opponents ducked back inside their rooms and Mark moved up, but after Jarrod's shots, the gunmen stepped out into the hall to fire back.

Mark shot the man on the left from behind before he got off a shot. His partner fired once but missed Jarrod. He tried to duck back in his room but Mark shot him twice in the chest. Jarrod kept on running until he got next to Mark. His breaths came in ragged gasps. He was hunched over with his hands on his knees, gulping air like it was water. "I was hoping you was a good shot, or I'd a been a dead dog."

"Jesus, Jarrod. That was the craziest thing I ever saw. You could've been killed."

"Sometimes crazy is the best way to do things. It worked didn't it?"

"Yeah, but one of them got off a shot. You were lucky."

"Well, I had to try something. Those were my last two shells." He sucked in a breath. "Whooee, I need to get in shape."

Mark had the five women come in and do the same thing as before. Jarrod informed him he had ten more women waiting for him in the stairwell at the other end. By the time they finished the seventh floor, they had found two dozen women and one teenage boy.

They left them crowded together in the stairwell closest to the street and insisted they stay quiet. Mark picked up the two handguns from the dead men and gave one to Jarrod. The other one he gave to one of the women.

"If you see anyone coming up the stairs shoot them. Can you do that?"

"You bet your ass I can. I'll shoot them dead and then some."

"Try not to use up all your bullets on one guy. And don't shoot anyone coming from above. It could be us."

On the top floor, Mark looked through the window and saw the same two guards he'd seen before. Both had guns in their hands. They'd obviously heard the shots and were ready. Mark and Jarrod had a long unprotected approach to get within range. He'd been surprised at how little resistance they'd run up against so far. Either a very large percentage of the defenders left to chase Caleb or there weren't as many of them as he feared.

"Damn!" Jarrod said. "They look ready for us."

"We can't both approach from the same side. It's too long and there's no cover. I'll do the long walk from here if you go around to the other side. When they turn toward me open fire."

Jarrod nodded. "I suppose that means you want me to run the whole way to get there, huh?"

"You want me to go?"

"Hell, no."

"Well, just don't do anything crazy."

"Me? You're the one walking down the hall with no protection." He patted Mark's shoulder and went down the stairs.

Mark gave the farmer five minutes to get into position. He slid one gun in his pants at the back, the other in the front. He hoped with no gun in hand he wouldn't appear as a threat and the guards wouldn't shoot him on sight. Taking a deep breath, and hoping it wasn't his last, he pulled open the door and stepped into the hallway like he belonged there.

As the door clicked shut the guards looked toward him, their guns coming up. Mark swallowed hard, but so far no bullets came his way. He closed the distance steadily on unsteady legs. One guard raised his gun to eye level. "Stop right there."

Mark took one extra step and stopped. He'd covered a quarter of the distance, still too far. *Any time now, Jarrod.*

"Why are you up here?"

The second guard stepped away from the door and had his gun on target too.

"Uh, I, uh," he didn't know what to say. "I was just going to report the intruder was killed."

"Okay, you've done that, now get off this floor."

"Wait a minute," the second guard said. "I don't recognize this guy. Who are you?"

Uh-oh. Mark took one step backward.

Behind his two would-be killers the fire door cracked open. Jarrod slid enough of his body through to be able to take an accurate shot, yet still have some cover. Mark dove as the first shots were fired. The heat from one bullet touched his cheek; a second grazed his arm. His body slammed to the hard floor as he struggled to free the gun in the front. One of the guards pitched forward. The second man turned to return fire at Jarrod.

Jarrod emitted a grunt. The remaining guard fired with one hand while trying to open the door with the other. Mark got off a round, striking the defender in the leg before falling inside the room.

Mark raced to the door, knowing he needed to get there before the man locked it. If Buster or more of his guards were inside, it wouldn't be easy to dislodge them. As the door closed, Mark fired into it at different angles then kicked it open. It bounced back at him and he had to use his gun to keep the door from closing. Someone screamed. A lot of commotion and chaos came from inside but so far, no one had shot at him.

Poking his head around the door he found the body of the second guard blocking the door. Putting a shoulder into the door, he pushed it enough to slip through.

He was in a large suite with two doors on each side of a spacious living room and kitchen. The room was empty. A noise behind him made him spin and almost shoot Jarrod, who was fighting his way past the body. He was holding his shoulder, which was bleeding.

"Jarrod, you okay?"

"Well, not exactly, boss, I kinda been shot."

Knowing he had to get Jarrod out of there before he bled to death, Mark said, "Why don't you round up the women and get them out of here?"

"You may need me."

Mark knew better than to waste time arguing with the big man. Still, he was surprised when the farmer raised his gun and appeared to be lining up a shot at his head.

Jarrod closed one eye and said, "Duck."

Mark barely had time to register the word and act

before Jarrod pulled the trigger. Mark could feel the heat from the discharge as the bullet passed over his head. Turning at the sound of something hitting the ground, Mark watched the body of a man fall over one of the sofas.

"Shit, you scared me."

"You shoulda been scared. I'm not very good with one of these when I'm not wounded. Anyway better scared than dead."

"Yeah. Thanks."

"Sure thing, but maybe we best be moving along."

"Cover the other side while I check these doors."

Mark took the first room on the right. Inside was a king-sized bed with two dressers. A closet lined the far wall. He sidestepped around the bed and found a woman in a sheer negligee hiding behind it.

"Please, don't shoot me," she cried.

"I'm not here for you. Where's Buster?"

"He left with the others a while ago."

Mark didn't remember seeing him leave. At his size, he would have been easy to recognize.

"Are there others in here?"

She nodded.

"Come out here and call them for me. We're not going to hurt you. In fact, you can go free if you choose."

She hesitated, but Mark was out of patience. He grabbed her by the arm and pulled her out of the room. He went to the next door and opened it.

"Tell whoever's in there to come out."

"Darlene, come out. It's all right. They're only here for Buster."

The closet door opened and a tall attractive woman came out wearing a red satin teddy with a matching jacket.

They repeated the process until he had four beautiful women, all scantily clad, in the main room.

246

"I need to know where Buster is. Do any of you know?"

"He left a long time ago," a blonde with a squeaky voice said.

"Some boy came in and told him where some people were hiding," Darlene said. "He took off out of here with the other two guards in a real hurry."

Mark got a sinking feeling in the pit of his stomach. "Jarrod, we need to go now. Maggie and Darren are in danger. You ladies can come with us if you want or you can go off on your own. You just can't stay here."

"What if we don't want to go?" the blonde said.

Mark was shocked.

"Then go stand in the parking lot and wait for them to come back. But you can't stay here cause there's about to be a fire."

"Can we get some clothes first?"

"Yeah, please. You have two minutes."

Behind him Jarrod muttered, "Darn."

Thirty-Nine

MARK LED THE WAY and Jarrod brought up the rear. As they descended the stairs with their stolen harem, Mark noticed people in one hallway. They might already be too late to escape. They had used the last of the gasoline in Buster's suite and set it ablaze, which changed the blonde's mind about staying. They hustled down the stairs, slowing only to set the hallways on fire. When they reached the landing between the first and second floors, the outside door opened and two men came in, dragging two of the original freed women.

"You wait until I get you back to the room, you stupid bitch. I'll teach you to try to escape." He had his hand wrapped in her hair and was dragging her to the stairs.

The second man hauled his captive by the arm.

Mark and party froze as they saw the new arrivals enter. The captors stopped as they saw the two bodies of their mates lying on the floor. Their heads swung up.

The first man opened his mouth and said, "Hey," before Mark shot him in the face. Screams escaped several of the women, the echoes filling the stairwell. Some tried to flee back up the stairs, but Jarrod blocked them.

The second man pressed a gun against his woman's

head and pulled her tight in front of him. He backed up against the wall next to the outside door.

"You make a move and I blow her brains out," he shouted.

"Go ahead. Who cares? We've got plenty." Mark stepped down the stairs. He was halfway down when the threat was repeated.

"You can have her. Just get out of our way so we can go. But you should know that she's the only thing keeping you alive. So if you shoot her, there's nothing stopping me from shooting you." Mark walked toward the fire door. "Excuse me a second."

He opened the door and pulled a throw-away lighter from his back pocket. He let the door close behind him and bent down to light the gasoline-soaked carpet. Down the hall, a group of people talked with animated gestures. One of them saw Mark and pointed. Mark flicked the lighter several times before he got the flame to ignite. Two of the Horde down the hall started running toward him. He waved to the group and held the flame to the carpet. The carpet caught in a blaze along the line of flammable liquid. The others who had been watching ran for the front door. The two runners stopped when they saw the flames grow. Mark fired down the hall taking one down. The other man backed away.

Stepping back inside the stairwell, he faced the lone captor still holding his gun to the woman's head. "We need to leave now before the fire spreads."

"You set it on fire?"

Mark stepped forward as if leaving through the outer door. He stopped, standing next to the man and pointed toward the fire door. "Yeah, big fire."

As he'd hoped, the man turned his eyes in that direction. Mark lifted his gun and shot. The victim had seen the movement too late and tried to duck, but the bullet struck the top of his head and down he went. The gunshot was loud in the confined space.

"When I open the door, go left and down into the creek. Do as I say and we may get away."

One woman asked, "You're really going to set us free? No strings?"

"No strings, but you have to move now. Follow me. Jarrod, you still okay?"

"Still standing."

"You, with the gun, stay toward the rear to help Jarrod watch our backs." She nodded.

Mark pushed open the door into a darkening sky and stepped aside. He motioned toward the creek. "Go! Hurry!" The women filed out while Jarrod ushered them from behind. He looked at the procession. Several of the first group of freed women stood in the creek, waiting for them. It swelled their numbers even more.

Mark ran to the corner of the building to cover their escape. A shot kicked up dirt behind the last woman descending the bank. A shooter had found the escapees. More of the Horde ran around the corner. Four shooters advanced on the group of women, who now pushed the group in front to hurry.

Mark stepped from around the corner and fired. The first two shooters went down in the initial barrage. The other two ducked back around the opposite corner as the last round left Mark's gun. He stepped back behind the hotel to reload. His fingers fumbled the magazine and it fell to the ground. He stooped to pick it up and that saved his life. A bullet whistled over his head coming from behind him. Another gunman had gone all the way around the building and ran toward him, firing as he came.

Mark slammed his last magazine into the 9mm and ran for the creek. He jumped and slid down the bank, stopping below eye level. The two shooters left their cover and chased him. The killer from behind the hotel jumped down the bank about twenty yards from Mark.

The two pursuers were now in the open. When he popped up, gun leveled, they tried to shoot him, but since they were moving, had little control over their shots. Mark pumped two rounds into each target, then ducked back down.

Looking over his shoulder, he watched the last of the women enter the drain pipe under the street. Mark crawled to a tree and waited. The last shooter had also taken cover behind a tree, only ten yards away. Mark didn't have time to wait. Stepping backward, but keeping the tree between them, Mark made his way to the tunnel. Once there, he was out of cover. He ducked and dashed through, out of sight.

The long train of women had just reached the next crossing. They were almost to the truck. Mark had to give them enough time to get to safety, but time was a weight pressing on him. He had to hurry. Peeking back through the tunnel, he couldn't see any signs of pursuit. It made him wonder.

A chill ran down his back. The sound of a small stone skittering across the road above made him slide down into the creek and duck back through the pipe emerging on the opposite side of the road.

From there he crawled up the bank, staying close to the concrete side rail of the bridge. He peeked around the bridge, his face at street level. Leaning over the rail on the far side was his pursuer. If not for that pebble, Mark would have been ambushed from above. Mark aimed through the decorative concrete spindles of the rail and fired until the body pitched over the rail and splashed down into the creek.

As Mark slid back down, he looked at the hotel. Smoke poured out of some of the upper windows. He wished he had time to set the lower rooms ablaze, but all he could hope for now was that the fire would spread.

251

He jogged through the pipe and picked up his rifle, then ran to catch up to the others. Night had finally fallen, which gave them the cover they needed. Behind him, an orange glow filled the sky, letting him know the hotel was burning bright. Hopefully, the fire would grow stronger. Mark had fully expected there to be more men inside than there were. What concerned Mark most was not knowing where Buster and his troop went. If he did go out to the farmhouse, he might have taken a large contingent with him.

"We have to go faster. We could have company any minute." He encouraged the caravan to move with more urgency. He passed them and ran up next to the lumbering Jarrod.

"Mark, how are we gonna transport all of these women?" Jarrod asked.

"Jarrod, you'll have to worry about that when you get to the truck. Squeeze in as many as you can Find a second ride if necessary. Take them to your place. I have to go. Buster is going to the farm. Maggie and Darren are in danger."

Without waiting for a reply, Mark ran ahead. When he got to the truck Mark passed it. Stopping at the first car on the street he used the butt of the rifle to break the passenger window and unlocked the door. Running around the car he slid in, broke open the steering column and searched desperately for the right wires.

Trying to work too fast Mark kept fumbling the wires. He stomped his feet in frustration. Mark took two deep breaths and tried again. This time he crossed the stripped wires and the car started. Flooring the pedal, Mark raced furiously not worrying about being seen.

The farmhouse was five miles away. The drive went fast but to Mark's mind every second was too long. He thought of the others. Had they made it to safety? Would he ever know? He pictured each one as if saying goodbye. If Buster were at the farmhouse, he would kill him, but he also knew the big man wouldn't be alone.

Keeping the headlights off, Mark turned on the road about a half mile from the farmhouse. He parked on the far side of the cornfield. Taking the magazine out of the 9mm, he pulled rounds from the other weapons he had gathered until he had a full one. Then he combined whatever bullets were left into a spare. He dropped the empty gun and slid the extra magazine into his pocket. Even though the rifle was empty, he took it with him so he could use the scope. He stood up on the car and sighted over the corn. If anyone was there, they were either in the house or hiding.

Mark decided to approach the house through the cornfield. As he drew closer to the barn, he slowed his pace and started taking stock of his surroundings. If Buster was here, would he kill whoever was inside and leave? Would he take them captive and leave?

Or would he lie in wait for Mark, the man who had caused Buster so much trouble over the past week?

No, if Buster *had* come, he'd still be waiting for him and he would have guards stationed around the property. Mark scanned the grounds again. There would be one man in the pine trees near the road, watching east and west; another to the right of the house, near the cross street, looking north and south; and one or two more out back to prevent an approach through the cornfield.

But, where would he place the sentry watching the rear?

His gaze went to the barn. It was the building closest to the field and offered complete cover. A spotter placed there would be in a position to come up behind Mark if he tried for the house.

Mark moved to his right. He followed the rows of corn past the outhouse and around the back of the barn before breaking cover. There was a large sliding door on the back that matched the front one. The trouble was that it

253

was heavy and old. It was likely to make noise. He stepped to the side of the door and tried to peek through, but it was too dark to see anything.

Mark slid the door open. It creaked announcing his presence. He rushed in and squatted behind a car; a car that hadn't been there before. The darkness was deep enough to hide him without having to seek cover. Unless whoever might be in there had a flashlight.

He waited, listening to the stillness. A scraping, the sound of a shoe against the dirt floor told Mark someone was on the other side of the car. Mark crept forward. When he reached the bumper, he tried to slip to the other side of the car but found another bumper against the first. Then the flashlight snapped on.

A cone of light appeared at the opposite end of the car. The light crossed behind the car. Mark pulled his knife and duck-walked toward the guard. Mark had to take him silently. The light was almost around the trunk when Mark lunged blade first. Aiming for a spot just above the light, the knife slipped into the body and the flashlight fell.

The impaled guard let out a cry which Mark smothered with his hand. Two hands clasped around Mark's trying to free the blade. Shoving his opponent against the car he pushed hard on the knife. The guard tried to fight but his efforts grew weaker until he could no longer support his weight. Mark guided the body to the floor and stayed on him until he stopped breathing.

There had been no time to close the door. If anyone went to check on the source of the squeak, he would be able to see the door was ajar. The beam of faint moonlight that poured through provided scant illumination. It wasn't much, but maybe enough that he could see if someone went near to check.

Feeling his way along the vehicles Mark made it to the front of the barn. The front door was open a slit to enable the watcher to see outside. He looked through the slit and waited. No one came to investigate the noise. Using the scope, Mark scanned the grounds. If there were another guard out there, he couldn't find him. Nor could he see anyone moving in the house. Mark found the small flashlight. Without fear of being seen now, Mark swept the cone of light over the middle of the barn, counting four cars crammed together. Mark assumed Buster had instructed his troops to hide them so they wouldn't give away their presence.

Five cars with four per vehicle would be twenty with nineteen remaining. Figuring two men to a car, minus one, Mark estimated nine more. Either way, he would have to take them out one by one.

Holding the light close to the floor, Mark went back to the body. The dead man's weapon was a .40 caliber. He couldn't use the bullets. He didn't want to carry too many guns, fearing they would drop or clatter together when he needed to move silently, but he brought it with him for the moment. Putting the flashlight in a rear pocket, he waited to let his eyes adjust again to the darkness. Then, he slipped out the back and moved through the cornfield toward the street, in search of his next victim.

Forty

ONCE MORE, MARK followed the cornfield, stopping at the last row before the north/south street running in front of the house. A line of three large boulders marked the edge of the property. They were about ten feet from the cornfield, perpendicular to the street. On the closest and largest one squatted a man with his knees pulled up to his chest. He rocked back and forth as if he was listening to good music in his head. His gun was on the rock next to him.

Mark doubted he would be able to approach the watcher undetected. He decided a straight, fast run was his best option. He set the extra gun and rifle down, and knife in hand, burst from the corn. He was halfway to the boulder before the man stopped rocking and cocked his head like a dog hearing a strange noise. He turned as his hand reached for the gun. But the initial hesitation gave Mark a chance to leap for the boulder. He tackled the man, driving him head first to the ground between the two boulders. A snapping sound occurred as the two men hit. Mark scrambled to his feet, expecting his opponent to do the same, but he didn't move. Looking closer, Mark noticed the angle of the man's head. His neck was broken.

Mark took the gun and placed it in the cornfield with the others. In order to get to the sentry in the trees, he had to cross either behind or in front of the house. He was tempted to leave him and try for the house, but he didn't want anyone coming up behind him. To have a reasonable chance at saving Maggie and Darren, he needed the element of surprise. The men in the house could not be aware he was on the grounds. Besides, there could be another guard on the far side of the house. Mark might run right into him.

Mark chose the long route. Returning to the cornstalks, he raced a good distance back the way he'd come before turning toward the tree-lined road. The corn rows ran to within ten feet of the trees. Keeping low, once more he darted between pine tree branches and waited for signs that he'd been seen. After a minute, he found it hard to control the urge to move. He forced himself to wait another minute. Mark then moved from tree to tree, staying on the cornfield side. Mark assumed the watcher would be on the street side, otherwise he wouldn't be able to see anyone coming up the road.

With each tree he rounded, Mark paused to make sure no one was positioned there. He found his foe five trees later, turned around facing the fields as he was relieving himself. He had just zipped up his pants when Mark appeared around the tree. The surprise factor had frozen each man for a second before each moved.

The sentry reached for the gun stuck in his belt, while Mark made a desperate lunge to reach him with the knife before he could get off a shot. The man sidestepped Mark, hitting him with a double fist between the shoulder blades and driving him to the ground.

Perhaps sensing he had the advantage, the man opted to jump on Mark rather than try for his gun or shout for help. He landed on Mark's back, sitting on him. Grabbing the back of Mark's head, he slammed it into the ground several times.

Pulling his knees under him, Mark reached back, grabbed a wrist and pushed up into a shoulder roll. He landed on top of his combatant with both of them facing up. Wrapping strong arms around Mark's chest, the man squeezed, then his arms slid up around his throat. Mark struggled for breath. Managing to grasp one finger, Mark yanked back as hard as he could and heard it snap.

His foe howled and the stranglehold slackened. Getting a small space to move, Mark rammed his head backward, smashing the man in the face, shutting him up for a moment, but sending bright light bulbs flashing in his own head. He latched on a second finger, but the man released his grip before it broke. Mark spun on top and drilled his right fist into the bloody face, taking the fight out of him.

Mark hit him two more solid blows to make sure he wouldn't get up again.

Stripping him of his weapons, Mark stood up, hands on knees and tried to catch his breath. He stared down at the unconscious man, thinking he should finish him, but he couldn't do it. Instead, he opted for pistol whipping him to ensure he wouldn't wake up anytime soon.

Forty-One

THREE DOWN. NOW came the hard part. Still bent over, Mark directed his attention toward the house. There were two doors, front and back, and they would be watched. The only other way in was to break a window, which would announce his arrival. Nothing he could think of would work. His brain was too tired to come up with anything else. He studied the possible entry ways again and again dismissed them all as suicidal.

Mark raced for the blind spot at the rear of the house, pressed against the wall and waited.

Maybe I can create a diversion to draw them out while I sneak in another way.

He was still squatting there, thinking, when the guard in the trees crawled out into the open and tried to scream for help. He choked on blood, then tried again. Mark saw no way of getting to the man before he issued a cry of alarm, but maybe he was the diversion he needed.

No, I have to shut the man up. I should have done it right the first time.

The guard started to run back when he found his voice, the shout rang out. It was too late now. The man collapsed to the ground, coughing, trying to clear his throat.

As long as they were alerted, maybe he could at least even the odds a bit. He needed their attention focused away from him. Taking the flashlight out of his pocket, he turned it on, and tossed it toward the struggling body, hoping the light would stay on. The flashlight bounced once and rolled under a tree, but light could still be seen through the branches.

He didn't have long to wait. The rear door opened and footsteps descended the wooden stairs. Mark crouched around the corner.

"Over there," one of them whispered. "Go that way and stay wide. I'll go through the trees and come up behind him."

There was no response. Mark guessed there were two of them. Staying where he was, he brought the gun up near his face in a two-handed grip and sighted, watching for the first person to come into view. A lone gunman appeared beyond the corner. His gun was up and ready. But his eyes were focused in the direction of the light.

Farther out, a second man stepped into sight. Mark could now track them both. As the first gunman moved past, Mark shot him in the back. As soon as he pulled the trigger, Mark swung the gun toward his partner, haloed by the flashlight, giving Mark a perfect shot. He pulled the trigger twice more. The man spun but did not go down. Taking no chances, Mark moved closer and fired twice more, putting him down for good.

Turning toward the fallen guard, Mark pumped one round into him, then went back to the wall and crouched. He moved toward the front of the house. The windows were high above him. Making it to the front porch unseen, he climbed over the wrought-iron railing and crawled below the front windows to the opposite end. There, he pressed his back against the wall between the windows and the front door.

Inside, overlapping voices made it difficult to

determine how many people there were. One voice rose above the others, "Did they get that bastard?"

Someone approached the front windows. He lay on his back and slid backward, keeping himself as close to the wall under the windows as possible. A face pressed against the pane with his hands on each side. Mark slid the gun up against the wall to the bottom of the window. Angling the barrel toward the face, he sat up and pulled the trigger twice.

The glass erupted and the face inside disappeared. Someone screamed in agony. Mark rose up above the broken window and searched for a target. It was difficult to see details, but he guessed anyone moving was most likely a bad guy. He shot three times at fleeting figures, not sure if he hit anyone.

The window next to him exploded as someone fired back. Mark dropped to his belly and crawled down the steps as bullets shattered the remaining windows.

To the side of the steps, Mark found a good-sized decorative stone. He pitched it through the glass storm door, hoping it would serve as a distraction. As it crashed through, he bolted for the back door. A lot of fire was directed toward the front. He guessed there must be five or six shooters. The windows were too high to allow him a view inside. If anyone were looking, they could see him, but unless he could step up on something, he had no angle to see them.

He passed a spigot on the side of the house and stopped. Testing his weight on it, he stepped up, rising slowly. He might not be able to hit anyone or even see them, but he had to keep them off balance, guessing where he was. With any luck, whoever was in the house might think more than one person was attacking them and they were surrounded. Two small windows were side-by-side above him with a six-inch wooden frame between them, where Mark slid his head as he rose above the window.

Voices and movement came from within. He took a quick peek trying to spot Maggie or Darren, but the windows were high and didn't allow an angle to look downward. He could only see the tops of a few heads. He dropped to the ground as the front door opened. A tall man leaned out over the railing and spied him. They exchanged fire, but Mark was in the open and about to retreat to the back of the house when the telltale click of a slide locking back sounded louder than a gunshot. Mark raced forward and got off one shot. The shooter fell back and managed to crawl into the house. Someone else started shooting through the front door, preventing Mark from gaining entry.

Mark scampered to the back door. He climbed the steps and listened. He had to be almost out of bullets, so he switched weapons. He was about to make an entrance when a deep booming voice called out.

"Hey. I know you're close enough to hear me. I got your friends in here. You need to drop your weapon and step into the open, or I'm gonna kill one of them. You hear me? I ain't playing with you. You got one minute, then it's your fault when one dies."

That was the one thing Mark could not fight against. He had hoped by keeping them guessing and occupied they would be too confused and disorganized to think. He had no real choice and no doubt Buster would carry out his threat.

To put his gun down and surrender though, would lead to all their deaths, but he could not live knowing he was responsible for getting Darren and Maggie killed.

He tried to negotiate, hoping to buy some time and maybe gather some information about how many of them were left. "You're the ones trapped inside that house. You can't stay in there forever. I can wait you out and pick you off one by one. And if you kill them, you no longer have leverage against me."

"Then while you're waiting you can listen to this boy and this old woman scream."

Just then, someone did scream. Darren, who was like a miracle son. Even if it cost him his life, he had to at least get Darren free.

"I'll trade myself for them. You let them go and I'll give myself up."

He heard whispering, but it wasn't enough to tell him anything, other than there were at least two of them.

"This ain't no negotiation. The only chance they got of living is for you to give up."

"You're just gonna kill us all anyway."

An evil laugh erupted from within. "Yeah, well, you're dead for sure. But I'll tell you, we may keep the woman alive. She's a bit old, but she's still got some use left." He laughed again. "And I got a guy who likes young boys so I might spare him too. What's it gonna be?"

"Damn," he muttered. Maybe being shot would be a better choice than allowing Darren to spend his life as some pervert's sex toy. He sucked in a deep breath. "All right, here's my gun." He tossed it through the window. "I'm coming in."

Taking the knife from its sheath, he stuck it in his pants under his shirt and threw the sheath away. He replaced the backup gun in his belt outside the shirt and over the knife. They would no doubt search him, if they didn't just shoot him as soon as he walked inside. Hopefully, the gun would conceal the knife.

"You come in slow with your hands out in front of you. I want to see hands first, or I shoot right away."

Mark did as instructed. He showed his hands in the doorway then stepped in slowly. One solid-looking man waited in the kitchen to the left, his arm bandaged with some torn clothing. The wound had bled through. On the floor behind him was the body of Buddy. Mark hoped the dog got in some vicious bites before he went down.

Using the gun, he motioned Mark forward. Seeing the gun as Mark went by, he lunged forward and snatched it from Mark's belt. Mark jumped, not so much from the move, but because the contact caused the knife to slice his skin. He turned, facing the killer to keep the bulge of the knife from view.

"Look what I found," he exalted, as if he had found buried treasure. He pushed Mark into the dining room. "He was trying to sneak in with a gun." He held the weapon up like he had to prove his statement. He brought it down on Mark's head. It wasn't hard enough to knock him down or out, but it hurt a lot.

Mark lifted his head to look at his opponents. He locked his hands behind his head, not so much to show he was no threat, as to keep his shirt loose in the back, hiding the shape of the knife. To his right, against the wall, a tall skinny guy, with long straggly hair, held Darren in front of him with a gun pressed against the side of his head. A welt shone brightly on Darren's face.

The big man – *Buster* – sat at the far end of the dining room table, rocking back and forth with a smug look on his face. Maggie was tied to a chair with the front of her blouse open. She had a red marks on her chest, but otherwise looked unhurt. Her gaze was hard and meaningful, as though she were trying to convey something. He broke eye contact before Buster noticed.

A body lay under the table. One of his blind shots through the window must have connected. Two more were near the front door. Unless someone else was upstairs, only the three of them remained. Now all he had to do was figure out how to take them out.

He risked another glance at Maggie. Her eyes flicked toward Buster. She nodded her head toward him. The look in her eyes made him think she was trying to send a message, but he had no idea what it was.

"So you're the one been causing me all this trouble. You don't look like much." He laughed and stood up, upsetting the chair. Mark tried not to show emotion as Buster came to his full height ... but it wasn't easy. He was larger than Mark had thought, standing at least six-foot-eight and probably topping three hundred pounds.

"I suppose you must have something going for you though 'cause it took real balls to waltz into my home and take something that belonged to me. Yep, could have used someone like you."

"You never asked," Mark said.

"Huh?"

"You don't ask people to join you. You just move in and kill anyone you can't use."

"Don't need old folks, they just get in the way. Besides, I got all the men I need. You get too big,
it's harder to control them."

"Guess you're gonna have to start recruiting, 'cause you're down a few."

Buster chuckled. "The ones you killed here? I got plenty of men to replace them."

"Not so many ..."

Buster walked up to Mark, his eyes narrowed. Mark, looking up, held the gaze as calmly as he could.

"What're you talking about? You killed a few when you stole your woman back, but you saw I got a whole lot more at the base."

"Not now."

Buster snatched his shirt and yanked Mark to him. Buster roared, "What're you trying to say?"

Mark let his hands drop to his sides. He needed to make his move soon before the big man put him out of commission or the man behind him saw the knife.

"I took *all* the women back. Then, there was a fire. Your home burned up and your men with it."

265

A transformation occurred in Buster's expression flashing from annoyance to rage. He drew his massive arm back and drove it hard into Mark's face. Mark turned and lowered his head as the blow landed, taking the brunt of it on the top side. Still, a burst of light exploded inside his head. He catapulted over the table, landing at the feet of the man holding Darren.

Mark rolled to a stop facing Buster. He couldn't take another punch like that. Pushing to a sitting position with his right arm behind him, he cleared his head and readied to attack. Buster stormed after him, pitching chairs out of the way, shoving the table against the far wall, pinning Maggie there. The skinny guy behind Mark backed up.

Mark slid the knife out and started to rise, trying to keep it hidden behind him. The blade caused another cut on his backside as it came free. Buster lifted his arms like a huge bear, but before he could bring them down, Mark lunged up and swiped the knife at the big bear's enormous stomach.

Mark couldn't believe how fast Buster stopped and jumped backward. Even having the advantage of surprise, Mark was only able to make a shallow cut across his belly.

Mark pivoted and changed targets to long-hair holding Darren. His neck was a good twelve inches above Darren's head. Mark had plenty of room to scythe the blade across, slicing his throat open. Blood spurted. Letting go of the gun and Darren, he clutched desperately at the wound.

Mark grabbed Darren by his shirt and pitched him into the living room. "Run!" he yelled. With only a brief look back, Darren turned and fled through the broken front door.

Buster turned to his last man. "Get the boy and kill him." Buster turned on him, picking up a chair while the killer disappeared out the back door.

Mark reached for the gun the tall guy had dropped, but Buster swung the chair, forcing him back. Buster kicked the gun behind him.

"I'm gonna enjoy killing you."

The dying assailant sagged to the floor between the two men. Mark backed into the living room. Buster advanced, using the chair like a lion tamer, trying to herd Mark into a corner. Mark thought about following Darren, but he couldn't leave Maggie alone with Buster.

Buster jabbed the chair's legs at him. The thrusts were hard, backing Mark up. Mark countered with stabs over the chair, but Buster was beyond his reach, his long arms keeping him away.

Mark was fast running out of room to maneuver and having trouble dodging the thrusts.

From somewhere outside, the sound of a gunshot stopped them for a second.

Buster smiled. "Say goodbye to your kid."

More gunshots followed, one after another, and Mark's heart sank. With renewed fervor, Buster came at Mark, who had more difficulty fending off the attacks. With a wall to his right and a couch on the left, Mark knew he had to make a move.

As Buster pulled the chair back, Mark lunged, leaping into the air and trying to stab Buster in the face. Buster countered with surprising speed, stepping back and angling the chair up. Before Mark could regroup for another thrust, Buster swept his leg under the chair, catching Mark as he landed from his leap, tripping him. He fell backward onto the couch. Buster advanced in a flash, pinning Mark under the chair, his arms caught under the wooden crossbar. Mark tried to sink deeper into the cushions to gain enough space to slide his arms out, but Buster leaned his massive body on the chair, giving Mark no chance to pull free.

Mark wiggled frantically, kicking as hard as he could under the chair, but Buster gave no signs the kicks affected him. Keeping his bulk pressed against the chair, he lifted one of his huge arms over the chair and pounded his fist on top of Mark's head. With each blow, Buster took bigger and harder chops. Mark was having difficulty staying focused.

Then Buster rose higher to punch harder and Mark was able to slide his left arm out. Mark attempted to block the punches with his arm but Buster landed another one with stunning force. Buster hurled the chair away, smashing it into pieces against the wall. Mark made a feeble attempt to stab him, his effort slowed by the beating he had taken. Buster smacked his knife hand to the side and slammed his body down on Mark like a giant wrestler going for a pin. Even with his arm now free, Mark could not raise it enough to damage the behemoth. The knife barely pricked his side. With his weight crushing Mark underneath, all air exploded from his lungs. Darkness crept in around the edges of his vision.

Using his weight advantage to keep Mark in place, Buster rotated his trunk so both hands could wrap around the knife hand. The slight rotation was enough for Mark to draw in a breath. Even knowing he would lose the knife, breathing seemed more important.

Mark fought with renewed vigor, sending weak punches to the side of Buster's head. He squeezed the knife tighter, but in the end he didn't have enough strength left to prevent Buster from taking it. With a snap Buster broke one of Mark's fingers. The pain blinded him; yet still, Mark struggled on. When Buster broke the second finger, the battle was over.

Buster ripped the knife from Mark's shattered hand. Mark attempted to keep the knife away, but Buster sliced away at Mark's arms, chest, and shoulders. Then Buster smiled, holding the knife pointing downwards. With both hands, he began lowering the tip towards Mark's eye. Mark put up both hands to stop the knife, but Buster simply put his weight into it. Mark strained futilely as the tip got closer, but he had little hope other than delay the inevitable. Buster was too strong and Mark had little left.

Then, something solid struck Buster on the head. A second blow split the skin, and blood flowed down the monster's face. Maggie stood to the side, a leg from the broken chair in her hand. She tried a third swing but Buster blocked it and then knocked her away. Something crashed to the floor.

Mark had trouble breathing as pain and Buster's weight fought against every rise of his chest. Refocusing on Mark, a furious snarl on his face, he put both hands on the knife and lowered his weight toward Mark's chest. Mark grasped the doubled wrists and pushed up with all his might. The blade only slowed its descent as Mark's vision darkened at the edges.

One shot and then another rang out. Buster flinched and arched backward. With Buster's body on top of him Mark couldn't see what was happening. The big man looked down at Mark, pain now replacing anger. He drew the knife back and Mark found that he was now too weak to even raise his arms.

Another shot fired, Buster fell forward, the blade embedding into the sofa inches from Mark's face. Buster pushed upward and turned his head.

From over Buster's left shoulder, Mark saw, coming out of the darkness, a thin beam of moonlight through the window highlighting an angel. She touched a gun to Buster's forehead. "Remember me, bitch?" she said and pulled the trigger. Mark slipped into darkness.

Forty-Two

MARK AWOKE. It was dark, and as his eyes adjusted, he could see someone was sitting in a chair positioned next to the bed.

"Hi," Lynn said in a soft voice.

"Hey," He swallowed hard, his throat dry.

He heard her move. "Water?"

"Yes."

She held the bottle for him, placing a hand behind his head to help him rise to drink. He felt a sharp pain in his left side as he did and let out a gasp.

"Careful, I think you have a broken rib or two."

He sipped, feeling pain every time he swallowed.

"How long have I been sleeping?"

"A full day. You took quite a beating."

"The others ..." He stopped, afraid to hear what happened to Darren. He tried again, "Is everyone all right?"

She leaned over him and looked into his eyes.

"We lost James," she said. "We did such a great job of stopping them. I'm not sure how many we killed or wounded, but a few did follow us. The three girls and I waited in the house while Caleb and James patrolled the grounds. Four of them found us and sneaked up through the woods. They jumped Caleb and took his gun. James heard and came to help … he shot two of them before they realized he was there. They let go of Caleb to shoot back and James managed to wound a third before they shot him. But Caleb was able to get to his spare gun and shoot the last two. I assume he got the idea of a spare from you."

"Maggie?"

"Obviously, she took it hard, but James saved Caleb and I think that helps. We buried James out behind the barn next to the other graves you dug."

"Darren?"

She smiled. "Darren's just fine. He's been pacing at your door all day, hoping to see you."

Tears of relief flowed down Mark's face. "I thought he was dead when I heard the gunshots."

Lynn stroked his face and wiped the tears. "No, Darren ran out to the cornfield past the boulders and apparently tripped over some guns. By the time his pursuer caught up to him, Darren picked up a pistol. He fired until the gun was empty. He got him. Darren was naturally upset about it, but he's been more concerned about you."

Mark realized that he and Darren had truly become father and son.

"You killed Buster?" He reached out and took her hand as he saw her eyes get a faraway haunted look. "You okay?"

"Yes, the pig deserved to die." She fought back tears. "I only wish I could kill him again. Maggie pounded him over the head with a chair leg and then I finished it. He won't hurt anyone else."

They sat without speaking for a while.

Lynn stood up and played at tucking him in. She leaned forward and hugged him then kissed his forehead. "Get some rest."

Lynn took good care of him. Darren hardly left his side. It took two days before he wanted to get out of bed and

271

another before he could. Lynn had set and splinted his fingers, but they hurt like hell. He had bandages all over his body from cuts, scrapes, and bullets. His head ached constantly as did every muscle in his body.

But for the first time in a long time, he felt relaxed.

Epilogue

A FEW DAYS LATER, at Mark's insistence, they went to see how Jarrod and the rescued women were. One of the ladies was a doctor and two others were nurses, taken when the Horde raided the hospital. They'd managed to piece Jarrod back together. Much to his delight, they were nursing him back to health.

After a while, life as they now knew it became the new normal. They ran the farm, planting an assortment of crops both outside and in the greenhouses. Jarrod found two more small windmills and over time they added them to the first one. With the windmills working, they had electricity for the important things and were able to pump water from the well, so they no longer had to use the outhouse. Mallory had worked in a bookstore in a previous life. She led Mark there one day and they loaded up on do-it-yourself books. Mark started reading about solar panels.

Jarrod gave them a rooster, some chickens and a couple of pigs and soon they had fresh eggs. It was like living back in the days of pioneers, but with a lot more knowledge. They struggled with things at times and fought like families do, but they adjusted to their new lives.

Mark knew that Lynn was getting past her ordeal when she came to his room one night and stayed. Maggie, after months of mourning, moved in with Jarrod and the rescued women. Caleb and Alyssa continued to develop their relationship. But when they showed up at lunch one day with straw in their hair and on their clothes, Lynn decided it was time to slow them down.

The boy who'd escaped from the barn showed up one day, looking almost as starved as Buddy had when they'd found him. He begged to join the family and willingly told them about the Horde. After the hotel had burned down, fewer than ten remained and went their separate ways. Lynn put him on probation and made him live in the barn. She assigned Ruth as his boss. He did anything she told him to do, and over time, they became a good couple.

As time went by, they discovered others like them and set up a small community. They helped each other with planting and harvesting, as well as building windmills and barns. Of all the women they had rescued, only five stayed. The others left over time to their own groups and families.

More than a week after the end of the Horde, Mark returned to his house. He knelt by the graves of his son and wife and told them the story of his new family's survival. Promising to check on them again, Mark stood up to leave, then thinking of Becca and Bobby, took out a knife and carved them a message on the back of the two crosses.

If they were still alive, they would come home. They would find the graves. Now they would know how to find him. Mark looked from the graves to the shell that was the house. He dug up the buried mementos, then, turning his head to the sky, made the sign of the cross and walked away. It was time to move on.

Perhaps they would never know what caused the

plague that killed so many, or why they were the lucky ones who survived. But they had, and they did what they had to do to keep it that way. It was time to face forward and create a new future.

And some day, when they stood in front of their God, maybe then they might know the reason.

Acknowledgements

I'd like to thank the staff at Larchmont Elementary for their support over the years.

My family and friends for their encouragement.

My many co-workers at the casino and the Toledo Mud Hens for spreading the word.

Jim MacCambridge for guidance on some of the weapons aspects.

And EJ, Bill and Jayne from Rebel ePublishers for taking a chance and making this project possible.

About the Author

Having spent 35 years as a teacher and 25 years as the owner/operator of an Italian Restaurant, Ray now spends his time, reading, writing, hiking, cooking, and playing the harmonica.

You can reach him on the Rebel ePublishers website, or at raywenck.com.

Also by Ray Wenck

Teammates, Teamwork, Home Team, Warriors of the Court

And for more from Ray Wenck …

Please turn the page for a preview of the next book in the Random Survival series, *The Long Search for Home*.

The
Long
Search
for Home

Ray Wenck

One

The chill that ran down her spine was all the warning Becca needed. They were getting closer. Her breaths came in deep painful gulps, but to quit would be the end. Knowing what they would do if they caught her, she raced on, ignoring the pain. But the outcome was inevitable. They were bigger, stronger, and more numerous.

Sprinting hard over the open high grass of what had once been a golf course, she reached down and found the handle of the long survival knife her father had given her many years before. In mid-stride, she yanked it free of the sheath strapped along her thigh. With the blade now rising and falling in her hand like a relay racer's baton, her father flashed through her mind. He was the reason for this journey. If she was going down, she would make him proud.

The pain in her side was almost unbearable, like a knife being pushed deeper with each stride. The thundering footsteps of her pursuers echoed behind her in time with the pounding in her chest. Becca would have to make her stand soon. She would not reach the potential safety of the trees ahead.

As she readied for the battle, she thought of her

brother. *Where the hell was Bobby?* He had gone ahead while she rested, before the men found her and gave chase. If she survived this attack and found he was watching her from a distance, with one swipe of her knife, Becca would make him her sister.

Her pursuers grunted as they pushed harder to overtake her. It was time to face them, before they could take her down.

Stopping took three hard steps to slow and turn. With a savage scream, she whipped the blade in a high arcing backhand swing. The honed edge tore through the first assailant's throat. The man clutched at his neck as blood spurted into the air in a crimson fountain.

The dying man's body bumped her as he fell. The second man launched at her. Becca just managed to face him when he struck her high on the chest. The blade impaled the man's large bare gut, but his momentum drove her over backward. They rolled in a heap, coming to a stop with her hand still clutching the blade, but the man's body pinned them both to the ground.

The third and fourth men arrived together, hooting at their captured prize. With a huge evil smile, the first man reached for her. She raised a foot to kick him away, but he grabbed it and laughed. That was when the third eye appeared on his forehead wiping the smile off his face. His body stood for a second as if to say, "Damn, so close," before collapsing.

Bobby!

As the body fell, the fourth man stood gaping. He stopped unfastening his pants, a frantic, almost deranged look on his bearded face. Given the brief gift of time, Becca threw a shoulder into the corpse that still trapped her knife. The body slid and started to roll.

Another shot snapped the man's attention from Becca, causing him to duck. After a third, he screamed, yet still he stood, unharmed, frozen in place, his manhood clutched tightly in his hand.

He looked behind him. Becca watched him as she freed one leg, pressed her foot against the weight, and pushed. He snarled, focused his wild eyes back on Becca, and pulled his knife. "Bitch," he spat.

With the blade forward like a spear, he lunged to skewer her. Becca slid free from the body, emitting her own growl. Yanking her blade free, she rolled. Rather than immobilize her, as her fear would've done just weeks before, she used the angst to spur movement. The knife wielder was unable to stop his thrust as Becca moved. The downward jab threw his weight forward and off balance. Her heart racing, Becca spun on her bottom. Before her assailant could right himself and turn for a second attack, she screamed and dived at his leg, slicing clean through his Achilles tendon.

The man screamed and hobbled on one leg. Becca rolled clear as the wounded man dropped the knife and fell to the ground, clutching his injured foot. Becca stood and glared down at him. She ignored the sweat burning her eyes. Her breaths came in short, harsh gulps, exploding from her. Her victim rolled from side to side. Two bodies lay a few yards back. *I should've known Bobby wouldn't have missed.*

The wounded man whimpered. She stood over him, void of emotion. The man pleaded, first for his life, and then for help with his wound.

Steps thundered from behind. Becca spun and crouched, ready again to do battle.

"Becca." A concerned young man, rifle in hand stopped ten feet from her. "Are you all right?"

All Becca saw was another enemy. With great effort, she sucked in a deep breath and blew it out. She relaxed and lowered the knife. Bobby came closer, and then she nailed her brother with a punch to the chest that rocked him back a step.

"Ow!"

"That's for taking your time shooting those assholes."

"I wasn't taking my time. I was in those woods scouting on the other side. I didn't even know those hounds had picked up your scent."

She snorted at the appropriate use of terms. She shuddered at the thought of what they would have done to her had they managed to take her down.

Bobby stepped forward to put an arm around Becca's shoulders. "Hey, Sis, I'm sorry. You know I wouldn't play games with your safety. Are you all right?"

Becca cringed. She hated being comforted by him. She wanted to shake him off to show she didn't need his sympathy, but in truth she did need him. She wanted to cry and bury her head in his chest, but this new world had stolen any real emotion from her weeks ago. Everyone she had ever cared about had died– everyone but Bobby and, hopefully, her father, mother, and little brother.

She was so different now and struggled with the conflict within her as if she were two separate people inhabiting one body. Gone was the spoiled, self-absorbed young woman, leaving a shell driven by some strange wild creature. Confused and angry, with each passing day Becca seemed to lose more of her previous identity.

No, she didn't want to be coddled by her brother, but the small part of her old self that still existed craved the simple comfort.

BOBBY HELD HIS SISTER, but not too close. He was well aware of the knife still hanging at her side. Becca was capable of instant and violent reactions. He feared he was losing her, and the thought scared him. When he had seen that pack of animals closing in on her, the fear of failing made keeping his hands steady difficult. He had to stop once, take two quick calming breaths to chase away any emotion, before acquiring his target. He had almost been too late. He fought off his own shudder for fear Becca would feel it too.

Pressing ahead of his sister to scout their path had been stupid. That decision had almost cost Becca her life. He vowed never to make that mistake again. Twice today his poor judgment had cost them. They were lucky to be alive. This new world did not allow too many second chances.

With a sigh, Bobby gave his sister a squeeze and whispered, "I'm sorry, Sis, but we need to get away from here before someone else finds us."

Becca moved away from him and wiped her face. "You can't go wandering off like that anymore. You hear me?"

Bobby nodded. "I know. I'm sorry." To change the subject and avoid her accusing look, he added, "Let's see if they have anything of value and get moving."

Ignoring the wounded man, they went through the nearest bodies finding very little that was useful. Four handguns, four knives, and two granola bars. The two dead men farther back yielded another handgun and a shotgun.

"Ready?" Bobby asked.

"Yep." Becca started back the way they had come.

"Wait! Where you going?"

"Back to get our stuff."

"No, wait." Bobby ran to catch up with her. "We'll be walking right back into trouble."

His sister continued walking.

"I don't care. I want our things."

"Becca, listen. By now those scavengers have taken everything of value."

"No, they haven't. They've taken all the food and water, but not what was valuable."

287

"Food and water are the most valuable commodities now. They're long gone. It's not worth the risk to go back there. You're only asking to attract more trouble."

"No, Bobby, they're the ones who asked for trouble when they tried to carjack us." She whirled on him.

He stopped abruptly to avoid running into her.

"And for your information, the pictures and scrapbooks are the most valuable things we brought with us. They are the only things we have to remind us of our past, of our family. They are important to me. I will not lose them."

"But, Sis—"

"No!" she screamed, turning on him. Her nostrils flared and eyes narrowed. "I need them. I need them to remind me of better times. I need them because they give me hope that perhaps one day life could be as good again as they were in those pictures. They may be all that's left of what our family was once like. I can't leave them, Bobby. I won't."

She spun around, walking briskly again.

Behind them the injured man yelled, "Please, you can't leave me here."

In an instant, Becca pivoted, let out a war cry, and sprinted toward the lone survivor.

Fearing the carnage, Bobby tried to stop her, but she busted through his arms driving an elbow into his chest. When she reached the man she kicked him twice as he cried out in pain. Then, as Bobby watched in shock, she lifted her foot and stomped on the man's head. He no longer cried.

"Bastard!" She spat on him and stormed back toward Bobby.

As she passed him, her face appeared unlined and calm. She smiled. "Come on, baby brother, let's go get our stuff." She laughed, pushed an arm in the air and released a triumphant shout.

Bobby followed. He marveled at the changes in his sister. She had always been beautiful, smart, and popular, but she had been so lost in herself she seldom noticed others. Now her beautiful face had sunken cheeks, dark-circled eyes, and she had lost the extra pounds her sedentary lifestyle had gathered. She was a hardened, lean woman who had killed several times to survive. Bobby liked this new version of Becca much better, but he was also afraid of and for her. Volatile and often unpredictable, she was strong now and he could rely on her in dangerous situations.

He jogged to catch up to her. "Becca, did you forget they would also have control of our arsenal as well? We didn't get a good look at how many of them there were. But if they got their hands on the weapons we stashed, it's gonna be real hard trying to get your pictures back."

Again she turned on him, this time advancing. "Our pictures, Bobby. They're *our* pictures, of *our* family. How are you going to feel if we get home and find" – she choked – "that they're all dead?"

"Don't say that, Becca. Don't even think it." Bobby swallowed hard and looked away. He didn't want to think about that possibility. Pushing her words from his mind, he softened his voice, "Becca, we have to hope."

"Dead. Dead. Dead. What if this entire trip is for nothing? Won't you wish you had those scrapbooks then to remind you of who they were and what they looked like?"

Crying, she turned and stormed off. "Well, I'm going even if I have to go alone."

Bobby stood while she lengthened the distance between them. She really pissed him off sometimes. But her words had struck home. What if their parents were dead? His throat constricted, but just as fast he said aloud, "No! I won't think about this now." A quick backhand across his eyes removed any potential tears.

Frowning he ran after her. Without a word he pulled up in stride next to her.

"Okay, but follow my lead when we get there."

"Dream on, dumb jock."

"God, you can really be annoying."

"And you can really be a pain in the ass."

"Bitch."

"Prick."

Within three steps, they were both laughing.

"Let's do this, Sis."

"You know it, little brother. And I better not find anyone wearing my new shoes or I'm really going to have to hurt someone."

Bobby smiled. That was the old Becca.

Made in the USA
Columbia, SC
14 February 2018